THE COLOR OF LIES

THE COLOR OF LIES

CJ LYONS

BLINK®

B L I N K

The Color of Lies
Copyright © 2018 by CJ Lyons LLC

Requests for information should be addressed to:
Blink, *3900 Sparks Dr. SE, Grand Rapids, Michigan 49546*

Hardcover ISBN: 978-0-310-76535-6

Audio ISBN: 978-0-310-76591-2

Ebook ISBN: 978-0-310-76537-0

Cover design: Darren Welch
Interior design: Denise Froehlich

Printed in the United States of America

18 19 20 21 22 / LSC / 10 9 8 7 6 5 4 3 2 1

To Evan:

like Alec, you are a true

Gentleman and Scholar

"We don't see things as they are, we see them as we are."

—Anaïs Nin

"Art is the lie that enables us to realize the truth."

—Pablo Picasso

CHAPTER 1

Ella

I hate birthdays.

Birthdays taste of burnt toast and sour milk and smell of parched grass and frozen steel. Especially here in Cambria City, a place cold and ironbound, with shadows so thick the sun runs and hides for weeks at a time. I yearn for the soft embrace of the sea, the sweet jasmine whisper of salt air.

Funny, because I've never been to the ocean.

Today I'm eighteen. Officially an adult. So I decide to celebrate my birthday my way. I ditched my morning classes at the high school, showed up for my advanced composition and photo-collage class early at Cambria College, and now, instead of heading home like I'm supposed to after my studio time, I'm relaxing at the bottom of a swimming pool in the college's natatorium. As usual, I'm alone; this narrow lap pool is too small for any classes or swim team practices, and it's in one of the back rooms of the nat, hardly ever remembered.

Every year on this November day, my gram Helen, who raised me, laughs and sings and dances—usually she's a hermit, so I know the effort costs her dearly. That's exactly why I make sure to thank her, as much as I'd prefer to ignore the date circled on the calendar. I can't let her down. Because behind her façade of giddiness, she weeps silent tears.

So many tears you could salt an ocean with them. Every single time Gram Helen wishes me a happy birthday, it's with the shadow of death clinging to her.

It's a story never told, not from start to end, but so many bits and pieces have been filled in by so many voices. Helen's voice and Uncle Joe's and even Darrin's. Never mine, though.

I can't remember anything from back then. A blessing, Helen says, they all say. A few years ago, I mustered the courage to check out the newspaper article about the fire, but I didn't make it past the picture below the screaming headline, flames reaching out to me from my laptop, heat singeing my face before I even reached the reporter's words. It left me sick for a day after, my imagination conjuring horror and pain, worse than if I'd been there in person.

So lucky I wasn't there, everyone tells me. So lucky I was only three, too young to remember. So lucky my parents decided to leave me with Helen so they could take their first vacation in years. So lucky to have been hundreds of miles from that small cottage on a remote beach . . . lucky to have been nowhere near the blaze that killed them.

Which is why I'm here now. Hiding from Helen's false smiles.

I hover a few inches above the pool's floor. Swishing my fingers above my face, I use the crystalline water and softly shimmering light to paint images invisible to anyone except me. A mom and dad cradling a baby, love shining gold all around them. A little girl, dancing and running and jumping into their arms for hugs, and her parents are so happy, so proud of her. They join hands, the girl swinging from their arms, knowing, certain, trusting that they will never, ever let her fall.

The perfect family. Smoke and flames fill my vision, vanquishing the sheltering calm of the water, engulfing my imaginary family. They vanish, ripples of a dream that never lived to see the light of day.

I throw my body to one side but the flames reach out for me, greedy, grabbing. Fire stole my parents and now it's come for me. I huddle, my legs scraping the rough surface of the bottom of the pool. Black tendrils of smoke bind me, choking my breath. They lead back to a fiery figure standing high above me at the far side of the pool, the nightmare demon who terrorizes my dreams. When I was little, I used to have this nightmare almost every night. But now, the memories only haunt me on this day—my birthday.

The day the fire took my parents.

I struggle to re-create my peaceful happy birthday wish. But the spell of the water is broken and my lungs burn with need. I exhale, push off the bottom, and rise to steal a breath, the air slapping at my face. I inhale, then immediately return below the surface, using only my flutter kick to propel me faster than most people can swim using both arms and legs.

I reach the far end of the pool and come up, ready to flip into my next lap, but as I break the water my motion stutters and I fall back, flailing my arms. For a moment, all I can see is fire and smoke. My chest tightens and I can't breathe past my panic.

Then I blink and there's a guy standing above me—a real one, not my nightmare fire-demon.

He's fully clothed, a messenger bag across his chest, watching me with eyes magnified by horn-rimmed glasses, eyes so green they mirror the water surrounding me.

"Nora Cleary, right?" he asks.

I splash in confusion, getting the tops of his shoes wet, yet he doesn't retreat. *Nora?* No one calls me that, not since I was a child—he must have the wrong girl. Unless . . . maybe something's happened to Gram Helen. Why else would a stranger be searching me out? "Is something wrong? Who are you?"

I squint at him, the water's reflection dancing over his clean-cut features. He can't be the police or campus security—he's only a year or two older than me, dark-skinned with hair as black as mine, dressed like a student in jeans and a Carhartt jacket.

"I'm Alec Ravenell. There's a project I'm working on. Could we go someplace? Talk? I could really use your help." His words are soft, lilting, carried by an accent hailing from someplace *else*, far from ironbound central Pennsylvania. Virginia or the Carolinas?

The bitter taste of fear slowly ebbs, replaced by curiosity as I realize it's not solely his accent that sets him apart from other guys. Usually by now, I'd be seeing colors and scenes conjured by whoever I was talking to—I wouldn't have to guess where his accent is from, I'd *see* it in his words. But the air around Alec remains calm. No shimmers of color, no images ghosting over reality.

I blink. Look again. Nothing. That has never, ever happened before. Not with anyone. "My help?"

"Yes. Unless . . . Is this a bad time?"

"N-no," I stammer, still staring past him, waiting for the empty air to come to life and show me what he's really talking about.

I'm not used to taking anyone's words at face value—I've

never needed to. Like most everyone on my mom's side of the family, I have synesthesia. It means my senses get tangled up, confusing what I hear with how my brain translates another person's words, all combining to form auras of brilliant colors and pictures in my mind. Images so vivid, I've spent my whole life coloring, drawing, painting, trying to reproduce them.

But not with Alec. No sparks of color, no ghostly images to reveal the truth behind his words. Suddenly, I feel as if I've become half-blind, tone-deaf, and lost the use of three of my four limbs. I struggle to remember what he even asked me only a few seconds ago. Words without any colors to ground them slip by so fast; mere sounds, virtually without meaning.

Following my gaze, he turns to glance over his shoulder. There's nothing there except stacks of unused race blocks and lane floats. Then he looks back at me, curiosity lighting his eyes. Bewildered and uncertain, I duck below the surface and swim to the ladder. When I climb out, he's there to hand me my towel.

"Thanks."

"I've never seen anyone swim like that. You should try out for the team."

As I towel my hair—water slipping from the dark strands to create a puddle at my feet until I straitjacket them with the terry cloth—I parse his words, seeking their hidden meaning. Usually so-called small talk reveals everything I'd ever want to know about a person's true intentions—auras don't hide behind small talk. But now I'm drowning, with no clue what truth lurks beneath Alec's words.

"I don't go here." I wrap a second towel over my swim-suit, adding an additional layer of protection to combat my sudden vulnerability. I'm not feeling underdressed—I'm feeling naked.

Alec says nothing. He's still shrouded in an aura-less mystery of blankness. An empty canvas waiting for me to gather the courage to create that first splash of color that will change everything.

"To college. Not yet. I mean, I do take classes here, and I have permission to use the pool . . ." I'm rambling. I never ramble. I never chat. I watch and listen, let others do the talking. But I can't stop myself. It's as if the empty space around him is a black hole and I need to fill the void. "Besides, Cambria High doesn't have a swim team." I clamp my lips shut, immediately regretting the confession that I'm still in high school. But I have the feeling he already knows everything I've just told him.

Grabbing my bag and stepping into my sandals, I stumble toward the women's locker room.

"I'll meet you out front," he calls after me.

I haven't agreed to anything, but I feel like my fate has already been sealed.

CHAPTER 2

At least she didn't scream, is all I can think as I make my way down the hall from the swimming pool where I found Nora Cleary. I trudge back to the natatorium's main lobby. The look on her face when she came out of the water and saw me standing there—sheer terror.

This was a mistake. A huge mistake. I should just leave now.

I almost do, but I catch the eye of the blonde manning the reception desk and pure, stubborn pride stops me. She's watching me but pretending not to, her expression filled with curiosity. Given how fast I went into the pool area and came back out, not to mention the way I'm loitering now, I guess it's rather obvious I didn't come here to swim. My stare goes on too long and she edges her hand up onto the phone.

Had Nora's friends set me up? Did they call campus security? They seemed nice enough, genuinely pleased to tell me where to find Nora once I explained I needed her help for a school project; I even showed the guy, Max, my student ID. Maybe they thought it was a harmless prank, sending a strange guy to surprise their friend?

Except Nora had been more than startled. She'd been panicked by the sight of me.

No. I can't put the blame on Nora's friends. It's my fault. I should have thought this through, planned better. But it's taken me three months to find the courage to approach Nora at all. I never expected it would turn into such a mess so quickly.

I turn away from the girl at the desk, forcing my rigid spine to ease into a less threatening slump, and pretend to study the bulletin board. I need to regain control—my first meeting with the girl who might change my life could only be described as a train wreck on steroids.

That look. I can't erase it from my mind. Unadulterated primal fear. I edge a glance at the receptionist. She's still wary, I can tell by her posture, but at least she's no longer gripping the phone like a lifeline. Did Nora see me the same way? As a threat?

It was a mistake. Coming here. I'd been thinking of privacy when I should have been considering how a girl swimming alone in a deserted pool would feel if a strange guy suddenly showed up, knowing her name—knowing so much more about her, more than she could imagine—and wanting to talk.

I pull my phone free and pretend to be fascinated by what I'm reading. Really, I'm debating if I should call Professor Winston. Tell him I can't get the interview, that I've blown it. Without what he calls the "human face of tragedy," he won't use my story in his book.

No. The chance to have a publishing credential like that is too good to pass up. It will make my career, open doors I could never dream of otherwise. I slide my phone back into my pocket. Dr. Winston and Nora Cleary are the only reasons I left home to come to this third-rate, cold-all-the-time, rust-belt college.

No way am I going to give up. Not after so many years, so many miles. So very many questions. Nora is my chance to finally have answers. Answers I've been seeking most of my life. Answers I need.

The outside door opens and a chilly breeze brings in the smell of wood smoke along with a trio of white guys carrying gym bags. The smoke makes the hair on the back of my neck stand at attention, reminding me of the first time I laid eyes on Nora.

Fifteen years ago, I'd pulled her from the sea like a treasure from a shipwreck. Despite the salt water soaking her to the skin, she smelled of smoke and ash. And that look of terror—almost identical to one she gave me at the pool just now.

Did she recognize me? After so many years, does she remember who I am?

I push my glasses higher on my nose. Goosebumps pepper my arms as a shiver ripples over my skin. Remembering that night always does that to me. It was the first time I'd ever seen death. Smelled it. Felt it reach out and try to take someone I loved. Even now, fifteen years later, I've never been as terrified as I was that night.

Suddenly, I have the urge to call home. To hear familiar voices as soothing and calm as sunrise on the ocean. Anything to feel normal and accepted by people with whom I can let my guard down, not have to worry about what I think they think I am, or wonder if they're afraid I'm a threat instead of just a guy trying to figure out his past and future.

This was such a huge, huge mistake . . .

CHAPTER 3

Ella

I shower and change into my jeans and a cowl-neck, then pull a fleece top over it. Gram Helen says I dress in more layers than an Eskimo, but since she almost never leaves the house, she's not one to judge how best to stay warm in a Pennsylvania winter. As I lace up my boots, I can't help but wonder why Alec sought me out. What kind of project could I possibly help him with? He didn't have the look of an art student—the only classes I take here at the college.

How had he found me? Why was he using my childhood nickname?

A guy I couldn't read past his actual words . . .

I glance at the locker room's side exit, half tempted to head home to whatever cringe-worthy birthday surprise Gram Helen has waiting and pretend this encounter with Alec never happened.

I text Rory, knowing she'll be with Max and my gram. She and Max have been my best friends since the first day of third grade when Rory, with her waves of violet effusiveness, gathered us two misfits into her orbit. We've been inseparable ever since.

Usually I would have had lunch with them before coming to the college for my art classes, but not today, when I'd see all their secrets spilling out in a rainbow of colors whenever they thought about whatever they had planned for tonight.

Met a guy on campus, I type. *Alec Ravenell. Needs my help?* I'm hoping I got the spelling of his name somewhat close.

Helen's freaking, comes Rory's almost instantaneous reply. I swear she'd have her phone surgically implanted if she could—unlike Max, who's as likely to forget his on the charger as have it with him. He's like me, feels no need to stay connected simply so others can intrude whenever it's convenient for them. That means the two of us are usually a step behind when it comes to gossip or current events, but that's why we have Rory to catch us up.

Before I can type a response, my phone rings. Rory. Of course. "Don't worry, I'll be home soon," I answer. "Helen will still get her birthday torture."

"You're on speaker," Max's voice comes through.

Ouch. I hope Helen didn't hear—but she probably has her noise-cancelling headphones on if Max and Rory are in the house.

"Don't worry, it's just us," Rory adds, to my relief. "Helen's in the kitchen, putting the final touches on your cake."

"Not sparklers again?" Last year, she set the curtains on fire. They were ugly curtains, so not a bad thing, until the smoke alarm began blaring and poor Helen had to retreat to her soundproof studio in the basement while we cleaned up the mess.

Although everyone on my mom's side of the family has synesthesia, we all have different forms. Gram Helen feels sounds—not as fun as you might think, and it's driven her to work alone from home, where she can control her environment, barely coming into contact with any other humans. But it's also given her the most wonderful voice—she can pitch it to create any emotion she wants, which is why audio publishers pay her top dollar as a voice talent. If she could survive the outside world, she could have been a movie star, she's that good.

My uncle Joe, my mom's baby brother, he tastes words— also not always a very fun gift, not unless you like filling your mouth with day-old baby poop every time you hear or see the word "sugar."

Even my mom had it, they say. She saw colors with numbers. It allowed her to check calculations really fast, because all she had to do was scan the colors, look at the answer, and she'd know if it was right or not. A good thing for an insurance fraud investigator, which is how she met my dad when she joined the family business: Cleary and Sons, Insurance and Financial Advisors, established 1947. *Protecting your past, present, and future.*

It's still our business, but now, with Dad gone, it's run by Uncle Joe along with Darrin West—not a Cleary or a son, but my dad's college roommate and a financial genius. Joe hates insurance, is always telling me that he's only watching over things until I can grow up and take over the firm. They all expect me to get a degree in accounting or actuarial science and keep the Cleary in Cleary and Sons like my father and his father and his father before him would have wanted.

So many dead people controlling my future. Given that this is November and it's my senior year and college applications are due, like, *now*, where I want to go and what I'll be majoring in will be the first question everyone will be asking me tonight.

"No open flames," Max answers. "Something even better. But you need to stay away, give us a little longer to get ready." I don't need to see the bright excitement coloring his words to know he's loving this, keeping me in suspense.

"Are Uncle Joe and Darrin there yet?" Joe's hopeless—he'll wander off by himself until forced to play at being social—but Darrin's good at keeping Helen from fussing and worrying too much. His Texan drawl doesn't spark her synesthesia as much as other people's voices, and despite their differences in age, he always treats her like she's the one who got away, flirting and charming her until she can't help but laugh. It's weirdly adorable.

"Not yet, but Darrin texted Helen to say they won't be long."

Rory breaks in. "So who's this guy? Alec something? Is he cute? What color is his aura? Where are you going?"

I smile. Only five questions in one breath; she's restraining herself. We know each other so well I don't even need to be with her to see the colors of the emotions behind her words. They're like a laser show overflowing from my phone: sunflash-yellow excitement, aubergine anxiety, rosy hope, cerulean curiosity, more rosy hope . . . the last erupts like fireworks surrounding an image of two people kissing.

Both she and Max work harder on my love life than I ever will. I've tried to explain how hard it is to get to know someone when you can see their lies and evasions and hidden moods spelled out before they even finish chatting about the weather, but they just don't get it. Worse is when I misinterpret what I see and hear. There are so many layers of truth, I don't always see the right one. But my friends assume it's something I can turn off or ignore, with no clue I'd have better luck learning how to breathe underwater.

"So," Rory continues. "Did he pass the aura test? I mean, with those gorgeous green eyes—"

"Wait. How do you know what color his eyes are? You set me up," I accuse them.

"Didn't you get my texts?" Max says. "I warned you he was coming—"

"Max!" Rory's aura flashes bright from the phone. "I told you to keep it a surprise. Now you ruined everything."

"I was in the pool," I interject. "Missed your texts." So typical of Rory, with her exuberant love of grand gestures, never even thinking of how uncomfortable it might make an introvert like me feel to have a strange guy show up out of nowhere. To Rory, life plays out on a stage more dramatic than any Hollywood set. Thankfully, I have Max to run interference, even if his warning didn't reach me in time.

"When did you meet him? How long have you two been planning this?"

Max answers. "Since he came to the house about an hour ago. Helen said our job is to keep you occupied until she has everything ready . . ."

"My idea, of course," Rory adds.

"I'm the one who got all the info while you distracted him with your jibber-jabber chit-chat. He's a journalism major. Lives at Weaver Hall."

"It's called having a conversation, and I got just as much info as you did from your precious computer. He's a junior at Cambria College but only nineteen because he graduated

THE COLOR OF LIES

high school with his associate's degree, so he got to skip two years. He's from South Carolina, in case you couldn't tell from that delicious accent. Speaking of delicious, I'm sure you already noticed that for yourself—he has that kind of quiet cuteness that you like. And—"

"Guys, guys, what does he want?" I'm just outside the locker room, ready to go through the doors to the lobby where Alec is waiting.

Max jumps in. "Your help with a project he's working on with Professor Winston. Didn't you say your graphic design teacher was assigning you non-design students so you can see what it's like to work with a client?"

"Right. Yeah." I'd hoped my turn wouldn't come up until later in the semester—the students who have already gone, the real college students who have years more experience than I do, have set the bar spectacularly high.

"What's his aura like?" Rory is fascinated by my gift— funny, because there are times she's totally blind to the emotions right in front of her.

With Max, for instance. Half the school thinks he's gay because he doesn't date and hangs out with us all the time. No one except me sees the way his aura shimmers to Valentine red and pulses in time with his heartbeat anytime he's near Rory. He and I have never spoken about it, though I'm sure he knows I know. Of course, I'd never break his trust and tell Rory the truth.

Rory's still chattering. "Go, have coffee. Find out about his project. Flirt a little. Then maybe after, you can bring him here for the party."

"What? Are you crazy?" I twist away from the door and huddle beside the bulletin board bristling with notices for roommates, ride-shares, yard sales, and party fliers. Seeing the random detritus of college life always makes me feel as if I'm trespassing, pretending to be someone I'm not just because I'm lucky enough to be able to take a few classes here instead of being locked up inside the high school all day.

"I can't bring a college guy I don't even know home, and especially not to my birthday party." Talk about embarrassing—my family goes all out, and not in a good way, when over-celebrating my birthday. Case in point: last year's sparkler birthday cake disaster. Who knows what they—and Rory and Max—are cooking up this year given the amount of trouble they've gone to in order to keep me out of the house.

"No. It'll be fun," Rory assures me. "Only if you like him, of course. But I have a good feeling about this Alec Ravenell."

"Or not," Max puts in, his tone radiating a deep umber of concern—he's an introvert like me, understands how difficult it is to let a stranger trespass into my life. "If you're uncomfortable meeting this guy, we can join you there. Then bring you home to the party. Alone."

As usual, my two friends are pulling me in opposite directions. It's up to me to decide my fate.

Still on the phone, I gather my courage and push through the door to the main lobby where I find Alec bouncing on his toes with jerky, nervous motions, his face lighting up when he sees me.

"I thought maybe you ran out the back," he admits. "Didn't mean to come on all stalkerish or anything."

It's so weird, words that are mere sounds. I find myself opening and closing my free hand as if straining his words, testing their meaning. Not just his words but his body language—it's like trying to listen to two foreign languages at once with no dictionary to help.

I guess that's what my synesthesia really does: translate people. Not their empty words and gestures, but what Gram Helen would call their essence. Otherwise, who are we? Random islands of thought and emotion wandering through this world, occasionally ricocheting into each other's lives?

Is this how everyone else sees each other? Is this how the rest of the world sees me? Flat, colorless, superficial. Even the people who should know me best like Rory and Max? The revelation shakes me to my core. I know my gift is unusual, but I've never before experienced what it might be like to live without it.

I thrust the phone at Alec. "My friends would like to know what to tell the police if you turn out to be a serial killer."

"Sure, of course." His smile widens, creasing his eyes. I try to memorize their shade of blue-green so I can capture it in paint later. Azure? No, they're more green than blue. Aquamarine? I can't remember ever seeing eyes so vivid in someone with skin as dark as his. It's stunning, the contrast.

He takes my phone. "Uh, hi again. It's Alec."

"And where are you taking our Ella?" Max sounds possessive and much older than he really is.

Alec glances at me. "How about Java Joe's? Nice and public, plenty of witnesses and security cameras. That work for you?"

I nod and take the phone back, holding it to my ear so Alec can't hear. "Keep an eye on Helen, try to get her to relax. When do you want me home?"

"We should be ready by five," Max says. "Text if you need us to come rescue you—we can be there in ten minutes."

"Have fun." Rory, of course, needs to have the last word. "Don't do anything I wouldn't do."

I hang up, hiding my sudden blush as I pocket my phone. When I look up, Alec's holding the door open, the November wind rushing in to ambush us. I still can't believe I'm doing this, going out for coffee with a total stranger.

This isn't me. Watching is easy. Talking, interacting, the whole give-and-take of an actual conversation—that's hard. Virtually impossible with the constant distraction of the other person's ebb and flow of emotions and wants and needs underlying their actual words. Every time I open my mouth, I need to decide whether to respond to what someone says or what they actually mean.

But those powers of observation, they're what makes me a good artist, combined with my gift of reading emotions. Turns out a lot of creatives have synesthesia, people like Wassily Kandinsky, one of my artistic inspirations. It effects about four percent of the population—that's twice the percentage of people who have red hair, which also runs on my mother's side of the family and which I failed to inherit. Instead, I have my dad's black hair . . . so boring compared to the bright copper both Gram Helen and Uncle Joe have. Or my mom's gorgeous auburn curls.

As I walk with Alec in his oasis of colorless calm, I wonder if it might be possible for me to pretend to be normal, to be in the world instead of merely observing it, at least for this one day.

Normal has always been so far out of my grasp, I've never had a hope of reaching it; easier to try to catch the moon by standing on a ladder with a fishing pole and a thousand yards of line spinning out across the sky.

But maybe, just for today—with this guy and his invisible aura—maybe I could actually try for normal? After all, Gram Helen says birthdays are made for wishes.

CHAPTER 4

Ella

Alec says nothing as we walk away from the nat, and his silence is almost as confusing as when he's talking. Finally, I muster up the courage to begin the conversation.

"What—" I start to say, ready to ask about the mysterious project he needs help with, at the same time he says, "Why—"

We laugh awkwardly, and I motion for him to go on. "You first."

"Why do your friends call you Ella? I thought your name was Nora." He sounds uncertain, as if maybe he has the wrong girl. Maybe he does. I hope not.

I could take the easy way out, explain that both are short for Eleanor—it's the truth but not the important part. I sense Alec's more interested in the why behind the truth. "I used to be Nora. Short for Eleanor. But everyone's called me

Ella since I was little. Why did you call me Nora? Where did you hear that?"

We've crossed the street to the other side before he answers. "Eleanor seemed too formal. To me, you'll always be Nora."

It's an answer but not one that makes much sense—he talks as if we've met before. I would definitely remember meeting someone like Alec. "But—"

"Why'd you change to Ella? Did something happen?" he asks.

When Gram Helen tells this story, it's colored in shades of blue and green with the occasional flash of the dark purple that black silk becomes when it's wet and held up to the sun.

I take a breath, drinking in the silver wash of winter air, swallowing it down until I feel my toes tingle with the cold. "We have a cabin, up in the mountains near a lake. Maybe not a lake, more like a big pond. But to me, when I was a little kid, the water was home—more home than any bed inside a room inside a house. I could hold my breath so long that I'd sit there, below the water, the world perfectly calm and still—it was heaven. One time, I stayed under so long my uncle and gram panicked, thinking I was lost. Or worse."

"I'll bet you scared the daylights out of them."

"Yes, but not on purpose. I didn't understand why they

were so scared—which scared me. My uncle hauled me out and my gram, she told me it was too dangerous, that I couldn't go into the water alone ever again. Not ever." I throw a hint of Gram Helen's fear into my voice, the way her usual bright tangerine had shriveled to the brown of an orange forgotten and left to rot in the sun.

"But you didn't listen, did you?" His voice is without color, but his eyes gleam with certain knowledge.

"It was like telling me not to breathe or to give up eating. My uncle sells insurance—it's the family business—and one day I heard him talking about an umbrella policy that would protect people from almost anything. I was only four. The next morning that water was calling to me, and I knew I couldn't resist, so I took the biggest umbrella I could find and I ran down the dock, and the wind gathered in the umbrella, about ready to launch me into space, and I jumped . . ."

"The girl with the umbrella that could protect her from anything . . . Ella."

"Exactly. It started out just family and friends, until an art teacher asked us to create a self-portrait to introduce ourselves."

"You painted yourself with the umbrella? In the lake?" His smile crinkles his eyes, making them look old and wise through the thick lenses of his glasses. "I'll bet they didn't see that coming."

"The teacher loved it, thought it was whimsical, until she asked me why the girl with the umbrella looked so calm even as the waves washed over her and pulled her deeper down into the water. I made the mistake of telling the truth: that she was calm because she felt safe there, underwater. That she wasn't afraid of drowning—she was afraid of when she had to come up for air."

His smile fades, and he slows his pace as he regards me. "Not good."

I like how he fills in the blanks—almost as if he can see the colors and images swirling around me as I give voice to the memory. "The teacher told the counselor, who told the principal, who called Gram Helen."

I stop, a wall thicker than a glacier blocking my words. Because this part isn't mine to tell, it's Gram Helen's. Helen did what she always does when the world comes knocking: she refused to answer. Instead, after hearing the message the principal left, wanting to schedule a meeting to "discuss concerns," Helen unplugged the phone and locked it in the basement freezer, insulated by ice and metal to keep the world at bay.

It worked. That's the thing: people call Helen dysfunctional and passive-aggressive, but her methods succeed. Not as safe as being underwater, watching the world through a soft blanket of blue-green, but about as good as you can get here in this jangly, sharp-edged city where everyone seems to think they have the right to waltz into your life whether you like it or not. Like a strange guy showing up while I'm swimming alone. Even if he is kind of cute.

Maybe it's a mistake to trust Alec too much. I flick my eyes at him, glancing as far sideways as they'll go, but still nothing. I can't even read his expression, let alone his real intentions.

"But you really were okay, right?" I like how his accent lilts and curves as if not bound by the same rock-iron gravity we locals are. I can almost feel the wash of ocean waves in his voice. "I mean, nothing bad was happening?"

Even without an aura, I sense the concern coloring his voice. I quicken my stride, the spell of his voice broken by the pragmatism of his words.

"Of course not. Why would you even think that?" Especially as he's a total stranger who I've foolishly just bared my heart to.

He shrugs and we keep walking. "Your friends seem nice. But why were they at your house and you weren't?" He squints into the late afternoon sun. "This isn't part of some joke or prank, is it? I don't want—"

"No," I hasten to reassure him, cursing Rory and her love of melodrama. "I'm sorry if you thought that. They just wanted to surprise me. In a good way."

"By sending a stranger to where you're swimming alone?"

"Well, it's not like you're a stalker or anything," I try to turn it into a joke, but neither of us laugh. "You see, I live with my grandmother, and she has a hard time leaving the house or dealing with strangers. So, that means I pretty much have school and home and that's it. Thankfully, she's okay with Rory and Max, so the last couple of years we've all kinda hung out at my house most times—that way if I need or want to get away for a few hours, there are people I trust there to take care of Gram Helen, and she doesn't feel like we're babysitting her."

"But you are, aren't you? Does she have Alzheimer's or something? Seems like a pretty big burden to put on a kid. Can't anyone else help?"

I'm not a kid and there's no one else except Joe and Darrin—but there's no way I'm going to tell him that.

Java Joe's is around the corner. I'm so embarrassed by my over-sharing that I debate ditching him there. But he said he needed my help, and I'm still curious enough about him that I want to know why.

I fiddle with my parka zipper before I ask, "So, what's this project you need help with?"

I really hope this is about the graphic design class. I need a good grade in design if I'm going to get into art school. *If* I ever find the courage to apply, that is. I'm confident in my art, just not so sure about leaving home and destroying my family's hopes and dreams for my future. Despite Alec's implications, it's not a burden watching over Helen and Joe. I owe them everything. And they're my only family left. Without them, I'd have no one.

Before Alec can answer, we reach Java Joe's—one of those battered old silver diners that look like they could be hitched to a truck and steered away on a cloud of diesel fuel and coffee grounds and then set back down on any random corner of any random city and fit right in. I beat him to the door and hold it open, inhaling the tangy scent of burnt bacon grease, cinnamon, and strong, strong coffee.

He grins and nods his thanks as he passes over the threshold. I follow him to an empty booth against the windows at the far back wall. Some people think Java Joe's is striving to be shabby chic with its retro decor, but Rory says it's really only shabby cheap. It hasn't changed since her parents were students. Same red-topped, metal-rimmed tables, same booths with their peeling fake leather upholstery that sports the occasional duct-tape patch, even the same menus with the same coffee stains permanently laminated in place.

Here's the thing about people: They come in all sizes, colors, shapes, and sounds. But the sizes, colors, and shapes I "see" have very little to do with reality. It's part of the reason why I hang back and stay quiet—it's too hard to figure out which is which, especially when you're in a crowd, like a jingle-jangly classroom or a bright-sparking-fireworks-waiting-to-explode school cafeteria. Or, nightmare of nightmares, a mall. Forget watching a movie in a theater, torn between the auras the actors fling about with such abandon and those of the people reacting in the crowd.

Usually I don't like restaurants—too many people with too many stories grabbing at my attention. But Java Joe's is never crowded and we've picked a good time; there are only two other customers, both sitting alone at tables and working on laptops. I ignore the menu and the water-speckled silverware to twirl the song list caged inside the ancient jukebox selector. The jukebox is dead and gone—there's a freezer of to-go ice cream where it once sat—but the songs it played remain behind. I'm never sure if that's sad or kind of cool. Bittersweet; maybe that's the word.

Alec buries his face in the menu, the words reflected in his glasses. He suddenly seems nervous, which surprises me since I'm the one out of my element.

Then the waitress is there with her stoplight amber waves of anxiety. As if getting our order exactly right will save the world. Or more likely, given the way she keeps flicking her eyes toward the glass-walled office with its open door behind the counter, save her job. "What'll you have?"

I order tea and a cinnamon bun—they grill them until they're sticky, gooey globs of sheer caramelized heaven, the main reason why Java Joe's is still in business—while Alec gets coffee.

"Your project?" I remind him once she leaves us in peace.

"Well—" Suddenly he's the one who seems shy and tongue-tied. "I'm a journalism major, and I'm working with Professor Winston on a true-crime story."

True crime? Now I see the challenge—photos, large chunks of text woven between them without distracting a reader, maybe graphs and charts or maps as well. Difficult, but much easier than creating a business logo from scratch. Alec's story will be perfect for my graphic design class—it plays to my forte, seeing the big picture of how individual items fit together rather than focusing on picayune details. Pretty much how I'm forced to navigate the world because of my synesthesia. "When's it due?"

He seems taken aback, as if he hasn't factored a deadline into things. "He wants it as soon as possible. But I still need to do several in-depth interviews and finish writing them up."

"Can you give me what you have to start working with? That way I could mock up a layout, see if you like it. Are we talking print, online, or both?" I'm itching to grab pen and paper, start sketching, but I don't want to shift my attention away from him.

I never realized before exactly how much effort it takes to understand a person when their auras aren't filling in the missing pieces of their truth. Besides, I like watching him, the way he runs a finger up his nose to straighten his glasses, the subtle shift in his eyes when he's looking at me but trying not to stare too forcibly, the play of color across his dark skin as the light through the window shifts with the breeze.

"Both," he finally says. "But I can't let you see it."

"I don't care if it's a draft. I just need to figure out the design elements."

He frowns. "Design elements? I don't think you understand—" He quits talking when the waitress arrives with my food and his coffee. His lips purse tightly together and I feel as if I've somehow upset him.

I think back to my design class, try to remember what the teacher said about working with clients. "Let them lead," she'd told us. "Your job is to listen, not judge or assume. Even though they're coming to you for your expertise, they'll have a good idea of how they see their final vision coming to life. You need to respect and honor that."

Listen. Respect. Honor the client's vision. Everything I haven't done.

I stare at the waitress's hands as she shuffles the plates in front of us. Have I already blown my chance with Alec?

CHAPTER 5

Alec

I can't even imagine how I could have screwed this up worse than I've done already. Thankfully, the waitress brings our food before I can dig myself in deeper. What was I thinking, bringing Nora here to interview?

The waitress has overfilled my coffee mug. At least it's a decent-sized mug instead of one of those too-thin, skinny cups that let the coffee scald your hands even as it cools much too fast. Coffee is practically a religion back home—my father mainstreams it black while my mother considers it one of the few real pleasures modern civilization has left to savor.

She uses a French press and grinds her own beans. I'm not that fussy. Although I don't actually like coffee itself, I began drinking it when I first started taking college classes two years ago, because instead of hopping on the regular high school bus, I had to get up at 4:30 to take the city bus to campus. I learned to appreciate the hit of caffeine, if not the taste. Now I slurp about a third of the cup down, then fill it back up to the brim with cream. The diner specializes in all-day breakfast, so they have cinnamon sitting here at the table, and I sprinkle a healthy dose into the mix.

I glance up to see Nora—Ella—watching me as she dunks her tea bag and waits for her grilled sticky bun to cool. We exchange a smile, but then I feel my face flush with guilt. We're having such a nice time and I'm about to ruin it, and she has absolutely no clue.

"You're from South Carolina?" she asks, holding her tea cup with both hands as if it's made of precious rare porcelain rather than cheap restaurant-stock china.

"What gave it away? After three months here, I've learned not to say y'all—although I still refuse to acknowledge youn's as the proper form of the second person plural."

Her smile deepens. Her face isn't quite symmetrical, making her smile seem somehow more engaging. Or maybe it's her eyes, so deep set and dark. I'm not at all certain what it is. I just might need to make her smile again to be sure.

"It's your hands."

"Excuse me?"

"Your hands. They gave you away. While we were walking, every person we passed, you started to raise a hand to wave to them."

I close my eyes for a moment to suppress my laughter—I don't want her to think I'm laughing at her, when really I'm laughing at me. "You are so right. When I first got here, I never even realized that I was saying 'Hey' to everyone I passed until a couple of guys almost jumped me. Asking me who the heck I was and did I know them and why was I messing in their business. I stopped real fast after that, but guess my hands can't quit the habit so easily."

"It's not that we're not friendly up here." She's quick to defend her home. I like that about her. "Imagine what it'd be like for one of us down there, surrounded by strangers calling 'Hey!' to us as we're minding our own business walking down the street. A person could get whiplash trying to keep all those strangers in sight, make sure they're not up to no good."

I shake my head at her logic. "Are all you city folk so paranoid?"

"Basic survival instinct," she says solemnly.

"So that's why you're so observant, watching everyone's hands? You know that's where any threat comes from." Dad taught me that, along with how to take out someone twice my size, when to run and when to hit, and most importantly when to simply look confident enough that you're too much trouble for anyone to bother messing with in the first place. Command presence, he calls it. It doesn't work so much here at school, not for me. I guess I stand out too much—I'm the only black guy in my dorm and most of my classes—but it's still good to know.

Though it makes me wonder who taught Ella. And why she had to learn that lesson—had someone hurt her? I remember her story about the girl with the umbrella, the teacher's concerns, and my hands tighten around my mug.

"No. I just like watching people." Now it's her turn to blush and focus on her food.

I relax. "Right. Because you're an artist."

She jerks her head up and I know I've said something wrong, but I'm not sure what. "I'll never be a real artist, go to school for it or anything." Her tone turns wistful, and I wonder if she even realizes she's lying to herself.

"So what are you going to school to study?" I add more cream to my coffee, and finally have it exactly where I like it.

She glances down at the sugar bowl like she's staring into a crystal ball or something. "Probably accounting. Or actuarial science."

"Wow. Talk about intense. You must have mad math skills. Are you going to Wharton or one of those high-powered business schools?"

She shakes her head. "Actually, I hate math. But it doesn't matter because I'll never leave home. I can get the basics here at Cambria College, learn the rest on the job."

"You already have a job?"

"Don't sound so impressed. It's the family business. Cleary and Sons, Insurance and Financial Advisors. Our original office is here in Cambria City, but now we have branches in Philly, New York, and also London and Paris."

I lean back in my seat. How did I not know this? My research was so focused on what happened fifteen years ago, I never bothered to check into the family business, just assumed it had died when her parents did. Dr. Winston would say that was sloppy reporting, not learning how the past impacts the present. My dad would simply call it down-right lazy.

"I don't understand. Why does having a family business with offices all over the world mean you can't leave Cambria City? Don't you want to see New York, London, Paris?"

"Don't forget Philadelphia." She's trying to make a joke of it, but fails. Her expression is so sorrowful, it's all I can do to keep from reaching out to her. She's a subject. I can't get involved—at least not more than I already am.

"Right. You can't miss out on those cheesesteaks. It'd be a crime." I choose my last word carefully, hoping to edge into what I came here for.

"It's only a few hours away, so I'm sure I can find time in my busy schedule for Philly." She offers this as if her compromise just brokered world peace.

I lean forward, unable to resist the pull of her longing. "It's because of your grandmother?"

"Not just her. My uncle Joe too. They need me here. I have to stay, take care of them. I can't abandon them. They're all I have left." She looks past me, out the window, but it's not the gorgeous autumn afternoon she's seeing, I'm certain. For a moment, I wonder if she's thinking of the same thing I am—the fire.

A shudder runs through her body and I'm certain she is. I can't help it; I lay my hand on hers and squeeze it gently, pull her back to me.

"You're not what I expected," I tell her.

Her attention abruptly shifts to the approaching wait-ress, and I remove my hand, disappointed. I think back to the receptionist at the nat. Did Ella see me like she had? An outsider, an intruder?

As usual, I've come on too intense. I need to slow down, give her space. Professor Winston says the key to a good interview is to earn the subject's trust. Once upon a time, I was the only person Nora trusted, but this isn't Nora, this is Ella. I need to start all over with her.

Ella makes a small sound of sympathy, her focus still on the waitress. "She's just been fired," she whispers in a low voice I barely hear.

As far as I can tell, the waitress has the same surly expres-sion she had when she originally greeted us. She slaps the check on the table between us. "Have a nice day."

And then she's gone. But Ella is still watching her, her

forehead wrinkled in concern. "Poor thing. It's not her fault." She glances at the check and cringes. "You might want to double-check the math. She's dyslexic." She shifts in her seat, pulling back from the piece of paper between us as if it's making her physically ill.

I slap my saucer over it, hiding the check, and Ella visibly relaxes. "You must come here often to know all that."

She gives a little shake of her head, staring at the waitress who's now behind the counter arguing with a man who must be her boss. "No. I can just see it. In her voice, in everything she touches, in the air around her. He was yelling at her earlier—back in that glass-walled office, before she brought the check. And then when she was adding it up . . ." Finally, she tears her gaze away from the drama behind the counter and glances at me. "It's hard to explain."

I think about that as I slide the check from beneath the saucer, pull it into my lap to shield her from the sight of it, and use my phone to check the math. "She listed your tea as $9.25 when it should be $2.95. But the total is right." I raise my eyes up from the check, looking at her over the rims of my glasses. She appears suddenly soft and fuzzy as if not from this world, the not-quite-setting sun casting her in a warm glow. "How did you know?"

"It's something that runs in my family." She's moved to the edge of the booth, and seems eager to leave.

I pay the check, tip the waitress twice what I should—

least I can do if she just lost her job—and slide out of the booth. I offer Ella my hand and she takes it without hesitation. As I help her to her feet and on with her coat, I realize I was a jerk for thinking she was worried what people thought, seeing us together. I have a feeling Ella sees way past skin color.

But I'm also a jerk, because now I think there's more to her story than I'd originally thought. Dr. Winston loves any "color" that adds to a story and I suspect I've just hit pay dirt. The thought excites me—just a little—but mainly what I feel is relief as the dread of telling her the truth is lifted. If I can avoid that, even for a little while, it's worth it.

"Let's take a walk and you can tell me all about it."

CHAPTER 6

Ella

It's moments like this that challenge me every single day, each new person a cliff begging for a leap of faith.

Nearly always, I shy away. Maybe because of some tainted shadow in their aura. Most likely, it's that I've finally learned my lesson after tumbling off that cliff far too many times, more times than Wile E. Coyote chasing his roadrunner. Roadrunners can fly, coyotes can't. And neither can girls, not even when clutching an umbrella with both hands—they can sink, they can swim, they can fall . . . but they cannot soar free.

Alec is patient, waiting until we're outside, squinting as our eyes adjust to the late-afternoon sun hanging just above the treetops. "You watch people—but it's more than reading body language, right?"

I nod. "I see their stories."

He blinks. Slowly. Deciding whether to run or pause long enough to call 9-1-1.

"I'm not crazy," I insist, knowing all too well that people who need to resort to declaring their lack of insanity are the ones most likely to be wrong.

"Didn't say you were. Tell me more. About these . . . stories. What triggers them? Do you hear words with them?"

I quicken my pace, ready to bolt if he's mocking me. "I don't hear voices. At least not ones that aren't already there. They aren't that kind of story. Not like 'Once upon a time . . .' or anything like that." I pause. "More like pictures. When I see or hear words, they turn into light and colors."

He half turns away from me, scanning the sidewalk. Seeking out his escape route, I'm sure. I'm thinking I'll never see him again, not after the way I've flubbed this—and he never even got a chance to tell me about the project he needs help with.

But then he turns back and his eyes lock with mine, less aquamarine now, more azure. Set against his dark skin—I'm still trying to decide the right shade of brown to describe it—they almost glow. A stray gust of wind blows against us. I shiver and he angles his body to shield me from it in a move filled with old-fashioned gallantry that is too charming for words. But what I like even better is that he did it without thought—to him, it wasn't a gesture guided by chivalry but simply his nature.

He sighs a little, like he's trying to shake off the intensity of our conversation. When he finally turns to look at me, he's trying to smile. "So, tell me more about your—"

"The medical word for it is synesthesia. My gram calls it our family gift." Curse is more like it, but I don't tell him that.

"Does she have the same thing as you?"

"No. She feels things whenever she hears sounds or voices."

"Feels things?"

How to explain? "For Gram Helen, some sounds are like a dentist drilling or worse. Others are like a warm bubble bath, soothing. Some are so bad, she collapses, can't even get out of bed for a day or two."

He pauses and I think I've lost him for good. But then he nods slowly. "No wonder she can't leave the house. You're like her lifeline to the outside world."

I've never thought of it quite that way, but he's right. Not that Gram Helen doesn't do a lot for me. We're kind of partners, I guess. Darrin helps when he can, but he's busy with Cleary and Sons, always traveling. And Uncle Joe—in some ways, he's worse off than Gram, stays mostly up at the house on the lake, alone. It can be weeks between visits.

Alec continues, "And you see colors when checks are wrong?" He frowns, shakes his head. "No. When someone is lying or upset?"

"I see colors all the time—" I can tell he doesn't understand. But his earnest expression says he's trying. "The waitress. Her colors from when we first walked in were pulsing with anxiety. Then the manager was radiating anger—in him it was an ugly shade of neon green. Like he enjoyed making her feel bad."

"But you couldn't hear what he was saying."

"No, but I heard the tone of his voice. Didn't you? Before he shut the door to the office?"

He appears to think about that. "Yeah. I blocked it out—"

"That's what most people do. But once I hear someone's voice, I can't help it. I see everything they're feeling in their auras."

"Auras? Not like a psychic?" He sounds doubtful, and I don't blame him.

"No. It's just my name for the colors and pictures I see."

He slowly nods his head, though I can tell he doesn't really understand.

"That's okay," I tell him. "I've been living with this all my life and I don't really understand it, either."

"I want to." He sounds wistful. "You make the world sound magical."

"It is. People are so busy rushing around, faces buried in their phones or looking to the next thing on their to-do list that they don't take the time to see—really see what's all around them. The world is filled with magic. You just have to look and listen."

"So my aura." He stumbles a bit over the word. "It must not be too ugly—I mean, for you to hang out with a total stranger and share all this with them."

I can only smile and shake my head. How can I explain to him that he has no aura when I've only just convinced him that they exist? We reach the parking lot behind the natatorium where my car's parked. His too, I'm guessing. "I'm sorry. I started talking about me and we never had the chance to talk about your project, this true-crime story. I'm assuming you need some design formatting? Maybe a map or graph?"

Suddenly, I feel off-balance, like the first time I went skating, my ankles wobbly and the ice slick with surprises. Because I can't believe that I'm about to invite an almost total stranger to go out with me. Even if it is just for a school project.

My own aura betrays me, blossoming with magenta hope and gushing over with non-academic feelings. But Alec is so different from anyone I've met before. He's obviously smart, but also able to listen without judging, and he's so easy to talk to. I've never told anyone so much about myself—and never, ever about my synesthesia—on a first meeting. Something about Alec makes me trust him. As if, somehow deep inside, I know he'll never let me down. I'm not sure I can trust that feeling, not without seeing his aura, but somehow I find the courage to try. "Maybe we could talk some more? Tomorrow?"

His body twists away from me so I barely catch the dip of his chin as his shoulders hunch almost to his ears. A sigh empties his chest and his shoulders sag back down. And my own hope withers, turning to ashes. How could I be so naïve as to think he might be interested in me?

"Ella." His mouth twists the syllables of my name as if they're foreign, uncomfortable to shape. "I'm sorry for the confusion. I don't need any graphic design help." He turns back to face me, his gaze as heavy as a sodden wool blanket. His eyes have gone gray, the color of a winter lake before the ice forms. "I wanted to interview you about your parents. About how they died. Specifically about your mother's murder."

CHAPTER 7

Ella

I skid to a stop so fast, my backpack falls from my shoulder. Alec reaches for it, for me, but I back away, dragging it along the pavement. Suddenly, I want to run to my car and get far, far away from here.

"What did you say?" I haul the bag up, pressing it against my chest like a shield.

He opens his mouth to answer but I hold my hand up to stop him. I'm shaking my head, taking baby steps backward, putting distance between me and Alec's words.

"No. You're wrong." Each syllable leaks black ink, slithering through the air around me. "My parents died in an accident." Last thing I want is to explain the fire. *Accident* is vague, a much safer word.

He's watching me. Behind him, the November sky is the strange gold-violet that lies in limbo between sunset and complete nightfall. It's the closest thing to an aura I've seen around Alec, clinging to him like a shroud.

"Accident?" His voice echoes my own confusion. "Mia Cleary, she was your mother, right?"

"Don't you say her name," I snap. Electricity crackles through my body, a weird sensation of wanting to touch a live wire, if only to push it away and make the world safe again.

Run! Now, before it's too late, my brain screams. At first my body doesn't obey. My eyes are locked on his, across the blacktop separating us, our lungs exhaling ghostly mists as the air grows chill.

"But . . . she was your mother." He hasn't taken a step closer, yet his voice feels as if it's right in my ear. Intimate. Seductive. The temptation of wanting, needing to know . . . the temptation that he might be speaking the truth. Ridiculous; I know how my own mother died.

"You have the wrong girl." The words break the spell and I spin away, heading toward my Subaru.

The cheerful little red Impreza, battered and bruised but never beaten by its eleven years of Pennsylvania potholes, is my escape from this madness. I lurch toward it, fumbling in my pocket for my key, to get the door open. As I twist to toss my bag behind the front seat, I keep my eyes on Alec. Keep the threat in sight. He hasn't moved. Still stands in the exact same spot. Still watches me with that look of concern. Still with a silent, invisible aura, unreadable, unknowable.

"Just stay away from me." I slam the door on him, my fingers jabbing the key in the ignition, and screech toward the exit, leaving him alone in the gathering dark.

A stop sign blares up, a flash of neon red. I slam my brakes, the Subaru skidding to a halt. I'm jolted forward, my body tense with anger and sorrow and confusion. Flames swirl around me: blazing red, raging orange, searing yellow. Finally, I give in to them and collapse, my body quaking and my arms hugging the steering wheel, wishing they held someone real. Alec is wrong. A fire at an old beach cottage, a faulty heating system, a random spark—there's no murder in that.

Why would he think my mother was killed? And murder? Impossible. Insane. The very way he'd phrased the question shows how very wrong he is.

A different Mia Cleary, that must be it. Somewhere out there is another woman with another tragic story that anchors her life, spinning out an iron chain binding past to present. No other possible answer.

But he called me Nora . . . The whisper slithers through my mind. No one calls me Nora. Not since my parents died.

"No." The word startles me, echoing through the dark and empty car. "He's wrong."

Then why did his words hurt so badly? Wounding some part of me I didn't even know existed. Is it simply because he chose this day of all days to find me?

Even though I can't remember my parents and have pretty much gotten used to the idea of their not being around, I still think of them all the time. But that doesn't mean every time I remember them I curl up in a quivering mass of tears. My life is happy, filled with love and fun and joy.

When I think of my parents, it's not because I miss them—how can I miss what I never knew? Rather, I wonder what life would have been like if they had been here with me. When I was little, I used to imagine them hovering over me, watching and smiling like angels or ghosts. Then I got older and realized that instead of wondering what could have been, life was more about enjoying what I had. And what I had, what I *have*, is pretty fantastic, despite all of life's quirks. A home that shelters me from every storm, a family who loves and needs me.

So why am I now hyperventilating in my car? All because of a boy who's wrong, wrong, wrong . . .

A hesitant tap on the opposite window jerks me out of my sob fest. I look away, swipe my face with the back of one hand, sniff and swallow, then glance to the passenger side where Alec is leaning forward, his face pressed against the glass.

"Are you all right?" He cups his hands to see inside, then vanishes. The night envelops us the way winter nights can, falling so hard and fast you can almost pinpoint the precise moment the day surrenders. "I'm sorry. I didn't mean to—I thought you knew."

I fumble for the headlights. By the time I turn them on, he's now at my side of the car. The lights reflect from his glasses, hiding his eyes.

No aura to read, I can't see his face clearly in the dark; how can I trust anything he says?

CHAPTER 8

Ella

Alec taps on the glass. "Please, roll down the window. I just want to make sure you're okay."

His voice is kind, gentle—it almost makes up for his having no aura. I want to tell him to go away, that I'm fine, that I don't need him, I don't need anyone . . . but somehow I find my finger stabbing the button to lower the window. The temperature has dropped but it's not too cold, not for November. Still, I'm shivering.

"Who are you?" I ask. "Why do you think you know anything about my mother or how she died? Is this some kind of sick joke?"

Cold, so very cold that I can't feel my hands, my lips tingle, my breath comes short and fast. I'm a marionette whose strings have been cut, strangely disjointed from my body as it slumps in the seat. Not limp—lifeless. Cold and numb and far, far away from where I really am . . . imagining, like I always do on this day, worrying at what I'll never know . . . What if I'd been there? Would anything be different? Would they still be alive?

Or would I have died with them?

I had just turned three that day, so I would have been walking—no, running—excited by my first trip to the beach, first view of the ocean. Sand beneath my bare feet, though cold, because it would have been night by the time we arrived and it was November. Walking, walking, walking, the fog so thick it curled around me like a cat taking a nap, soft as fur and warm as well, but it didn't purr. Instead there was another sound, a soft rush of water lapping at my feet . . .

"Nora?" Alec's voice brings me back to the present and I almost automatically tell him to call me Ella. The wind gusts through the open window—that must have been the rushing noise I imagined—not water, of course not. "Should I call someone? I'm sorry, I never meant to—I thought you knew."

"Knew what?" My voice is a ghost of its normal self, barely makes it through the window to reach him on the other side. "I know what happened to my parents." That's better, a little life returning, like thawing out after walking in the sleet or rain. "You're the one who doesn't know anything."

"Right. Of course. I must have gotten my facts wrong." I don't need to see his aura to know he doesn't believe a word—he's that transparent. "I never should have—I do that sometimes, I'm sorry. I just get so caught up in things, I forget to think about the people . . ."

"Why would you even say that to me? You don't know me, don't know my family." My words whip through the space between us, crackling and snapping, sparks flying free. "Is that why you came to find me today? Not for a project, but to . . . to tell me some insane, horrible theory about my mother and how she died?"

"It really is for school. Professor Winston. He's the whole reason I came here for college, to study under him. He won two Pulitzers for his investigative reporting when he worked for the *Baltimore Sun*." He continues, "I'm so very, very sorry. Rule number one of good journalism is to check your sources. I really thought I was right." He thinks for a second. "June twenty-first—that's your mother's birthday, right?"

I jolt upright in my seat. "How did you know that?"

"It was in the file—" This time he stops himself, but the damage's already done. "Never mind. In fact, let's forget all this ever happened. I mean this conversation—don't forget about having coffee, that was kind of nice."

It was, but any niceness has been ruined by this conversation. I reach for the gearshift but my fingers are still frozen. I calm my breathing, slow it down, then realize I'm in no shape to drive.

"Could you drive me home?" I hate asking, it makes me feel weak—and I'm still not sure I entirely trust him. Except . . . something inside me already does. As if I've known him much longer than a single day. It's weird and I can't explain it—wish I could—but I don't want to leave him.

He nods and holds the door open for me as I climb out of the driver's seat. He walks me over to the passenger side. My knees are wobbly, and I try to cover it by wrenching the door open myself before he can reach for it. Then I sink into the seat, gravity too great a force for me to fight.

"Go left. Larchmont Street. Third house on the right, across from the park." I huddle in my seat as he drives. He's smart enough not to try to talk to me—the way my emotions are swirling around the car, filling it to the brim, if he added any more, we'd surely drown.

He rocks his head against the headrest. I glance over and realize his knees are jutting up, braced against the wheel; he forgot to slide the seat back before he started driving. He slouches forward then back again, trying to get comfortable. Watching his contortions, I almost feel sorry for him.

"It's that one," I say dully, pointing to my house.

He pulls up in front of the small house my gram and I share. It's technically called a bungalow, but I think it looks like one of those cute cottages you'd see at the beach. Or at least what I imagine a beach cottage would look like.

"Nora—"

"My name is Ella." This time, I do correct him. "And you're wrong about my mother, okay? You're just wrong. So thanks for the coffee and everything, but I have to go." I wrap my fingers around the door handle.

Alec turns to me, threatening to twist his spine into a permanent corkscrew. "Could we start over? Please? I didn't mean to—I must have gotten the facts mixed up somehow."

I'm torn. I like him. At least the him I met before he got all weird, talking about mothers being murdered. What he said, the things he knew that he couldn't know, calling me Nora, plus the other things he said that I know can't be true . . . It makes me feel queasy, that sick feeling you get when you're too close to the edge of a cliff and you can't help but look down, and some small part of you wants to jump, just to see what flying feels like.

Before I can say anything, the front porch light blazes on and Gram Helen appears, running down the steps wearing a conical birthday hat, ribbons streaming behind her, and carrying a rhinestone tiara in her hand.

"It's your birthday?" Alec says, slumping back in his seat, surrendering. "I must have the absolute worse timing in the whole wide world."

Gram Helen spies him, races to the driver's door, and yanks it open. "You're home! And you brought a friend!"

Her words swirl through the air, a musty shade of bile green. I know she's pretending to be happy, but isn't—the stress of social gatherings even with family and friends she's comfortable with will do that to her, much less introducing a total stranger to the mix.

"I'm sorry," I start to say, but Alec interrupts. "I'm Alec Ravenell," he says as he climbs free of the car and takes Gram's hand. "It's so nice to meet you, Mrs. Cleary."

It's actually Mrs. Crveno, since Helen is my mother's mother. Mom's side of the family is Croatian, originally from Sarajevo before they escaped during the war. Neither of us corrects Alec, but that's when I realize his mistake: he's looking for a murder victim named Mia Cleary. Because of her work, my mom used her maiden name—the only time I've seen her listed as Mia Cleary instead of Mia Crveno was in her obituary. Alec is looking for another woman altogether.

But with my mom's birthday? Then I realize we've both made a mistake. Names and birthdays—two of the most easily stolen pieces of identification. So if someone with my mother's name and birthday was murdered, it means some other woman was pretending to be my mother, stole her identity.

Finally, I can breathe again. Of course; dead people are

the most frequently targeted victims of identity theft. And things were laxer back when my parents died. That has to be the answer.

As I'm relishing my epiphany, Helen stops, considers Alec's words, and relaxes the tiniest bit, a hint of lavender overlapping her anxious green.

"Nice to meet you, young man. You have the sweetest voice." She ducks her head inside the Impreza where I'm still working to unlatch my seat belt. "Ella, dear, your friend's voice is all warm and toasty like melted caramel." She turns back to Alec, interlocking her arm with his. "Come into the house and join us, Alec Ravenell."

He glances back over his shoulder at me. "I'm not sure—"

I rush to rescue him from Helen.

"I insist," she says, looking at me, not him, as she holds the tiara aloft.

Ducking my head, I allow her to place the sparkly birthday tiara in my hair. Somehow Helen always gets exactly what she wants, whether it's an embarrassing birthday tradition I long ago outgrew or inviting a total stranger into our sanctum simply because she likes his voice. "We'll be right there," I tell her. "I just need to talk to Alec for another quick second."

"Okay, but don't dawdle. Everyone's waiting." She goes back up the steps to the porch. I see Rory and Max watching us through the bay window, Rory grinning so wide her braces glint in the porch light, giving her a silvery shimmer, and Max with a forced half smile that reveals a touch of both concern and distrust as he stares at Alec.

I grab Alec's arm. "I don't need to come in," he says before I can open my mouth. "I can walk back to campus. Maybe we can talk more later? I'm really sorry about all this . . . mess."

"No. You'll disappoint Gram Helen if you don't stay now. But you have to promise not to talk about any of this, not here in front of my family. Not until we can figure out how your murder victim's and my mom's . . . identities got mixed up." My mind's whirling with conspiracy theories centered on Russian hackers. "Not a word tonight. Deal?"

He nods, seems relieved—as if my suggestion of identity theft has removed a weight from his shoulders. Using both his hands, he straightens my tiara, his eyes creasing as his smile finally returns. "Deal."

CHAPTER 9

Ella

Because Gram Helen has so much trouble going out into the world, the world has always come to us, right here in our little jewel box of a house. It might be just the two of us, but our house is bright and joyous, a safe haven.

Helen's sound sensitivity means she only tolerates "good" sounds—wind chimes and birdcalls and bangle bracelets and laughter. My friends are welcome, as long as their voices don't trigger her spells. Certain voices, music, or other sounds release a barrage of pain—she says it's like Fourth of July fireworks exploding inside her head—that will send her to her knees. Thanks to noise-cancelling headphones and her soundproof studio we've built in the basement, things aren't as bad as they were when I was little. Sometimes she'll even risk leaving the house for a walk around the block. It's a rare treat, the sight of her in her tie-dyed caftans, bobbing along to the "good" music streaming from her headphones as her copper curls escape their grip, oblivious to the sounds around her, arms outstretched, palms up, embracing the sunlight.

Now, as I lead Alec up the steps to my house, I'm nervous. He's already met Helen, got her seal of approval. Rory and Max basically know him from earlier. Although Rory will still flirt—she could have any boy in school if she'd only decide which one she wants. More than looks, it's the way—despite still having braces—she never hides her smile, and holds her chin up when she walks, and remembers everyone's name and the name of their dog and cat and little sister and what their parents do for a living. The whole world feels warmer when you're with Rory. Within two minutes she'll know everything worth knowing about Alec.

What little she doesn't discover as she wins him over—resistance is futile when it comes to Rory—Max will ferret out. He's one of those guys who's quiet, always watching, always listening, but not in a creepy way; more like because he's interested in what you have to say. He's not very big for a guy his age, which means he's no threat, but he's also no pushover. Solid. That's my word for Max.

No, Rory and Max won't be a problem. Neither will Darrin—who's not only the silent partner in Cleary and Sons, he's my godfather. More like my guardian angel. Anytime I've needed anything, from money for art classes to learning how to drive, Darrin's been there, taking care of me. He was best man at my parents' wedding and takes his godparenting duties extremely seriously.

Alec and I reach the front door. Before I can open it, it's yanked open for me. A tall, lean man with the same copper-bright hair as Helen blocks our path. Uncle Joe. He's all elbows and knees, his head perched on a skinny neck, his chin so sharp that when I was little, I'd run before I'd let him hug me for fear I'd get poked by it. As awkward as he looks, Joe's personality is even more prickly.

"Who's this, then?" he asks. Before either of us can answer, he holds a hand up to Alec, palm out in the universal gesture for stop. "Don't say a word. Ella, you talk. Does he know the rules? What does he want? It's your birthday. Friends and family only."

Again, not waiting for me to even take a breath, he twists his arms around me in a hug and kisses me on the forehead before releasing me. "Happy birthday, sweet girl." The words flash in shiny pink ribbons that twist and flow into the shape of a heart.

That's Joe. My mother's little brother. He was only ten when they all fled during the Siege of Sarajevo back in the 90s, after my grandfather was murdered by a Serbian sniper. Despite Joe's appearance and sharp-edged manners, he's a good man with a good heart. If you can stand to be in the same room long enough to get to know him.

I haul in a breath, very much aware of Alec's eyes on me. But his expression is calm, his feet are pointed toward the house and not the road, and his lips are fighting a smile that seems genuine. Hard to tell without seeing his aura, but I take a chance. After all, we've come this far.

"Alec, meet my uncle Joe. No, I haven't had a chance to explain the rules to him. But if you give us just a moment, I'll take care of everything, don't worry."

Joe's frown contorts his face. He glares at Alec, who takes it like a man, not even shifting his weight. Then Joe jerks his chin in a nod. "Friends and family, young man. Not many are invited to join that select group." He steps back from the door and starts to turn away, but then stops to look back over his shoulder—with his bony build and long neck, I see a six-foot pink flamingo twisted tighter than a corkscrew. "Even fewer are asked back a second time."

Thankfully, Rory arrives to rescue us. She beams at Alec, winks at me, tosses her blonde curls at Joe and takes his arm. "Got some new ones for you," she tells him, leading Joe away from us so we finally have space to step inside the door. "Melliferous."

Joe raises his nose as if sniffing. "Cotton candy still warm and wispy."

"Nice. How about raconteur?"

They round the corner into the dining room, leaving Alec and me in the foyer. It's a small, cozy space with light oak floors and wainscoting below pale peachy-cream walls—a color called "moonrise" that I simply could not resist based on its name alone—with a staircase leading up to one side, the archway to the dining room tucked behind it, and on the other side, another arch leading to the living room. The living room used to be two rooms, a front parlor and a rear family room that opens up into the kitchen, but Helen had the wall between them taken down, creating the warm, inviting space where we actually do most of our living.

"Can I take your coat?" I remember my manners, holding out my hands for Alec's jacket.

"Depends. Am I staying?" He's shrugging free of the coat as he asks, so I know his answer. "Tell me about these rules."

I turn to hang up his jacket on the ancient walnut coat stand—which has actual antique hats perched on the highest hooks as well as unique colorful umbrellas and parasols bristling from the ring at its foot, gifts from Darrin whenever he travels. He gets to go all over the world, places where, even if I join the insurance business like everyone wants, I know I'll never go. Too far from home. From family.

Before I can turn back, I feel Alec's hands on my shoulders, taking my parka. He's tall enough that he nudges a silk top hat askew as he hangs it up.

Then we're facing each other, so close I can see the curve of his eyelashes magnified by his glasses.

"The rules?" he asks again.

I tear my attention away and straighten my posture. "Right. You already passed the first hurdle—Gram Helen likes your voice."

"She says I'm warm and toasty." I have to fight not to mirror his grin. It's as if that awful conversation in the parking lot never happened. "I kind of like that. How old is your Gram?"

"Way too old for you. Anyway, that's the first rule, no sounds that hurt Helen." This is where it might get tough. "Would you mind turning your phone off? The ringers and even the vibrate mode all make her sick."

He slides his phone from his pocket and turns it off without protest. "Done. Next rule?"

"A bit trickier. Helen is sensitive to sounds, but Joe … with him, it's words."

"Spoken or written?" He leans forward, genuinely interested.

"Both. They trigger tastes." Alec grimaces and I realize that he gets it—you can shut out a noise, but how can you turn off a taste, especially a nasty one? "Good news is there are only a few you need to avoid that might come up tonight. Sugar. Napkin. You can say TV, but not television. Best to simply avoid mentioning politics at all. Or the Beatles—the musicians, not the bugs or cars. I know they seem the same, but—"

His gaze drifts away from mine. Have I lost him? But then from behind me, a man clears his throat. "This must be Alec."

I turn to smile at Darrin, who is holding out a hand to Alec. As always, he's dressed in a crisp off-white shirt and well-cut suit that's a shade between navy and indigo, almost exactly matching his aura. Confidence radiates from him, and I instantly feel calmer.

Most families divide child-raising duties between two parents. After my parents died, I was lucky enough to have three watching over me. Gram Helen, she's our spinner of tales and provider of comfort. Even though she's totally Americanized now, not even a hint of an accent except when she swears, she still makes a few traditional delicacies. Baklava that makes my mouth water as soon as I see her gathering the ingredients and *tufahije*, an apple cake that wraps the entire house in shimmering golden love.

Uncle Joe, despite his quirks, is the one to seek out if you want fun and adventures—he taught me how to walk silently in the woods and cook a s'more and cast a fishing line properly. He even helped me win a science fair when I was twelve—we relocated a colony of bats from the attic of the lake house to a bat house we built beside the dock. It took us weeks of research and preparation so we didn't disturb the babies who couldn't fly yet and were still dependent on their mothers.

But if you want something done and done right, if you want advice you can count on, if you want the warm, solid feeling that things will never change and everything is going to work out just fine, then you need a godfather like Darrin.

Darrin leads Alec through to the living room, pausing to show him Helen's awards for her audiobooks and signed photos of the famous authors she works with, all the while chatting about the architecture and something about the Steelers, easing Alec into our world slowly, letting him catch his breath.

I follow behind, watching Alec's reactions. I love our house, the way it feels and smells and sounds, the way it's filled with life. From the fresh flowers growing near every window to the comfy-worn overstuffed chintz couch and loveseat to the fireplace that takes up almost an entire wall back near the kitchen. And then there's the artwork—Joe calls it the "Gallery of Ella," and it includes pieces from when I was a little girl, which he and Helen will no doubt insist on showing Alec, leaving me dissolved into a puddle of embarrassment. After my parents died, Helen left her own home and moved here with me, so this house reflects her more than anything: a feeling of luxury and comfort without fussiness, a safe haven from the entire ugly world.

I'm nervous of how we appear to an outsider like Alec. I find myself holding my breath, waiting for his judgment—silly, I know, because usually I really don't care what anyone else thinks of me. After all, they can't see me—not the *real* me—not like I can see them.

Darrin and Alec turn the corner into what used to be the old family room, where the walls are exposed brick. They take a step, but then Alec stops and glances back at the painting nestled into an alcove tucked beside the fireplace. It's the umbrella painting I told him about earlier. The expression on his face morphs from polite attention to wonder.

"Ella," he whispers in awe. Then he turns to me, the weight of his stare forcing a blush from me. "You painted this? When you were how old?"

"Eleven," I mumble. The piece is okay for a kid—I'm actually quite proud of it, not because of the technique but because of the way I was able to capture both movement and stillness simultaneously. I love it when I can create that kind of visual tension.

"Dinner," Max calls to us, poking his head out from the kitchen where he's been helping Helen. He's the only one who hasn't come forward to greet Alec, but Helen can be a full-time job, especially with the sudden addition of a stranger. At least I hope that's all it is.

Alec walks past Max, disappearing into the kitchen, while Max waits for me.

"We need to talk," he whispers. His usual brick-colored

aura is brittle with sick yellow chiseling into the edges. "I did some more digging. There's something you need to know about your new friend. Starting with the fact that he's a liar."

CHAPTER 10

Alec

I follow the others into the dining room. Max gives me a strange look as I pass—I can't tell if he's angry or jealous or what. If he didn't want me hanging out with Nora— Ella—then why did he send me to her in the first place?

The table could hold eight but is set for seven. Darrin shows me to a seat at the end of one of the long sides, placing Ella's uncle Joe on one side of me while Darrin takes the seat at the head of the table on my other side, effectively pinning me in as far from Ella as possible. Across from me are Rory, Max, and Ella, with Helen swooping in with the final dish and taking the seat at the other head of the table.

I'm swamped by a sudden homesickness. This is the first family dinner I've been at since I left home three months ago, and it isn't my family. Out of habit, I raise my hands and place them palms up beside my place setting, but then quickly pull them back when I realize they aren't going to hold hands to say grace—they aren't giving thanks at all, just eating. It's a whirl of platters and bowls moving one way or the other, all of Ella's favorite foods, Darrin tells me as he hands me a plate of sweet potatoes. I take a small helping—no way can they ever match my mom's, but they do smell good, so I take some more along with a slice of spinach pie that Helen tells me is called *zeljanica*.

Despite Joe's problem with words and Helen's sound sensitivity, the conversation never slows. Most of it about the family business, which Darrin mainly answers, and questions about Ella's plans for college, which she deflects with the help of Max and Rory. The three make for a world-class dodgeball team.

The spotlight inevitably lands on me. The first barrage is launched by Darrin. "Alec, tell us about yourself. Where are you from?"

I swallow my bite of sweet potato and meet Darrin's eyes. "South Carolina." Then I turn to Helen. "Don't tell my mom, but these sweet potatoes are just as good as hers, Mrs. Cleary. Wait, I'm sorry. I know you're Ella's maternal grandmother, but—"

She smiles indulgently, already understanding my dilemma. "It's pronounced ser-vano. It means red in Croatian." She pats her thick auburn curls.

I try it out. "Mrs. Crveno." It's not quite right, but close enough that she nods. "I just know Mom would love the recipe for your sweet potatoes if y'all don't mind sharing."

"Call me Helen, please. It's nothing special—I grate fresh ginger on top, slow roast them, then put them under the broiler at the last minute so they're almost caramelized."

Darrin isn't deflected so easily. "Where in South Carolina? What brings you all the way here to Cambria City?"

Rory jumps in. "Alec's studying journalism at the college. He's a junior. And Ella's going to help him with one of his projects."

All three adults swivel to stare at me. My cheeks warm under the combined weight of their disapproval. I get it. From their point of view, I'm an interloper. If Ella had been my dad's daughter, he'd be conspicuously cleaning his guns at the table if a strange man intruded uninvited on such an intimate family gathering.

"Only technically a junior," I explain, trying to alleviate some of their worries. "I just turned nineteen last month. Our high school was so small we couldn't afford any advanced placement classes, so they made a deal with a local college. I spent my last two years of high school attending college classes and graduated with my associate's degree, then transferred my credits here."

Darrin leans back in his chair, assessing my story, while Helen beams and nods at me, and Joe reaches across the table for more spinach pie. "Guess that makes you some kind of genius," he says. "Why Cambria City for college? Why not one of the big schools down south?"

I steel myself against the lie. The best lies always begin in the truth, so I answer, "If I'd known how cold it was here, I might have. But one of my heroes, Dr. Winston, is on the faculty. I couldn't pass up the chance to study with him."

Max interrupts the joke he's telling Helen to turn to me. "So this project Ella will be working on is for Dr. Winston? That must be nice."

Somehow Max doesn't make it sound nice at all. Again, I try to figure out what his deal is.

"He did those stories on police corruption in Baltimore, right?" Nora—no, Ella, I need to remember to call her Ella—asks, trying to help out as the staring contest between Max and me grows uncomfortable.

"Won two Pulitzers. And he uncovered one of the largest cases of health insurance fraud in the country. Medical identity theft, fake procedures, even people receiving sugar water when they were being billed for chemotherapy. The FBI's still prosecuting."

"That's what you want to do?" Ella says, and suddenly it feels as if only the two of us are in the room.

I nod. "I think nowadays, given the world we live in, we never know who to believe. That makes the truth more important than ever."

Her smile banishes any doubts I had about leaving home and coming here. At least for the moment.

"And your family?" Darrin is still in inquisition mode. "What do they do?"

"My dad's a detective for the sheriff's department and my mom runs our family businesses. Shrimping, fishing tours, rental houses. Pretty much anything a tourist would want."

He stares at me for a long moment, then nods his approval. The conversation continues to swirl around me. Joe turns out to be a chatterbox, taking the spotlight with jokes, riddles, and funny stories that border on risqué, his copper hair blazing beneath the chandelier as he gestures broadly with his hands. The kind of man my dad would have tried to frown into silence while Mom would have said, "Hush, now," even as she laughed. Not that Dad isn't funny—there are times when he'll have everyone in tears with his stories—he's just always overprotective when women and children are around. Comes with the job.

What would Mom and Dad say if they knew what I've done to get here, and to this table tonight? Shame forces my gaze away from the others. I focus on my food, but have lost my appetite.

Darrin and Helen are mostly silent, exchanging serious glances as if they're holding a private, silent conversation. I have the feeling I'm the main topic of discussion.

Rory matches Joe in the chatterbox contest, filling any

silence left behind when he pauses to take a bite of food. Ella smiles and laughs and shakes her head at her uncle's antics, but whenever her gaze turns my way a shadow crosses her face—and her gaze seems to always fall my way, as if I'm a cosmic black hole stealing all her light and joy.

Could I have bungled this any worse? I thought I'd been so patient, so careful, waiting three long months before approaching her. How could I have been so stupid? Dad said to let it alone, told me to pick another college, to stay away, but I just couldn't. I was determined to get the answers to the questions that have haunted me all my life, even if my journey led me far from home into this land of wind and mountains.

I miss home. The pull of the tides, the excitement of seeing what's left behind in their wake, the ever-changing skies, the same stretch of beach and dunes that actually are never, ever the same. Here I'm more than a stranger, I'm an outsider—almost everywhere I go, I'm the only black guy; every class I take, I'm the youngest one there; as soon as I open my mouth, people stare at my accent.

I'd forsaken everything I love to find this girl. But now, sitting at her table, among her family and friends, watching her laugh and seeing the life she has, only now do I realize exactly how much my finding her will cost us both.

Her life will never be the same after tonight. And it's all my fault.

CHAPTER 11

Ella

I still have no idea what Max's problem with Alec is—
we got swept into the dining room before he could tell me why
Alec is a liar, and he obviously can't say anything with everyone
here at the dinner table—but it's pretty clear that if not for the
fact Max knows it would upset Gram Helen, he'd probably
challenge Alec to a duel right there above the *zeljanica*.

Thankfully, Rory intervenes. "Cake, cake," she chants,
clapping her hands. And the air of impending doom clears.

As if by magic, Joe and Darrin whisk away the plates
while Max and Helen disappear into the kitchen, streams
of happy birthday joy trailing behind them in bright shades
of pink and gold.

"Sure I don't need to grab the fire extinguisher?" I
ask Rory, who's grinning like a crazy person, practically
bouncing in her seat.

"Nope. And no presents until you eat your cake, either."

"Fire extinguisher?" Alec asks.

"Never substitute sparklers for birthday candles," I tell him.

"Well, not if you're lighting them beside a window with curtains," Rory puts in.

Before Alec can ask anything more, Darrin and Joe return and dramatically close the drapes and dim the lights. Then Helen arrives, humming a song from *Casablanca*—the French song that almost gets everyone fighting in Rick's cafe—followed by Max walking in from the kitchen, carefully balancing a large sheet cake with a chocolate miniature Eiffel Tower growing out of it. The icing has been lovingly sculpted to look just like the postcards of Paris Darrin sends whenever he goes. Around the base of the Tower is a circle of nineteen birthday candles: eighteen plus one to wish on. Now I know why they worked so hard to keep me out of the house all afternoon. It must have taken them hours to create this edible work of art.

"It's beautiful." I'm clapping and smiling and trying hard not to cry in front of Alec—and failing. The cake really is too lovely to even consider eating.

Helen finishes singing—we never do "Happy Birthday," not at my house, Helen hates that song—and everyone calls for me to blow out the candles.

I hold my hair back to keep it from falling into the icing

or the flames, and bend over the cake to get all the candles in one breath. What can I say? All that time underwater is put to good use; I always get my birthday wish. This year it's the same wish as every year, that everyone stay safe and healthy. Yeah, not a big fan of change. I'll take certain boredom over random chaos every time.

Everyone claps and we demolish the cake—banana chocolate chip, my favorite. As Joe and Helen clear the plates, Rory whips out a small parcel from below her chair. It's a box wrapped in Eiffel Tower gold foil paper, and I realize this birthday is going to have a theme. Sure enough, once Joe and Helen return and I open the gift, I see that it's a silk scarf with the label of a French designer. It's gorgeous— much too pretty for me to ever wear and risk staining with paint, but that's okay because I already know that Rory will end up borrowing it and forget to ever return it.

"It's beautiful," I tell her, rubbing the soft silk against my cheek. "I love it. Thank you."

"Here's mine." Max plops a bag from our favorite bookstore in front of me. I reach in and pull out a set of French language MP3s along with a French-English dictionary. Definitely better than last year's gift, a Howler personal alarm for my keychain, guaranteed to rupture any attacker's eardrums.

"You want me to learn French?" I have a feeling where this might be going. My aura dances like candlelight, excited but also colored by a touch of trepidation.

"Never know when you might need to order *pain au chocolat* or *café au lait*," he says with a fake French accent.

"Right," I say, not sure how to reply. I give him a quick sideways hug. "Thanks, Max."

"Wait, there's more," Helen says, clapping her hands as Joe beams and almost bounces out of his seat.

That's when I realize Alec is gone. Before I can say anything, he returns, shyly offering me a small, old-fashioned 35mm film canister.

"I didn't think I had a present, but then I remembered my mom just sent this."

"Alec, you didn't have to—"

"My mom would insist. Never show up at anyone's home without a gift, she always told me. Especially if you're an unexpected uninvited guest and it turns out to be their birthday." He thrusts the canister into my hand.

I shake it. It's not filled with film but instead feels like a saltshaker. I pop open the lid and spill a few grains into my hand. Not salt. Sand.

"I got homesick," he explains with a shrug. "That's from our beach."

"Thanks." I don't meet his eyes, too entranced by the myriad of colors dancing through the grains of sand, sparked by his words.

I feel the warmth of a mother's love, longing for a son far away, the magic of family picnics on the beach, of walking in the water scouring tidal pools for treasures . . . all conjured by his words. Alec might not have his own aura, but he can create them. A rare gift I'd only seen a few times before in certain artists, musicians, writers.

He mistakes my silence for disappointment. "Thought it might remind you of the ocean." His words are rushed, as if embarrassed by his gesture. I'm not. I'm truly touched by his gift. It's as if he's given me part of his heart.

Despite his mistake about my mom, I like him all the more for it. "I've never been to the ocean. Maybe you should keep it—it's from your home, after all."

"Mom can always send more." Then he does a double take. "You've never been to the ocean?"

"Ella's never been anywhere," Rory says with a laugh. "She's such a homebody."

"Hey," Max puts in. "Who needs to go to the ocean? We built our own beach up at the lake house."

"It's just a cabin," I explain. Alec looks even more puzzled. I wish I could read him better. "Up in the mountains. Near a lake." I trail off, no idea what to say.

Thankfully, Darrin chimes in, his Texas drawl more accentuated than usual. "Don't worry, son. I don't understand it either. These mountain folk think they can throw a few bags of sand down near a spit of water and call it a beach. They got no idea what they're missing out on."

"You've never seen the ocean?" Alec says again.

CJ Lyons

Then I realize. The woman who was killed, the one who stole my mom's identity—it must have happened near his home, maybe even on the beach. Another reason why he'd confused his Mia Cleary with my mom. He thought I'd been there when Mom died . . . which, of course I wasn't. How could I have been?

Yet, somehow, a rushing noise fills my head—more real than any movie soundtrack I might have heard and remembered. Waves crashing in the dark, fog swirling, my feet cold, wet sand and water surging around my toes. Not my memory . . . but then where had it come from?

Joe stands up so fast he almost overturns the table. "And now for the *pièce de résistance*," he says in a very Pennsylvanian, absolutely non-French French accent as he slides an envelope across to me.

My fingers shake as I unseal it and I'm not sure why. A travel brochure falls into my palm. I look up, stunned. Helen is clapping, Joe is beaming, and Darrin is sitting back in his chair looking like a CEO who just made the deal of a lifetime.

"It's five weeks in France," Helen explains.

"This summer," Joe adds.

"With private art classes and studio instruction," Darrin, ever practical, puts in.

Rory bounces with delight. "Paris! Think of it, Ella!"

Max is a bit more subdued. "We'll be here, toiling away

in the heat and humidity and you'll be in France, seeing the world."

I give a little shake of my head, quickly turn it into a nod and grin. "Wow. I'm—wow."

Overwhelmed is more like it. A trip to Paris? To paint? It's literally my dream come true.

And yet . . . I can't go, surely they all know that. How can they think I could leave? I never even made it to our sixth-grade class field trip to the science museum in Pittsburgh—was halfway out the door when Helen collapsed with one of her spells.

I can't do this—leave my home and my family—but how can I say no to such a thoughtful, wonderful, perfect present?

The cake that had been so yummy on the way down is now trying to scratch its way back up my throat like an animal escaping a cage. More than worry about leaving Helen and Joe, I'm overcome by this strange feeling of dread. A certain knowledge that if I leave the people I love behind, something awful will happen to them. My feet feel cold and wet, and the smell of salt water makes me dizzy. I clutch the edge of the table and try to fight my way back to my initial excitement and joy.

"Wow." I'm repeating myself. "Thanks, guys. I just can't believe it."

Alec catches my gaze, and I suspect he's the only one

who senses my turmoil. The others are all grinning, con-gratulating themselves on keeping the secret and really surprising me.

Suddenly, I'm choking on smoke and ash, flames billow-ing around me, reaching for me. In the distance, a woman's screams fill the air.

And I'm absolutely certain the woman shrieking in pain and terror is my mom.

CHAPTER 12

Alec

I can't keep from staring at Nora—Ella. *Ella.* How could she sit there and say she'd never seen the ocean? Why would she lie about something like that?

Except . . . she really does act as if she doesn't remember anything. It's difficult to fathom; something that forever changed my life, she's somehow erased from her memory. Maybe I should leave without telling her the truth?

The conversation continues without me. Ella definitely isn't as happy about her summer trip to Paris as she pretends to be. Another puzzle. I'd kill to go to France, to go anywhere. Imagine walking in Hemingway's footsteps, maybe following them all the way to Spain and beyond? I had the opportunity—both Clemson and UNC offered me scholarships and both have semester abroad programs—but instead I blew my one chance to leave my small, suffocating town by the ocean to come here, to another small, suffocating town swallowed up by mountains.

And everything is going horribly wrong.

Finally, the party breaks up. Rory offers to give me a ride back to the parking lot where I've left my bike—I've been saving to buy a car, but college expenses keep eating away at that money—with Max, of course, tagging along as chaperone. I make my good-byes, being sure to thank Helen for the gracious way she allowed a stranger to crash their party as well as for the first home-cooked meal I've had in months.

She puts her hands on her hips, looks me over like my own grandmother does, and gives her head a little shake. "Growing boy like you, you need more meat on your bones. You come back anytime, Alec Ravenell. I like the way you talk. Maybe you could come over, record a sample for me?"

I'm not sure what to say. Behind her Joe is raising his eyebrows in surprise, but Darrin passes me, a dish towel over the sleeve of his designer suit, and nudges me. "Say yes, young man. It's not many she invites."

"It'd be an honor," I stutter. Still, it feels weird. Something about this whole family feels weird. The way everyone caters and indulges Helen—I get that. Not only is she the matriarch, she has special needs because of her synesthesia. But Joe's place as her oldest son seems to have been totally usurped by Darrin—despite not being blood, he's clearly the man of the house, the one everyone turns to when there's a decision to be made. Maybe it's simply because he's older than Joe? Or since Joe seems to live practically as a hermit in the house up near the lake, Darrin fills the void in the family dynamics?

And where does Ella fit into all this? The entire family hovers around her, watching, listening to her every word, but mostly, I noticed, watching me, Rory, and Max. As if Ella needs protecting from us. I understand a bit of scrutiny for myself—the stranger suddenly invited home for no good reason. But Ella's oldest—and from their conversation, only—friends?

I nod my good-bye and join the others on the front porch. Ella walks with us out to Rory's car, a yellow VW Bug that suits her larger-than-life personality. Once we reach the driveway and are out of earshot of anyone inside the house, Max abruptly stops. "You want to tell them the truth, or should I?"

The challenge is meant for me, but since I have no idea which truth or lie Max is referring to, I say nothing and simply meet his gaze head on.

Rory fills the silence. "What are you talking about?"

"He said he wanted Ella's help for a project he was working on with Dr. Winston." Max leans forward. "But I checked. Dr. Winston isn't teaching this semester. He's on sabbatical, finishing his next book."

I almost laugh with relief. Before I can explain, Rory steps in to defend me. "If he was lying, Ella would have seen it in his aura."

She acts as if Ella's enhanced visual perceptions are more reliable than a polygraph. I wonder about that—was that why she'd acted so strangely after I told her about her mother? Has she seen my lies? Have I already lost her trust?

I think back to our conversation and realize I hadn't really lied. In fact, I'd mostly told her the truth, just not all of it. So how did this aura-reading work? As soon as I make it back to my dorm, I need to do some research on synesthesia.

"*Cold Cases Gone Hot*," I answer Max's accusation. "That's the name of the book. I'm working as Dr. Winston's research assistant and getting some independent study credits." I pull out my phone. "I've got his home number. Want me to call him so you can ask for yourself?"

But it's not Max who interests me right now. It's Ella. She doesn't seem to care about Dr. Winston's book at all—isn't even questioning how her mother's case might fit into things or why I'd want to interview her.

Instead, she's frowning in the direction of the house, making a shushing motion with her hands. "He's telling the truth," she says. "Alec told me about a case he's researching. It involves a woman who stole my mother's identity and was murdered."

That gets everyone's attention. Even Max relaxes his guard. A bit. But I know Ella's twisted what I told her, colored my facts with her own interpretation. Denial. So powerful a force that people can create entire new memories to shield themselves from pain. Dad taught me that, not Dr. Winston, but it applies just as well to journalism as it does to police investigations.

It's going to kill her when she learns the truth.

I almost walk away. Drop everything. School, the chance to be published, my need for answers. I would do that, to spare her. At least I want to be the kind of guy who would.

"Really?" Rory asks, gripping my arm as if the killer is waiting in the shadows. Her touch anchors me and earns me a death-glare from Max in the process. "Someone got killed? And they were pretending to be Ella's mother?"

"Why would anyone do that? Your mother's been dead for years," Max says.

I keep my mouth shut. No way in hell am I dragging everything out here. If I'd known that Ella had no clue what the truth really is, I'd never have approached her the way I did. Idiot. So many amateur mistakes. I cringe at the thought of what my dad would say if he knew how badly I've screwed things up. Worse, what would Mom think?

The front door opens and Helen appears, waving to Ella.

Ella flushes. "Let's talk about it tomorrow. Alec can show us his research and explain. Then maybe we can help him."

"We don't have school tomorrow. Veteran's Day," Rory jumps in, sounding intrigued.

Here's my chance. Drop the whole thing, tell them to enjoy their day off school, that I've made a mistake and Ella's right, I have the wrong woman.

I open my mouth. Ready to do it. Ready to walk away. Never look back.

But then I see the way Helen is staring at me, her arms crossed over her chest, distrust written all over her face. And Ella has somehow ended up standing beside me, close enough to almost brush against my body. She wants to help, is eager to help—despite the pain I caused her earlier with my clumsy attempt to explain.

Doesn't she deserve the truth as much as I do?

"We can meet at the student lounge on campus," I surprise myself by saying. "Ten o'clock, the meeting room beside the computer lab. It's usually empty that early in the day." I know because my roommate sleeps until noon—complete with snoring that rattles furniture—and I had to find a place to camp out and get work done.

Ella nods, then looks over at Helen. "I have to go." Then she turns back to me and flings her arms around me in a hug I am absolutely unprepared for. "Thank you for the gift of the ocean. I hope I can go there and see it myself someday. It was very thoughtful."

And she's gone, dashing up the steps to the house.

"Happy birthday," I call after her, ignoring the looks Rory and Max are giving me. Rory is beaming brighter than the streetlamps while Max looks ready for a fight—he still doesn't trust me, and why should he?

I reach into my pocket, the one that carried my sand from home. It's become my touchstone these past few weeks as the weather grew cold and the days short and dreary. Of course, it isn't there.

That night so long ago was a dark, chilly night, a lot like this one. Fog swirled at my feet as I ran from the fire. And found a scared little girl hiding in the ocean as if it could protect her from the evil behind us.

Ella doesn't remember any of it. But I do. I remember everything, despite trying my whole life to forget.

CHAPTER 13

Ella

When I get back inside, Helen is nowhere to be seen, but I can hear Joe and Darrin doing dishes in the kitchen. They're talking—I can't hear the words, but the murmur of their conversation flows around me in a swirl of wispy color. It always surprises me how much Joe opens up to Darrin—he's such a recluse by nature, which is why he lives in the house at the lake. Usually when he's around other people, he does all the talking, mainly so he doesn't risk hearing a word that will make his face go sour and leave him retching all night.

But he and Darrin have always gotten along, will have actual conversations. Two men with absolutely nothing in common—except me, I guess—and they'll chatter away for hours. I like that. Like that Joe has a friend. I worry about him all alone up at the lake. Sometimes we won't see him for weeks. He always claims he's busy with work, but we all know he's really just a figurehead at Cleary and Sons, counting down the days until I can take over for him. Lately, every time I see him, his aura sags with loneliness, worn patches of sadness rubbing it thin.

I close the front door and lean against it, listening to the house, checking, in a weird way, to make sure its aura is unchanged after everything that happened tonight. It feels solid, steady, no alarms except the one in my mind wondering how I suddenly ended up juggling so many things—no, not things, people—and which one I will drop first.

I reach into my pocket, but it isn't the Paris brochure I slide out. Instead it's Alec's sand. I still can't believe he gave it to me—or understand why it stirs such powerful emotions inside me. I've always longed to see new places, been drawn to the ocean even though I've never been, but this feels like so much more. Emotions tangle inside emotions to the point where I can't decipher them. Joy collides with dread, anxiety drowns beneath hope, fear dances with sorrow.

Sighing, I reach for the brochure. The mystery of Alec's sand and what it means will have to wait. Right now, I have to deal with a bigger problem: what to do about Paris?

I want to go, it's the chance of a lifetime. But there's no way I can leave Helen and Joe. And no way I'd ever be able to enjoy the trip if I did. The thought of leaving home fills me with a sick feeling that churns my stomach until

I'm sweating and shivering. I can't explain how, but I know something awful will happen if I leave my family. It's crazy, I realize, but I cannot deny this feeling. It's as if it's already happened, it's that certain, written in stone.

They'll ask why when I tell them I can't go to Paris and I won't be able to answer. Helen and Joe will feel mortified, blame themselves, and they'll all ask me about college, because surely I'll be leaving to go to some big school in some big anonymous city. Then I'll have to share my plan of staying here, taking classes at Cambria College. Which they will disapprove of. I deserve a world-class education, they'll say. My parents would want that for me, they'll tell me.

The dead parents guilt card—it gets played more often than expected. For something big like my future? Oh yeah, they'll slap it down for sure.

And then there's this dead woman who stole my mom's name. I'm not sure why, but she haunts me. I know it's just a weird coincidence, but I feel compelled to help Alec find her killer.

Or maybe, if I'm honest with myself, I'm just compelled to spend more time with Alec. It's been a long time since I've liked a guy, felt this nicely nervous flip-flop in my insides. Falling in crush, Rory calls it, and she ought to know since she does it as regularly as she brushes her teeth.

I leave the men to the cleanup—it is my birthday, after

all—and head upstairs to my room. Helen is waiting, sitting on my bed.

"You can't hide from me, you know," she says, patting my comforter. It's a patchwork quilt made of recycled saris; she bought it for me last Christmas and it's one of my favorite things. Not solely for its beauty, but because each square radiates the excitement of faraway lands and adventures.

I swallow my sigh and sit down, pulling my knees up and hugging my fluffy faux leopard-skin pillow that Rory bought to give my tranquil, pastel bedroom "an edge."

As I stroke its plush fur, Helen touches my arm. Not condemning, rather questioning. "You'd think we gave you an all-expense paid trip to Siberia instead of the artistic capital of the civilized world. What's up?"

"I can't go." There, it's out. In an almost inaudible murmur, but I've finally said the words I've been holding inside of me ever since last spring when the school counselor looked at my grades and portfolio and told me she could find me scholarships to places like the Rhode Island School of Design or NYU or even SCAD in Savannah if I wanted. The offer had at first made me float with joy that my work was good enough, that I might be able to make a living doing what I loved.

But that balloon deflated and crashed to earth when I walked outside the school and felt the weight of possibility crushing me. I could do anything, go anywhere, the counselor had beamed, her aura blindingly bright. She couldn't imagine anything more exciting—and I couldn't dream of anything more terrifying. She didn't know that I had family that needed me, had a responsibility to my dead parents and the business they loved. She just didn't know.

Then I'd arrived home, my safe, quiet, comforting nest of a home, and found Gram Helen in the midst of one of her spells after a new engineer had ruined a book she'd been working weeks on. I made her tea, baked her cookies, wrapped her in her favorite fleece bathrobe, made sure she had her lavender bath salts, and never felt so needed. My home. My family. My cocoon, soft and clingy and fitting just right.

That night I realized I had no wings, was no butterfly waiting to be set free, as much as I might yearn to fly. I am a caterpillar. Stuck right here.

My family needs me. Period. My need to stay exactly where I am has everything to do with them . . . and nothing at all to do with my irrational fears that something awful will happen if I leave. At least that's what I tell myself.

"It's not that boy, is it? The one you brought home tonight?"

I shake my head vigorously.

"Still, he must be something special to bring him to your birthday party."

Not special, just bad timing. Well, maybe special, but it's too early for me to even think that way. "It's not about Alec. I just met him."

Her gaze is penetrating, sees right through my skin and bones as if she could pluck the truth from the silence between each heartbeat. Her eyes narrow and she nods. "Then it's because of me. Because of us."

She says nothing for a long time, wrapping her arm around my shoulders and holding me tight. "You know, when I was your age, I dreamed of a life on the stage. London. Or Hollywood. I was going to be an actress who would never be forgotten. I'd outshine them all." She pauses. "Know what happened? First time I summoned up my courage and stepped onto a stage?"

I shake my head. Gram Helen never talks about her past, at least not her past before she inherited me. All I've ever learned is that she fled here from Sarajevo with my mother and Joe after her husband was killed. She never talks more about those days. It's as if her life before was erased once she arrived in America and began a new one.

But now her face turns dreamy as she tells her story. I close my eyes, letting her words wash through me, creating vivid images that flow through my mind like a movie.

"It wasn't even a performance, just an audition. But, oh how I'd practiced. Hours in front of the mirror. I was going to be the best Juliet our school had ever seen. I walk out onto the stage, the whole world turns to shadow and light as the spotlight finds me, and I've never felt so at home. And then . . ." Her voice shudders and shies away. "Some idiot backstage starts rolling out scenery. With one wheel squeaking and the other clanking."

Two of her worst sounds. I open my eyes, the spell broken. "Migraine?"

She nods. "Didn't even make it to the bathroom before I started puking. Ended up running out the back door of the auditorium, straight into the arms of a boy I'd never met before, and threw up all over his shoes."

"You never acted again." I don't make her say the words.

"Not in front of an audience. But I've played many roles." She means the books she brings to life as a voice talent. "Not the least of which is being your gram." She hugs me tighter. "And you know that boy? Ended up marrying him."

That makes me smile despite my misery. "So you're okay with me not going to Paris?"

"No. I most definitely am not. Because the point is, at least I tried. I stepped out onto that stage even though I knew how hard it would be, for someone like me, with my limitations. But I at least tried."

My head is shaking, *no, no, no.*

"I can't." My whisper is so thin I'm sure she can see right through it. "You need me. And Uncle Joe does as well."

Black smoke sweeps over her, curling around her throat, covering her head like a widow's veil. The sense of dread is so strong, so overwhelming that I clench my jaws against a sudden rush of nausea.

She leans away, her lips pursing in consideration. "We're adults. We love you. We love having you near. But we would never hold you back. You need to live your life, Ella."

I flinch before her next words, knowing exactly what's coming. It doesn't help, her words still hit their target: my heart.

"It's what your parents would want."

And there it is. My epitaph.

There's no winning. Not against ghosts. Two dead people I can't even remember, not really, more imaginary than real, and they're running my life from beyond the grave.

CHAPTER 14

Alec

As Rory and Max drive me to the parking lot where I left my bike, the silence is like one of those soundproof barriers between a limo driver and his boss. Only I'm alone in the back and they're both up front.

Thankfully, it's a short drive. Rory waves good-bye and shouts, "See you tomorrow!" while Max simply slouches in his seat.

I unlock my bike and somehow manage to avoid any encounters with campus security on my way to my dorm. Thankfully, my roommate is out partying—he'll wake me around two-thirty after the bars close and he stumbles his way back to the room—so I have a few hours of peace and quiet.

I want to call my dad but simply can't face him—he won't say he told me so, but he did and we both know it.

Instead, I call Dr. Winston to update him. I'm worried he'll be upset at my lack of progress and clumsy handling of my introduction to Nora—she'll be Nora in the book, if I can get the story to the point where it's publishable. But, instead, he's excited.

"Wait," he interrupts me. "So we have an orphaned toddler, two parents—one who killed the other and might have killed the girl if she hadn't run, a family with synesthesia . . . You definitely need to get into that research. Too bad it's not the dad's side, we could play that up with the mental illness angle ... Plus amnesia, and a family who's hidden the truth from the girl all these years?"

I hate the way he sounds almost gleeful. This is a real girl we're talking about—a girl I'm coming to like. A lot.

"And," he continues, "all that's before we get to the boy who saves the girl, then loses her, and spends his life searching for answers to why her parents died, to the point where he leaves home to find her again. Alec, I can't promise anything, but we might not use this story in my new collection—we might have enough material here for a complete book all on its own. If I can swing it, you wouldn't get only a byline. You'd have shared credit right on the cover."

I can't share his enthusiasm. Funny, because for the past three months, the thought of being published and jumpstarting my career has been the only thing keeping me sane in this strange city I find myself stranded in.

The next day, I get to the meeting room early, reserving it for the entire morning so we won't be disturbed. I stayed up most of the night preparing my case with the same care my father takes before appearing in court to testify.

You're not reciting mere facts, Dad would say. *You're telling a story. One that the jury wants to believe. Because if your facts are the truth, then the jury can go home and sleep soundly at night. If you're wrong, then not only did the system designed to protect them break down, but there's also a criminal still running free.*

I'm sure of my facts. But unlike most juries, my audience doesn't want to believe me. They'll twist and turn my words inside out, probe at them with denial and fear, anything to return to the ignorance that sheltered them before I blundered into their lives. Their lives? *Her* life. Ella's life.

The thought almost has me gathering my laptop and running all the way back home to South Carolina. What's the cost of dropping out, losing a semester's tuition, being humiliated before my parents, compared to destroying someone's life? Nothing.

I've pulled the plug on my laptop, ready to pack it up, when Max appears at the door.

"Where are you going?" His tone is challenging, as if I've already proven myself a failure.

"Nowhere," I tell him, my words driven more by male

pride than logic. I jerk the laptop cord to stretch to another outlet, jam it into place. I've been taking college classes for two years now, yet I've never before felt so anxious. But never before has so much been at stake.

Rory flounces into the room, her bright pink coat swirling around her like a wool cloud. "What's up?" she asks, eyeing Max and me with suspicion. "You guys doing some male bonding or something? Should I leave, or will there be chest baring and fist pounding?" Her eyes crinkle with delight. "Please tell me there'll be chest baring and fist pounding. I'll sell tickets, make a fortune."

Max frowns her into silence and she slides into a seat at the small conference table. He stalks around the table, ignoring me, and takes the seat opposite her.

"I've been thinking," he says, leaning toward Rory as if there's no one else in the room. "About what you said last night, about Ella's auras helping her see lies. I don't think that's true."

"Really?" She pouts as she considers. "How so?"

I stand at the end of the room and listen. Last night I'd stayed up late reading the research on synesthesia, and it's surprisingly vague for a phenomena so well documented. Scientists can see a person's brain making the misconnections along their sensory pathways by using functional MRI and PET scanners, but they have to rely on a person's individual interpretation as to how those misconnections reveal themselves.

In other words, each case is unique. There isn't even an easy way to prove someone has synesthesia—in fact, many people who claim to have it turn out not to have any verifiable changes in their MRIs. Yet, they still insist that they see the world differently—and that the world impacts them on a visceral level with every sensory experience. Are they faking their synesthesia? If so, why? Or does medical science simply not know how to find proof of it in every patient? It's a fascinating condition.

"Well, for one thing, not everyone's aura changes." Max sounds like a TV defense attorney, building his case—only I'm the one on trial. Max clearly thinks I've somehow conned Ella into letting me into her life. "Like Darrin. She says his aura is always solid indigo."

"Well, Darrin has the emotional range of a sea slug," Rory answers. "A handsome, elegant, well-dressed sea slug, but there's just not a lot for her to work with."

"Exactly. So unless a lie caused him extreme emotion, she wouldn't see a difference—and if she did, she wouldn't necessarily know *why* he was feeling emotion. The truth can cause as much emotion as a lie."

"Okay. So maybe that's true with someone like Darrin or a stranger like Alec who she doesn't have a baseline on." She smiles in my direction even as she shrugs one shoulder, not committing to coming to my defense. "Sorry, Alec."

"No, that's fine. I'm interested in how all this works.

So different people have different colors for their auras? But they always keep those colors? Or—"

"Yes and no," Max interrupts me. "Ella says some people have basically the same color but the shades and images change with their emotions. Like her uncle Joe, he's always somewhere in the brown-red-purple spectrum."

"But people like me, I'm every color of the rainbow," Rory puts in.

Of course she is. Rory practically glows with emotion, and I don't have Ella's gift.

"Speaking of Ella, it's ten past. Where is she?" I ask. Maybe she isn't coming? I'm not sure if I should feel relieved or worried.

"She'll be here." Max doesn't sound concerned. "But more importantly, what's this big mystery? And what's it to do with Ella?"

"Maybe you should tell us first," Rory adds in a soft tone. "Especially if it has something to do with her parents."

I hesitate. If Ella has no idea about what really happened to her parents, then it's not my place to tell her friends first. But they only want to protect her. I totally understand that.

I'm about to tell them when the door opens.

Ella.

CHAPTER 15

Ella

After a sleepless night, I'd gotten up and dressed in comfort clothes: sweatpants, a worn Dr. Who tee layered under a fleece top, and finally my warmest parka, the one with tons of pockets for pens, phone, paper, sketchpad. I arrive at the student center early—before Alec, even.

Too nervous to wait, I pace through the maze-like space with its hidden study nooks, specialty cafés, arcades, lounges, and media rooms. Midterms were last week, so the place is a lot less crowded than usual. For once, I feel like I fit in. Maybe because I'm not carrying my portfolio, banging into everyone. Or maybe it's because I have a reason to be here, beyond killing time before I could get into the art studio or use the pool.

And now I'm back where I started, at the meeting room. Alec and Max and Rory are inside, discussing my auras. I lean against the wall outside the door, listening. My auras aren't something we usually talk about—just like we never discuss Rory's braces or that she's the real reason why Max left the wrestling team two years ago.

I smile as they mention Darrin. They're right; my synesthesia doesn't tell me truths or lies, only emotions—and sometimes emotions are so nuanced that I misread them.

Other times they're not nuanced enough, which is why some people's auras are the same color all the time. Like Darrin. I've known him all my life and he's a really complicated man—he can talk about anything from the financial markets to obscure German philosophers to sports. I *have* seen strong emotions from Darrin—worry during the stock market crash, fear when I fell off my bike and skinned my knees—but for the most part, he's a steadfast, reliable indigo. One of the few stable things in my life.

Then I hear Max and Rory ask Alec about my mother, and I realize I can't keep hiding. Time to go inside and start solving this puzzle Alec has scrambled my life into.

"Morning," I say brightly, as if I just arrived.

Max doesn't buy my act—he knows I'm never late for anything. But Rory smiles her usual bright beam of greeting and Alec nods as if he's happy to see me. Or maybe relieved is a better word. I wish I could see his aura, so I could parse the difference.

Last night I'd gone online, intending to search for any

new details of my parents' deaths. I got as far as typing their names and the word *fatal* into the search bar before deleting it. I just couldn't face reading about the fire again; it'd been hard enough the first hundred times. Besides, after fifteen years, the case long closed and forgotten, what could possibly be new? If there were any developments, the police surely would have contacted my family before allowing a reporter to write about it.

Instead, I researched identity theft—and learned a lot of scary stuff. Like how easy it is, especially if the victims are already dead. In a warped way, it made me feel better, knowing my parents' names and vital statistics could have been stolen, even if the thief had apparently ended up dead. If Alec had even gotten that right. After all, I don't know anything about him. Can I trust him or his so-called facts at all?

His gaze catches mine. I wish I knew why, but something in me wants to trust him. No. That's wrong. Something in me has *always* trusted him. Yet, I'm also afraid of what he might say. More than afraid, panicked in that stomach-tossing way that leaves your lips chilled and fingers trembling.

I almost turn and run away but Rory slides out a chair and I sink into it, my stomach tying itself in several more knots. The woman Alec thinks is Mia Cleary isn't my mother, which means there's still a potential murder victim out there. And a killer.

"Okay," Rory says when I remain silent, a molten puddle of anxiety. "We're all here. What's this about a dead woman pretending to be Ella's mom?"

Alec grimaces, and I don't need to see his aura to know he's not convinced my mother was a victim of identity theft.

"Why don't you start by telling us about the case you're investigating with Professor Winston?" I ask him.

His lips tighten, but he nods and opens his laptop. I think he's going to turn it to face us—his hands are poised like he's about to—but he changes his mind and drops them to his sides. "I grew up on a small barrier island off the coast of South Carolina. Harbinger Cove."

Max scrapes his chair back to give him room to tilt back, stretch his legs. "What's that got to do with Ella?"

"Harbinger Cove is where my parents went on vacation," I answer slowly. "Where the fire was. In their rental cottage."

Max frowns and drops his chair back flat on the floor.

"It happened fifteen years ago, yesterday. I didn't realize it was your birthday," Alec adds quickly, as if apologizing. For what, I'm not sure.

"You think someone from Harbinger Cove stole Ella's mom's identity?" Rory asks. "Like maybe the paramedics or mortuary workers or someone with access to her social security number who knew she was dead?" We stare at her in surprise. "What? I can do research too. That's how thieves get your info. Then they open accounts in your name and get fake IDs, sometimes even real ones, saying they lost the originals. It's called social engineering."

Alec nods as if she's a star pupil. "That's how identity theft works. But I don't think that's what happened in this case."

"Why not?" Max challenges him.

"Because I checked with my father. He's a detective with the sheriff's department now—back then he was a patrol deputy."

"Why was your dad so interested? Did he help to investigate the fire that killed my parents?" I ask, my question leaving a trail of falling dust motes behind it.

For some reason, I reach for the film container of sand that Alec gave me last night. I have it in my pocket, intending to return it to him—it's much too personal a gift to keep. As my fingers wrap around it, I imagine what it would be like walking barefoot on the beach, and suddenly I can almost feel grains of sand rubbing between my toes, hear the rush and crash of the ocean.

"My mom's family owned the cottage. We rented it to your parents. And my dad called in the fire. He and his four-year-old son. The son who then found the only survivor. A little girl wandering alone on the beach."

Both Max and Rory look at me, light sparking from them both: concern, fear, curiosity.

"You said the woman you're researching was murdered. But the fire was an accident, right?" Rory asks breathlessly, her hand gripping mine. I can barely feel it, mine has gone cold.

Alec looks at each of us in turn. "Look, I didn't come to you to stir things up. I never dreamed you didn't know—" He snaps his laptop shut. "Maybe I shouldn't be the one telling you this. Maybe your family should—"

I don't want the answers . . . but I do need them. "The fire wasn't an accident, was it?"

He shakes his head. Pauses. Gives me time. I jerk my chin at him to continue.

"The fire was arson. Forensics indicate that it was started by your father. After he killed your mother and before he shot himself." His words emerge in one breath, spoken so fast they crowd together. Like he's pulling a Band-Aid off fast so it won't hurt as bad.

It doesn't work. I feel swamped, a tsunami of emotion drowning me.

"No way." The words escape Max with a wave of dark doubt and burnt worry.

"Are you certain it was Ella's parents?" Rory asks, searching for hope.

Alec continues, his voice as relentless as the crashing waves filling my head. "It was your parents. They were identified through DNA. It was them."

I'm shaking my head, trying to force his words away. Without an aura, they're invisible, but I can still feel their impact. Sharp seashells breaking beneath my feet as I run, flee in terror . . .

"No." The word emerges a thin whisper. "No." Louder, but still uncertain. "It's impossible. I've never been to Harbinger Cove."

Now he's the one shaking his head, each movement releasing the sound of a gunshot whipping toward me, making me flinch.

"I'm sorry. I really am. But you were there."

"How can you be so sure?" Max asks.

Alec's expression of sorrow is for me alone. "Because I'm the one who found you."

CHAPTER 16

Ella

"Prove it," Max says, climbing to his feet and moving to stand opposite Alec, the table between them. He leans his weight on his fists as if that's the only way to keep from using them. Red scorches through his aura, lashing across the table toward Alec.

Alec's green eyes have gone dark with sorrow. "If I knew you didn't know the truth, I never would have come, never would have found you, said anything."

"Prove it," Max repeats.

Alec gestures to the laptop. "It's all here. Photos, autopsy report, DNA analysis. I really don't think you want to see them." He's still talking to me, but Max stalks around the table and takes the seat in front of the laptop, his movement forcing Alec to step back until he's against the wall. As far away from me as possible.

Max clicks and scrolls, his face bathed in the harsh light of the computer screen. I don't need to read his aura to know Alec has told us the truth. It's written in the planes and angles of Max's face as his lips flatten and his eyes blink heavily, reluctant to meet my gaze. "How come no one ever mentioned that Ella was there?"

"We're a tiny island community—we don't even have a newspaper. Plus, my dad said they'd never mention a minor; not to the press, not after a sensitive incident like this. And they needed to locate and notify next of kin—by the time that was done, the story of a fire on a remote island wasn't going to rate another mention in the city paper. Remember, it would have taken days to weeks before all the forensic and pathology reports were done, before they had all the facts."

"They lied," I whisper. No need to explain who I mean.

Rory squeezes my hand. "Of course they did. They love you. Who'd tell a three-year-old little girl a thing like that?"

"But the fire—" I'm still wrapping my mind around all this. "I was there? How did it happen?"

Even as I say the words, memories begin to play out in my mind—soft, faded, shredded around the edges, swirling like fog. Ghosts of the past, telling a story I'm part of but not really; it feels like I'm watching someone else's life.

I clutch Alec's canister of sand hidden in my pocket and remember . . .

A little girl, far from home, lost and so very scared.

Mommy said run and hide, so that's what she did. But now Mommy was gone and it was dark and scary and why hadn't she come to find her?

Mommy said be quiet, don't make a sound, so that's what she did. Not a sound. Not even when she heard someone yell—someone who sounded a lot like Daddy.

Just like we play. Hide and seek, Mommy whispered. *Hide real good and don't make a sound.*

So that's what she did.

It was scary outside in the dark. She didn't understand why there was sand everywhere, so much more than in her narrow stretch of beach beside her lake back home. She didn't like this sand. It sneaked into her shoes and down her dress when she slipped and fell, and it pulled at her ankles, constantly trying to trip her up. There were plants growing in it, vines and prickly grass. Creepy-crawly things moved under and over the sand, brushing against her skin, making her want to fling them away.

But she couldn't move, had to hide. Like at home. She'd make herself really, really small and crawl under things Daddy couldn't see under, and he never found her until she'd sneak out when his back was turned and *Boo!* And he'd jump up in the air and spin around and scoop her up high until he was blowing raspberries on her belly, and they'd laugh and laugh and laugh and Mommy would declare, "Nora wins! She's the queen of hide and seek! The best ever!"

Then she'd join in on the Nora sandwich—best hug of all—and Daddy would dance Mommy around the room with Nora between them, and everything in the whole wide world was perfect right there in their safe house with her safe family and it wasn't scary at all, not like now, here in the sand, curled up tight, hands over her mouth, eyes squeezed shut so they couldn't see her, but she also couldn't see them and there was that strange sound, a roar and crash over and over, and the little sounds, the scuttling crackles, and most of all a man's voice shredded by the wind, calling her name.

And then the screaming started.

CHAPTER 17

Alec

My dad never talks about the bad parts of his job, at least not with me and Mom. Instead, we celebrate the good things and try our best not to worry about the dangers he faces every time he puts on his uniform and Kevlar. Now that he's a detective, he might face less physical danger, but he comes home silent and withdrawn more days than he used to. I know the part of his job he hates the most is telling families that the people they love are dead. And how they died.

I never dreamed I'd be doing that myself. It's one of the reasons why I didn't want to become a cop, why I want to pursue a career where instead of handling what's thrown at you on the streets like Dad, I can take my time to find the real truth buried under all the he said-she said. That's why I came here, to cold, gray Cambria City. To find truth, not crush people with it.

Now that I've exposed her truth, Ella will never look at me the way she had yesterday at the diner. How could she? I'll forever be the guy who walked into her perfect life only to shatter it.

"Tell me everything," she says, her eyes aimed at the opposite corner of the tiny room. Like she can't stand to look at my face, not even out of the corner of her eye. "Starting with why they think my dad killed my mom. Because that did not happen. He wouldn't have done it. He couldn't have."

"Ella," Max says, half rising from his chair, ready to protect her. I'm glad she has such good friends. She's going to need them.

"Maybe we should go," Rory suggests, stroking Ella's arm as if calming a wild animal.

Except Ella doesn't look wild or in need of protection. Finally, she turns her head the slightest bit, and is looking straight at me. It takes everything I have not to look away.

"I want to know everything. You said you were there. Tell me what happened." Her words are as heavy as a judge's gavel pronouncing sentence.

I nod, accepting the weight of responsibility. What would Dad do? Tell the truth. But in a way that will ease her into things, not do more harm.

"A sheriff's deputy doesn't make much," I begin. "But my mom's family has lived on the island for ages—one of the few families who haven't sold out to mainland developers. We rent out a few cottages to help make ends meet. That's why we were out there that night, my dad and I. We were prepping a last-minute rental for the Clearys."

"Last-minute?" Rory asks. "So Ella's parents hadn't planned their vacation in advance?"

I shrug. "I guess not."

She frowns, but I keep going, wanting to get through my story as fast as possible. Once I finish, they can dissect every fact and theory—after all, that's the whole reason I'd come here. All my life, I've been obsessed by one question: why? Why would a man do that to his wife, abandon his daughter, destroy her life before it even began? It was so cruel, so heartless, so . . . unfathomable. There has to be a reason why.

"I was only four. Loved to play at being my dad's helper. Of course, I wasn't much help, not really, but still it was nice when he let me hang with him."

Max grunts with impatience. I ignore him, and continue to ease into things. "It wasn't that cold, but there was some low-lying fog on the dunes. Other than that, the night was clear, the moon almost full."

Ella's head bobs, her expression absent as if she's walking through the sand with me.

"The cottage was dark when we arrived. The lights were off. But there was a strange car outside. Pennsylvania plates. We rang the bell and knocked. Figured maybe the visitors had arrived early and gone for a walk on the beach."

I stop there, despite the urge to plow on. I need to tread carefully. Silent tears slip down Rory's face as she clutches Ella's arm, but Ella's expression is more frightening—she looks right through me as if I'm not even there, as if none of us are. A blank screen. What images does she see in my words? Does she glimpse the truth?

Am I doing more harm than good, forcing her to remember, to relive something she'd buried so deep?

"My dad opened the door and a blast of smoke and heat came out. The alarms hadn't gone off—later, the forensics guys said someone had disabled them. My dad sent me to get help—there's no cell service out there—while he ran inside to try to find anyone who may have gotten trapped." My gut clenches just like it had that night when Dad vanished into the smoke. Except back then the smoke wasn't the only scent choking me.

I take a breath and swear I taste blood, just like that night when cold, bloody copper filled the air, clinging to everything. It was days later before I stopped smelling death.

"Before I got very far, the whole house suddenly went up. I ran back to find my dad. I thought he was dead, that the fire had taken him." My voice breaks but I'm not embarrassed, too caught up in the memories that have haunted me all my life. That fire could have killed my father—could have killed me.

"Finally, he came out coughing, clothing singed, dragging something—someone. But it was too late. We both barely made it away before the roof collapsed and flames shot up everywhere. He was having trouble breathing, so I ran to get help for real this time. The fastest way home was over the dunes and down the beach, but when I hit the sand I saw a girl. She was just a little kid, littler than me, alone in the water, the waves knocking her down. I remember feeling so grown up, like a superhero, racing to save her."

"You found me." Ella isn't asking a question; I nod anyway.

"You were in the water. The surf kept pulling you under, but you kept swimming farther out. Until I caught up with you."

"I was hiding. Not from you. From someone else."

I frown. "Your father? Did he—" Despite my best efforts to remain neutral, my voice is choked with rage. "Did he try to hurt you like he did your mother?"

"Her father?" Rory is aghast. Ella says nothing, just stares, unblinking.

Max makes a noise deep in his chest and stands, blocking my view of the girls. "Why are you doing this? What's in it for you? Dredging this all up. No one asked you to—"

"Stop it." Ella isn't shouting, yet her voice strikes like

a hammer. "Stop it. Max, Alec had no idea I didn't know about that night. What he and his father went through."

She isn't calling my version of events the truth. I can't really blame her; it's a lot to take in. Fifteen years of her life's history erased and rewritten with a few words.

She stares at me—no, around me, as if searching for something that isn't there. Finally she says, "But I know one thing. My father didn't do that. He didn't kill my mother or himself. My father is innocent."

I avoid Max and walk over to where Ella sits. There's no free chair near her so I crouch, getting down to her eye level just like I did when we were kids. "I'm sorry. I'm so, so sorry."

Back then, Nora never said a word. Not a word, not during the whole time she stayed with us—most of those eleven days were spent gripping my hand and hiding behind my legs—until the social worker and police finally found her grandmother and uncle and they'd come to take her home.

Then as my mom was bundling Nora into her new car seat and Dad was talking logistics with her new family, giving them his card, promising to follow up even though it wasn't officially his investigation—only then did she fling her arms around my neck and press her lips next to my ears and whisper to me.

Two words. "Promise me."

Promise her what, she never had a chance to tell me,

because her grandmother hustled her away before she could say another word.

Lord, how I wanted to keep her. Or go with her. Stay by her side, protect her. I'd blubbered, pretending it was just the wind blowing sand in my eyes. Stood out there staring at the dust trail kicked up by the car long after it had vanished. For months, I begged my parents to call Nora's family, to let me talk with her. I needed to know she was okay, that the monster who killed her mother hadn't scarred her as well. I needed her to be safe even as that night haunted me.

I'd wake two, sometimes three times a night with horrible dreams of her being burned alive—what if she'd been in the house, what if she hadn't escaped? Then the nightmares would escalate and it would be Dad killed or him and Mom or all of us, the fire grown to a demon intent on destroying everything I cared about. A cloud of dread clung to me for months. I didn't smile or laugh anymore; it was as if I was haunted, not by the dead but by a living girl.

And now, here she was. Alive and well. Until I blundered into her life and ruined everything. Stole her smile. Silenced her laughter.

I've become the boogeyman from my own nightmares. Haunting the girl I'd been so desperate to save.

Her eyes tug at mine, pleading, as desperate as that three-year-old begging me to make a promise I could never keep. "My dad was innocent, right?"

All I can do is close my eyes, shake my head. "I don't think so."

When I open my eyes, she's gone. Not physically, but her entire body has pulled back into the chair as if trying to disappear into the fabric, her arms are wrapped tight around her chest, protecting her heart and other vital organs, and her glassy stare is fixed on the door behind me.

Slowly, feeling a lot older than I had only moments before, I stand. Is this how Dad feels when he has to deliver a death notification? So empty, so helpless?

"Wait. That can't be all. Maybe someone else set the fire. Maybe the fire left evidence—I've heard of fingerprints being seared into objects, preserved." Max seems oblivious to Ella's pain, instead focusing on proving me wrong. "How could they be sure? I mean, after—" Finally, even his insensitivity finds its boundary as Rory *shush*s him with a glare.

"Nora's—Ella's—fingerprints and her parents' were the only ones they found, besides my mom's from when she cleaned. And before you ask, they found no fingerprints other than her father's on the gun or the gas can. No footprints or tire tracks." I sigh. "It was a thorough investigation, even if it did take a while to complete."

"Then why are you here? What do you want from Ella?" Rory, getting to the heart of things. I've noticed that about her. She's definitely keyed into what's most important, at least when it comes to protecting her friends.

"I thought she knew, remembered. I was interested—" I stop. Too clinical. Yes, journalists are meant to be objective observers, but this isn't only Ella's life, it's mine as well. How can I trust myself to get close to anyone, how can I ever trust anyone, if I can't understand why people do things like what happened to Ella's parents? The need to know the truth about that night has driven me all my life. Not just what was in the reports from the cops and the forensic scientists and the medical examiner. The real truth. What wasn't in any report. The why.

"Don't you see?" Max is facing me, hands balled into fists. "He wants to sell her story. Use it in this book his professor is writing."

"Yes, that's part of it. But there's more as well. I wanted, I needed—" I can't look at Max, meet the challenge in his glare. Instead, I focus on Ella. "I know the facts. What's more important to me is understanding why. I thought you might know—or want to know. Help me find the truth. About why your dad—"

Her eyes grow large, the pupils dilating with fear to the point where I see my face reflected in them. My features are warped, grotesque. I've become a monster.

"I can't help you." She shoves her chair back and gets to her feet, her body wavering until she draws in a breath and with it the strength to stand straight.

Before I can say anything to stop her, she turns and is

gone. Rory chases after her. Max moves more slowly, backing away toward the door, his eyes fixed on me. As if I'm the threat. Then he disappears through the door, slamming it shut behind him.

Leaving me alone. I slump into the chair near the computer. When I reach for the keyboard, blood from the crime scene photos on the screen stains my hands red.

The heat clanks on, filling the room with parched air that stinks vaguely of overcooked hot dogs. I shiver and long for home, for my beach, the crystal blue ocean that reflects the moods of the sky, my mom's cooking and warm glances, my dad's deep baritone that is always so certain about everything.

I thought that by chasing my night terrors, by finding the answers, I could finally exorcise my demons.

Now I'm wondering why I ever left home for this cold, barren city.

I reach for my phone, trying to remember Dad's work schedule. Mom would offer comfort and solace. As appealing as that sounds, it isn't what I need, not after bringing such pain to Nora. To Ella. More than pain, fear.

"Dad? I think I really screwed up. Bad."

CHAPTER 18

Ella

For the second time in as many days, a guy is driving me home in my own car. Unlike Alec, Max didn't ask; he simply slid my keys from my hand as soon as I took them from my pocket. Rory's behind us in her Bug. Somehow everything feels worse without her chatter providing background noise, her words painting a kaleidoscope of neon cheer, distracting me from grim, gray reality.

I sit in the passenger seat, knees up to my chest, and despite wearing my warmest clothes, I'm shivering. For me, the Subaru is filled with a damp, impenetrable fog, and the noise of the heater becomes the roar of the ocean. My layers of clothing drag on me as if they're soaked through; I can almost smell the salt water that drenches them.

Good thing Max is driving, because as we come to a halt I can't even see we're at my house, the fog surrounding me is so thick.

"We're here." He waits for me to do something. "Sure you don't want us to come in? Maybe we could help—"

I shake my head and press my weight against the door release. It pops open and the fog swirls out and I can see again. "No. Thanks. I'll be fine."

At least I think that's what I say as I tumble free of the car. He climbs out as well, walks around to my side and hands me back my keys. Rory's waiting at the curb, beaming encouragement despite the brown waves of concern emanating from her false smile. Leave it to Rory to turn worry into chocolate. The thought gives me the energy to wave back as she and Max drive off.

I eye the house suspiciously, but nothing has changed since I left this morning. Somehow this surprises me. How can my entire world have collapsed without anything else changing?

I glance up and down the block at the houses of families I've known since I was a little girl. What are their cheerful façades hiding? As my eyes seek out their secrets, I imagine couples betrayed by the ones they love, lost fortunes, terminal illnesses . . . a host of devastation silenced by an outward appearance of normalcy.

Before I make it to my front door, Darrin's Lexus purrs into the drive, parking behind Joe's rusted-out Tacoma. We have a separate garage out back, a building at the far end of the driveway that runs past the side of the house, but it's been my studio for so long that everyone, even Darrin, parks outside. Darrin eases out, his car door closing with a gentle whisper instead of the solid bang my Impreza makes.

"Hey there," he says in greeting. "Glad I caught you."

"Are you heading back to the city?" I ask. Darrin never stays here more than a night or two even though he has an apartment downtown. The original Cleary and Sons was in Cambria City, but over the years Darrin has expanded the business far beyond our tiny, landlocked rustbelt town. He spends most of his time, when he's not traveling, meeting with clients in either the Philly or Manhattan outposts.

I've never been to any of our other offices or Darrin's other homes. I imagine him in a penthouse, its windows filled with a vista of neon lights, entertaining Victoria Secret models or the like. After my parents' deaths, he's grown Cleary and Sons into an international, highly regarded boutique agency. It will be my inheritance, he always says. Something my father would be proud of. Darrin was my father's best friend. He must have known, seen . . . something. Why didn't he get Dad help? Warn my mom? Before it was too late.

"Yes, I'm heading out soon, but I wanted to speak with you first." He leans against his car without worrying about any dirt smudging his Burberry overcoat—no dirt would dare to attach itself to Darrin or his Lexus.

"Your gram told me you were hesitant about the trip to

Paris." He chooses his words carefully. That's the kind of man he is: careful, thoughtful, always with a plan. "I know you're worried about the money, but now that you're eighteen, the trust your parents set up for your education is open to you. Plus, you won't be going alone. I've arranged to meet with clients the first few weeks you're there, so I can help you get settled. And Joe will watch over Helen while you're gone."

More like Helen will watch over Joe, I suspect. But an imaginary future trip to Paris is the least of my concerns while I—we—need to face the truth of the past. Of my past.

"I'm glad you're here," I say, my voice sounding like one of Helen's documentary narrations, formal and distant. "I need to ask you about something." I open the front door. "All of you."

He gives me that "oh really?" raised eyebrow that he usually reserves for Joe, but follows me inside. Joe and Helen are in the kitchen heating up leftovers. "Ella," Helen says. "You're just in time for lunch."

"We need to talk." I know I'm sounding melodramatic, but I don't know any other way to approach this. I'm not even mad that they've lied to me for most of my life—deep down I know they only did it out of love, wanting to protect me. But now that I know the truth, I can't let the lies continue.

I take a seat in the living room, waiting for them to come in and sit down as well. Joe and Helen sit on the couch opposite me, Darrin remains standing behind them.

They're all staring at me, confusion and concern spiraling from their auras.

"I know the truth. About my parents. About how they really died." I close my eyes with relief as the words spill away from my lips, dripping crimson anxiety. When I open them again I see fear leaching into their auras—even Darrin's has turned from steadfast indigo to a bruised purple-black.

"How?" Helen asks, barely able to get the single syllable out.

"It was that boy, wasn't it?" Joe bounces from the couch; agitated air molecules spark and flare in their rush to get out of his way. "I knew he was trouble."

"Alec didn't mean any harm. Just like I know you all didn't. You were trying to protect me from the truth. I get that. I really do. But now I know, and . . ."

"Oh, honey." Gram Helen is at my side before I can find the strength to go on. Because I have no idea how this changes us, changes everything. I just know that it will. That today will mark an "after" we can never go back from. "I'm so sorry. Are you okay? What can we do to help?"

"What did that boy tell you?" This from Darrin, his voice calmer than calm.

"He said . . ." I falter. "He said my father shot my mother, then started the fire and killed himself. He said I was there when it happened, even if I can't remember anything. But he didn't say—I need to know—why? Why would my dad do that to me? To Mom? Why?"

I'm sobbing now, and even I can barely understand my words. Somehow, the rest of them know what I'm saying. And what to do about it. Gram Helen has her arms wrapped snug around me, a warm blanket of comfort despite the rotten egg despair swirling around her. Joe rushes into the hug, almost barreling us both over. Even Darrin comes around from behind the couch and hovers in the background.

"We don't know, baby," Helen croons. "We don't know why. No one does."

All my memories, my happy family, filled with hopes and dreams and wishes . . . were they all lies? Had my father ever loved us, ever loved me? I can't even bring myself to think such traitorous questions, much less ask them out loud.

"We were only trying to protect you," Joe says, worry and fear bleeding through his voice. "Will you forgive us?"

I can't trust my voice so I simply nod and let them hold me tight. Slowly, their auras quiet and my own softens, although it is still mourning black, a shroud that clings to me. But they hold on. Protecting me, supporting me. And I never want them to let go.

I have so many questions—yet I don't ask any of them. Not only because I'm terrified of the answers. I'm more afraid of the pain I've already caused, upsetting Joe and Helen and even Darrin. It's frightening to feel our little family rocked this way. I'm usually the one who keeps things calm, but this time I can't help. Except by waiting until they're ready to talk.

Which, actually, is kinda okay. It gives me time to process—something I do best with pad and pencil or paintbrush. So while they eat lunch—I have absolutely no appetite—I escape to my room and change into my paint- ing clothes: baggy denim overalls with tons of pockets for brushes and pencils and charcoals, and a paint-stained sweatshirt. Rory says just about every piece of clothing I own should be considered painting clothes since they're all stained with paint—except my swimsuits—and she's pretty close to being right. But these are my comfort clothes, and sliding into them feels like I'm putting on magical armor.

Before I leave the sanctuary of my room, I glance at my laptop. I can't resist. After all, what do I really know about Alec Ravenell? This guy who's turned my life inside out.

Sitting on my bed, I open the browser to a popular social media site. Even as I pull up Alec's profile, which Rory and Max have already examined, and click through to his mother's page—feeling like a total voyeur for doing so—I know Alec is exactly who he says he is.

He hasn't posted much on his own profile, but his mom has dozens of pictures of him with his family, celebrating in a big frame house that sits in the middle of a field of gorgeous feathery, purple grass with the ocean beyond. Scenes of them playing on the beach, out in fishing boats, and an entire stream documenting Alec's life: baby pictures of him snuggled in his parents' arms, Alec digging in the sand, Alec being chased by a bird twice as tall as he is—a whooping crane, I think—Alec bundled in a life jacket fishing at the rail of a boat.

And then everything changes. When he's about four or five, Alec the boy not only gets the glasses that older Alec still has, he also gains older Alec's serious, cautious expression. That look of always searching for something or someone.

I stop there, feeling like an intruder. Not only because

I know Alec hasn't lied, but also because I realize one thing about my own family: they never denied it. When I confronted them downstairs just now, no one said it wasn't my father who killed my mother and started the fire. No one said Alec was wrong.

I slam the laptop shut and lean back against my pillows. I feel . . . numb. Not anger, not depression, not any other emotion I can label . . . just numb. Why? Why would my mother go with him if Dad was so unstable? Why bring me? Why not get him help?

Was he sick for very long? Was it something new? Did he even know what he was doing, or was he delusional?

I close my eyes and try to remember anything. Anything to give me some idea who we were as a family. Were we ever as happy as Alec's family obviously is?

I push my thoughts aside, searching the black behind my eyelids for any trace of my parents. And I hear laughter. Joyous laughter—a woman. My mom, I'm certain.

In the background there's the hypnotic whisper of water lapping; soft, rhythmic slaps against the well-worn dock at the lake house where we lived when I was young. I feel feet thudding against warped, mismatched boards. And finally I see, just a glimpse. Bright sunshine rippling over the mountains, a hawk hovering overhead, watching our antics as I race my mother and father to leap together in faith, the three of us soaring into cold, soothing water.

I hold my breath, feel their hands grasp mine, keeping me safe, never letting me escape to the dark, magic kingdom hiding in the depths below. They always pulled me back, my lifeline to the sun and air and world above. They never once let me go.

But you ran. They were fighting for their lives and you ran. The recriminating voice in my head is my own. A misery of guilt and despair smother me, threaten to choke me with my own tears. Because it's true. That night, I ran. I abandoned my family.

And look what happened, the voice cackles. *Do you remember? Remember what happened after you ran away?*

Sand grits beneath my legs and I'm cold, so cold. I'm not me anymore, I'm Nora, scared little Nora who ran . . .

A crack came from behind her. Loud, like the grown-up movies on TV she wasn't supposed to watch. Then a woman screamed, but it wasn't on TV—it was her mommy. There was another crack and another, and now it was her daddy yelling, crying, not sounding at all like Daddy. He sounded angry and scared and she wanted to cry, but Mommy had said not to, so she swallowed hard until her crying was all inside her head, but that was still too loud and she had to be quiet, be quiet, so she held her breath and waited and waited and waited . . .

Everything went silent except the rushing noise that never stopped. Her chest was hot and felt about to burst, so she slowly let her breath out and even more slowly took a new one in, tasting the air, listening hard.

Nothing. She slit one eye open, peered into the night. Mountains of sand towered over her hiding spot where she'd crawled beneath a carpet of vines. Nothing, no one. Just a thick fog like when she'd piled her pillows on the floor and jumped off her bed and one of them burst open and let loose white, fluffy cloud-like stuff. Only this fog circling around her hiding place, it didn't fall away like her pillow stuffing—it stayed there, growing thicker and thicker, a white blanket draped beneath the black night sky.

She was alone. Carefully, still not making a sound like Mommy said, she crawled free of the vines and grass and stood. She had to find her mommy and daddy. Then everything would be okay, like it always was.

The screams and the sounds had come from somewhere in front of her, she thought—she wasn't certain, but she thought—so as much as it frightened her, she crept toward the hills made of sand, away from the rushing noise, the crash-quiet-crash noise that never stopped, only paused to catch its breath. The noise was somehow reassuring, an anchor as the fog blinded her steps and she stumbled through the strange white fog-black night.

She shouldn't be here, out in the night alone, lost, so far from Mommy and Daddy. It wasn't safe. She hugged her arms around her chest, let herself cry even though she still didn't make a sound—at least not one loud enough to be heard over the rush-crash-rush-crash. She just wanted Mommy and Daddy. She never should have run away. Never should have left them.

Once she found them, she'd never leave again. She'd be a good girl. Whatever made them bring her here, to this strange, frightening place, she'd never do it again, she promised.

She topped the hill of sand and suddenly it was bright light pushing her back with hot dragon's breath. Its smoke-filled wings spread black and furious, filling the sky as its mouth belched red and orange flames.

Panicked, she slipped and fell, tumbling down the hill and back into the prickly vines, sand filling her mouth and nose. This time when she got back up, she could barely breathe from the smoke choking her lungs; the entire night had roared into a raging cauldron of heat and stink and flames.

She ran. Away from the too-bright flames. Toward the rushing sound. Toward where the night was still and calm and black, two moons beckoning her with soft, silvery comfort. One was high in the sky, the other reflected in the water. So much water. Stretching far and wide, more than even her lake back home. Water, warm and safe, swirling around her ankles, tugging her forward, inviting her.

Sobbing, she fell into its embrace.

I'm still in the meeting room, hastily jotting down notes and a to-do list in my notebook. Dad hadn't been much comfort, but he was helpful. He's been a police officer for almost twenty years, first a deputy and now a detective, and has learned a lot about people during that time.

"You're a man now," he told me. "Step up. Take responsibility for your life. And for what you did to hers."

"Nothing is how I thought it would be." I hadn't intended that as a whine—although part of me would have liked to stew a little. But there was no time for self-pity. I needed to fix this. For Nora. "Where did I go wrong?"

"This is why you're not a cop. You're a storyteller. And you've been telling yourself this particular fairy tale for fifteen years. I mean, seriously, son, what did you think would happen?"

I braced myself; we'd had this conversation at least two dozen times since I told my folks I wouldn't be going to UNC or Clemson or even staying home to keep taking classes at USC-Beaufort. I'd given up on all the schools that wanted me in order to chisel my way into a tiny college in a small, obscure city in Pennsylvania where I knew no one. Except Nora.

"Was there any other way it could have gone?" Dad continued. Not ranting or haranguing, more like relieved his only child was finally accepting reality. "Did you think she'd want to help you investigate her own father's mental illness? Probe her family history—question her own sanity? Not to mention the fact she's only seventeen."

"Eighteen," I corrected without thinking. "Her birthday was yesterday."

There was a pause followed by a sigh. "You told the girl about all of this on her *birthday*?"

"I didn't realize—I just thought it was any other day. Plus, on Thursdays she's here at the college for class. I wanted her to feel comfortable, in a safe environment, when I introduced myself."

"And instead, you come off as the stalker of the century. You try that down here, y'all'd be lucky you didn't get a back end full of buckshot for your troubles." His voice dropped, low and serious. "Son, you need to get over this thing. It's ruining your life. And now hers."

"I can't leave until I make it right for her. That's why I called. I don't know what to do."

"Start with apologizing. Explain to her how you are when you get an idea in your head—like that time you were eight and decided it would be a good idea to climb the tallest pine around and see for yourself just what an osprey nest looked like. You planned that ill-fated expedition for what, a month?"

More like two months, not that I'd ever admit it. I'd made it to the top of the tree but there had been chicks in the nest, and the mother—or maybe the father, I couldn't tell, because all I'd seen was a tornado of feathers and talons and a beak that could snap my head right off my shoulders. So I'd made the strategic decision to retreat.

Which translated to falling. Branches catching and slowing me but also scratching and tearing, blinding me with flying needles, my hands flailing, grasping for a handhold, until finally I was on the ground. Fifty-four assorted stitches later and a cast on my broken arm—I'd snapped the bone right near the elbow, which ended any hope I had of throwing a ball straight ever again—and all I had to show for it was a cautionary tale my parents never let me forget.

That and first prize in the Pat Conroy Lowcountry Storyteller's contest—the first of many awards for my writing. But this wasn't a story. This was real life. I needed to stop trying to live out the fantasy I'd concocted and start fixing the damage I'd left in its wake.

"So I apologize. Should I tell her anything about the case?"

"Not unless she asks," Dad advised. "And then start with vague generalities. Don't get too specific, not until she's ready. And, son, she might never be ready. You've changed everything for her. She might not want to see you again. You need to respect her wishes. You understand?"

I sighed. "Yeah."

Dad's tone sharpened. "No, I don't think you do. You're used to wearing folks down or outsmarting them with an end run around them to get what you want. That's how you wound up there in Pennsylvania to start with, conning that teacher of yours to get you that job with his professor friend writing that tell-all true-crime trash."

"It's legitimate journalism—"

"It's voyeurism for profit." We'd had this conversation before as well. "My point is, you can't be dragging that poor girl and her family into your idea of how things should be. If she says no, if she slams the door in your face, you need to accept that and walk away. For good. Understand me, son?"

I grimaced as Dad's southern drawl thickened. After a few months up here—where everyone clips and skids their words together, bumper cars at a carnival slamming into each other and speeding away before you even knew what you'd been hit with—a voice from home sounds so welcome. But Dad wasn't saying what he was saying to assuage my homesickness or to make me feel better. No. This was Dad's "come to Jesus" tone. One you ignored at your peril.

"Yes, sir," I finally answered. "I understand."

"Good. Call your mother. She's worried about you."

Dad hung up, leaving me to plot out my apology. I was determined not to repeat the same mistakes I'd made yesterday. No ambushing Ella when she was alone. No hesitating about why I was there, giving her time to misconstrue everything. No lying to her, period.

That's about as far as I get before the meeting room door slams open and Max reappears. "I ought to deck you."

I fight to keep from rolling my eyes. Max is only a year younger than me, but somehow I feel like I've aged a decade, most of it in the past twenty-four hours. "Go ahead, if you think it will help Ella."

Max actually takes a stutter step forward, fists raised, before coming to his senses and instead kicking a chair away from the table and dropping into it. "You stay away from her."

"I intend to." It's the truth—kind of. I will stay away from Ella. Just as soon as I apologize and make sure she'll be okay. "Where is she now? With Rory?"

"No. We dropped her off back home. She's going to talk to her family. Tell them that she knows. That they don't have to lie to her anymore." He leans forward, one fist on top of the other, elbows splayed wide against the tabletop. Claiming more territory. Letting me know who's top dog here. "Do you have any idea what you've done?"

"How was I supposed to know she didn't know the truth? That her family had been lying to her for fifteen years?"

"Don't you dare! I wouldn't expect someone like you to understand what they did. They love her, they wanted to protect her from the ugly, awful truth for as long as they could." His words rush together as he becomes more agitated, until finally he spins back out of the chair, gesturing as he speaks. "That's real love. You've met Helen and Joe. Can you imagine how painful, how hard that was for them? Living a lie for so long? Until you come along and just, just—"

"Destroy everything?" I supply. I don't try to argue the point. How can I when Max is right?

"You're a freakin' human wrecking ball."

"I think I should go apologize. To Ella. And her family. I went too far, and I'm truly sorry." The words sound trite, too common by far for the size of my transgression, but they're a start.

Max paces, his steps jerky as he considers my words. I'm more than a little surprised that Max hasn't hit me—I wouldn't blame him if he had. But it's clear Max is much more of a thinker than a fighter. Just as it's clear that he is hopelessly in love with both Rory and Ella, although in different ways. I almost feel sorry for the guy.

Max whirls, obviously coming to a decision. "Yes. You need to apologize to everyone. But I know Ella. Now that she knows about this, she's going to pick at it like a scab until she's worried herself raw. You need to answer her questions in a way that will reassure her. Give her a sense of closure. Let her move on, not obsess over something she can't fix."

"How am I going to do that? Her dad murdered her mother, then shot himself. Who knows? He might have killed her as well if she hadn't run and hid."

"I don't know." Max plants himself in front of me. "But you need to make this right. And you have to promise me one thing. You cannot show her those photos of her folks. Not ever. I don't care what you tell her, you fix this. And then you stay out of her life."

I stand. "You mean you want me to lie to her? Isn't that what got us into this mess to start with?"

"*You* are what got us into this mess. And you're going to fix it, and then you're going to leave Ella alone. Forever."

"Okay." Max is the kind of guy who usually makes me want to argue, but there's no arguing about this. Only surrender. How did I screw up so badly? I turn to gather my stuff.

Max leans against the door, holding it closed. "Just make

sure you don't forget the last part. The part where you never see her again."

He yanks the door open and vanishes through it before I can say anything.

I sling my messenger bag over my shoulder and look around the empty room with regret. I don't care about Max or his stupid rules. But he's right about one thing—after I apologize to Ella, I need to let this go.

How can Ella look at me without remembering what I'd done? Without reliving the memory of her parents' deaths?

I came here because I thought she'd want me to, that it would fulfill the promise I'd made Nora so long ago, and had a crazy notion that she would remember me and together we'd discover the reason why her father had done what he'd done. But she didn't want me here. Didn't even remember who I was.

I wasn't helping her. Instead, I'd hurt her. Badly.

"Guess now, she's never going to forget you," I mutter. "Not after this."

I trudge from the room and snap the lights off.

CHAPTER 21

Ella

Feeling like a coward, my brain still trapped by memory combined with guilt and fear, I flee my room for the safe harbor that is my studio.

Years ago, I took over the detached garage behind our house as my studio. It's cold and drafty, but I have a space heater. Also, Joe found me these fantastic wool mittens with tops that snap back to turn them into fingerless gloves, and after I kept stealing Helen's lightweight but warm fleece sweater with deep pockets—not to mention snagging it on a canvas stretcher and smearing it with paint more than once—she deeded it to me.

The garage's overhead door is locked from the inside and I've blocked the bottom with rolled-up blankets to limit any drafts or rainwater leaks. I left the row of windows uncovered, and Joe and Darrin added two skylights, one on each side of the steeply pitched roof; plus, there's a window in the side door, so I get plenty of natural light.

As I step inside the studio, grabbing Helen's sweater from the peg beside the door, I push the button to lock the door behind me and sag against it, the soft fabric of Helen's sweater and comforting scent of her perfume—something expensive Darrin buys her in Paris—gathered around me. My mind feels shredded by unearthed shards of memory colored by the terror of that night so long ago and the guilt of abandoning my parents.

I press my palms against my eyes, but the shattered fragments of sights and sounds bombard me, colliding with my fears and doubts. Why was I there? Why didn't I remember? Why had Dad done it?

What if I've inherited what he had? Will I descend into violent madness, turn against the ones I love?

Forcing my eyes open, I scan my studio, deciding which project to use to drive away the pain. There's a collection of discarded bits and pieces of sheet metal and copper flashing for a multimedia project due next month, but I don't trust myself working with sharp edges and tools today.

Finished pieces—or nearly finished ones that I need a bit of time to ruminate on—hang from the rafters, floating in the breeze as I climb to my feet and turn on the space heater that stands just inside the door. Batik experiments from middle school are tacked over the windowless rear wall, adding bright color that most days I enjoy getting lost in.

There are seven easels with half-completed canvases—two are for class assignments, the rest are projects just for me. My imagination is always restless, never allowing me to focus on one project at a time, so I often rotate between them. There's one I've been struggling with for months—a swarm of bats spiraling out over the lake at twilight. I can never seem to capture the graceful chaos of their flight just right. They always come out either too rigid and controlled or too haphazard, as if they're crazed vampire bats from a horror movie, when the reality is more like a carefully choreographed ballet.

Finally, the largest canvas grabs my attention: a portrait of Rory that I want to finish by Christmas. I think—hope—it's my best work so far. Not that I'm a very good judge, but every time I walk in here and see it, I can't help but smile. If it gives her half the joy I've felt while painting it, then it will fulfill every dream I have for the piece.

I wind my way around Mason jars filled with brushes and cleaning fluids, different ones depending on the kind of brush and the medium. I should organize them on the workbench Joe built for me, but I like how the light sparks from the glazed concrete floor and catches in them—in fact, when I'm in a distracted mood like this, I'll often sketch or paint them as warm-up exercises.

Except today I'm in no mood to even do that—definitely not in the right mood to work on Rory's portrait. My space, always cluttered but never feeling crowded, suddenly feels chaotic and out of control. The easels and canvases block my view of the door, I almost trip over the sheet metal along with a pile of fabric I've been saving but can't remember why, and I have to catch a pickle jar of oversized brushes before it topples.

In the end, I grab a pencil just to keep my hand occupied, pull up one of my stools, and simply sit in the middle of my work and let the faint winter sunshine wash over me from the skylights. Then the sun shifts—this late in the year, it won't be long before it vanishes all together—and I'm left in shadow.

Holding a sketchpad on my lap, I keep my eyes half closed, focusing just beyond the paper so that the image is blurred. Then I slow my breathing and let my hand glide over the paper, without forcing it or looking at what I draw. One of my teachers starts every class this way—free drawing, she calls it, better than meditation for clearing the mind.

Usually she's right. But not today. Today my hand starts out slow, the pencil soft against the paper, but then memories begin to form. The crisp smell of the ocean combined with the sharp tang of decay from the dunes that surround me. I feel small, so very small. I cower in the grass, hiding from a man calling my name.

All I can think is: *What's happening to Mommy and Daddy?* The screams stop after the loud pops crack through the night, but the silence only makes me more terrified.

"Nora!" he shouts over the crash of the waves. "It's okay. Come out."

I don't. I'm not sure if it's because I don't recognize his voice—or if it's because I don't want to recognize it. Instead, I dig myself deeper into the grass and sand, ignoring the burrs digging into my flesh and the small creatures skittering around me. I carve out room for my face, my hands over my mouth and nose so I can breathe, but I don't breathe. I lie there, in the dark, and hold my breath, the only sound my heart pounding in time with the waves crashing.

Then footsteps come close and he calls my name again. I bite my lip, trembling like a mouse caught in a trap. "Nora!"

I try to pretend that I'm not there. That I never ran away, that I stayed with Mommy and Daddy. They'd keep me safe—or I could keep them safe, three-year-old me can't decipher the difference. All she knows is she's lost and alone and very, very scared.

The man's gone. I think. I risk opening one eye to scan the dunes above me. And freeze, my entire body gone rigid with fear. He's there. Standing in the moonlight. A strange orange glow surrounds him. The fire demon of my nightmares come to life.

My phone rings, vibrating from where it sits in the front

pocket of my overalls, thrumming into my heart. I startle, my pencil skids off the paper and I drop it. I blink, the spell broken. Unknown caller from a strange area code. "Hello?"

"It's Alec."

"How did you get my number?" My words curl around the phone in waves of cruel, scorched orange. Anger. A kind that's foreign to me.

"Rory."

I sit silent, stewing in a morass of emotions, my aura a bubbling cauldron.

"I called to apologize. Well, not to apologize—the apology I need to do in person." His accent draws out his words so they swim together. "Not just to you, I should probably apologize to your whole family. I can come over, answer any questions—"

"Not here," I interrupt him. "Darrin and Joe would kill you." Hyperbole of course—at least I hope so. But I remember the way Darrin's always-stable aura was disturbed, turning a violent shade of purple-black when I told them about Alec and how he'd told me the truth.

"Okay, right, sure." He's faltering, but I don't throw him a lifeline. My anger is cruel that way. Instantly, I feel ashamed. What my father did isn't Alec's fault; he's simply an easy target for my emotions. "But I want to answer your questions. Need to make sure you're all right. I never—I didn't—"

"Java Joe's," I decide. "Fifteen minutes."

"Okay. See you there. Thanks, I really—"

I hang up on him. Not from anger, but because I finally see what I drew. A silhouette of a man, his proportions askew, making him look monstrous. He's backlit by flames and smoke roils around him. All seen from the point of view of someone very small, below him. Like a little girl hiding below a sand dune, cowering in fear.

Is this monster what my father became when he surrendered to his demons?

Could this also be my destiny?

I jump off the stool and head for the door, forget to turn off the space heater and have to go back, then I'm in my car, not even telling anyone where I'm going or why. As I back out of the driveway, steering around Joe's truck and Darrin's Lexus, I feel like that little girl. Lost and afraid to look up for fear of what she'll find.

CHAPTER 22

Ella

Java Joe's is only a five-minute drive, so I'm expecting to beat Alec there, but I'm wrong. By the time I park and walk through the door, he's already at the table we shared last time, his back to the wall so he can see everybody. I catch him in the middle of his slurping routine, bitter black coffee twisting his face before he lowers the cup and adds the cream.

In a way I'm returning to the scene of the crime. The place where his lies began. Except he never really lied to me, did he? He just thought I knew more than I did. He had no idea he'd been lighting a fuse.

His hand with the metal cream container trembles a little as he sees me. He sets it down. I don't need to see his aura to know how uncertain and anxious he is. I slow my pace, let my eyes linger on his, unsure.

As I slide in, the waitress approaches with a pot of hot water, tea, and a steaming grilled sticky bun. She leaves and Alec and I sit in silence, the delicious scents of the food swirling between us. Once again, he's ordered nothing but coffee for himself. "Aren't you hungry?"

He shakes his head. "Not when I'm nervous."

"I make you nervous?"

His eyes go wide and he hides behind his coffee mug as he sips, his glasses fogging from the steam. For some reason, I feel like I suddenly have the upper hand—very different than the last time we sat here. I want to ask him why I make him nervous. Instead, I decide to be merciful and nibble at my sticky bun, not tasting as I swallow, surprised my topsy-turvy stomach doesn't rebel.

"I'm sorry," he finally says. He places his palms flat on the table, fingers splayed wide on either side of the coffee mug. I notice that he's aligned everything on his side of the table to line up; each piece of silverware, even his hands surrounding the mug, all equidistance apart.

"I know," I answer. "You thought you had the facts, thought I knew them as well. That part I get. What I don't understand is, what do you want? My permission to write about my parents in that book your professor is writing? Do you want to show me off to him, an example of your journalistic prowess?" My anger is coloring my words so I stop, take a breath, try to calm down. "Just tell me why you're even here."

His hands don't move from where they're planted on the table—not unlike the hands of a suspect before a police officer pats them down, I can't help but think. But the rest of his body recoils at my words, leaning back away from me, pressed against the booth's cushion.

"I screwed up," he finally says. "Sometimes I get so wrapped up in getting my questions answered, tying up all the loose ends, that I forget there are real people at the heart of every story. I should have left as soon as I realized that you didn't remember."

My sigh has a life of its own, spreading deep aubergine wings as it spirals through the space between us. "No. I'm glad you didn't. Leave, that is. I need to know the truth."

His eyes brighten. "That's all I want as well. It's why I'm here."

"Right. That and an eyewitness account for your professor's new book."

"That's not true. I mean, yes, he does want to publish your story, but I won't write it, not if you don't want me to."

"I don't."

"Okay." He breaks his careful arrangement of hands and eating utensils to slide one hand forward until his fingers are almost touching mine. "What do you want me to do?"

"I want the truth—not just your facts and forensics," I tell him before he can interrupt. "All of it. Because I think you and the police created a picture with the facts you have and decided it was the truth. But it's not."

He frowns, obviously not agreeing. I grab a napkin and a pencil from my overalls and quickly sketch a figure.

"What do you see?" I ask him.

"A duck."

"You sure?"

He peers at the napkin as if it's the Holy Grail. "No. Wait. A rabbit?" His gaze pops up to meet mine. "It's both."

"Exactly. Same lines, different truths."

A not-uncomfortable silence envelops us. My aura has calmed as my anger recedes, his agitation also fades as he takes a deep breath and releases it, not even noticing that his fork has tilted away from its plumb line. His anxiety must be contagious, because now my fingers itch to straighten the off-kilter utensil.

"We start over," he suggests. "Trust nobody, assume nothing." His smile is wistful. "That's what my dad always says when he's stuck during an investigation."

It takes me a moment before I nod in agreement. I don't like venturing into the unknown like this—not with so much at stake. But on the other hand, with so much at stake, how can I refuse?

"Where do we start?" I ask.

"I have all the police reports." He seems hesitant, and I remember his reluctance to show them to us earlier.

"From your father?"

He surprises me by chuckling. "No way. My dad hates that I'm looking into the case and that I've been obsessed with it since I was little. I filed a Freedom of Information request and gathered everything from the state, coroner, and local officials. Took me almost two years—government bureaucracy—but I used it as my college admission essay. Without naming you," he hastens to add. "I talked about the process, the quest for the truth, importance of a free and unfettered press. All that BS admission committees love if you're applying to a journalism program."

"You've been working on my parents' case for two years? Why?"

His eyes drift away from mine and his expression turns haunted. "I've been working this case all my life. You might have been too young to remember what happened that night, but I was too old to forget."

CHAPTER 23

Alec

I want to take the words back as soon as I say them. There is only one thing Dad and Dr. Winston agree on: feelings are a luxury you can't afford on the job. But how can I tell the real story, the real truth of what happened and why, without emotions?

My mouth goes dry and my chest tightens. My coffee has grown cold, but I take a sip, just to have something to occupy my hands. Still, she says nothing.

Finally, I find the courage to meet her eyes. She's watching me, her expression unreadable—maybe if I had her gift of auras, I'd know what she's thinking. I'm certain she can read me more easily than the neon signs that fill the diner's walls.

I realize I'm fiddling with the silverware, so I flatten my palms against the table, trying to still them. To my surprise, she covers my hand with hers. A stray memory startles me—a little girl's hand clutching mine, so very pale against my dark skin.

I glance up from our two hands pressed together against the old-fashioned red laminate tabletop. A strange smile quirks her lips.

"We start over," she says in a firm voice. "Start fresh. With everything."

Stunned, I nod. Does she mean it? A fresh start . . . for us?

She pulls her hand back, pushes her plate aside and sits up straight. "So. Two people dead. A suspicious fire. No assumptions. Where do we begin?"

I slide my hand back, lower it below the table, crush it into a fist. She means the case. And only the case. Idiot. When would I learn? No assumptions. She's so very right about that.

Before I can answer, the door to the diner opens and a group of college students barrels in, loud and boisterous. Ella turns in her seat to look at them, then turns back. "Too many people. Let's walk—someplace quiet, where we can think."

She scoots out of the booth and I follow, grabbing my bag and throwing money on the table. All I have is a twenty, twice the price of our food, but despite the fact it's my meal money for the next week, I don't stop to wait for change, too afraid she'll change her mind and keep going without me.

I rush out and catch up with her on the sidewalk. Her face is tilted to the sky as if searching for the sun. Not that there is much. Even though the sky is clear, ever since the clocks turned back it's felt as if the sun is playing hide and seek, out of alignment with the rest of the world. Definitely more so than back home, where I barely noticed the start or end of daylight savings time. There, even in November, the sun is always bright, reflecting from water and sand.

Or maybe those are simply the memories of home that I cling to. A lifeline to get me through this miserable gray Pennsylvanian winter.

A foursome of students crowd between me and Ella. As soon as they pass, I close the distance between us.

"Where to? Back to the student union?" It's almost one o'clock, but if no one else is using the meeting room I can extend my reservation.

"The duck pond," she declares. "I think better outside, away from people."

I let her lead me back to campus. We head behind the student union and take an empty paved path that winds into the trees between it and the science building. I've never been back here before—given the lack of trash, graffiti, and other student detritus, I'm guessing most students haven't found this particular section of campus either. The path turns to gravel then hard-packed dirt as it winds through sumac, oak, and pine trees. The smell of autumn is intoxicating, different than back home where the live oaks stay green and leafy year-round and the main indication of winter coming is the wood smoke drifting from chimneys and the sweet grass's feathery plumes turning purple, scenting the air with vanilla.

"You know where you're going?" I ask as the path branches once and then again, finally dwindling to the point where we have to walk one behind the other. She doesn't hesitate as the trees shiver in the breeze, scattering dead leaves like a benediction.

The trees give way as the path branches one final time, two arms embracing a shimmering body of water. There's a small dam at one end of the pond, water rippling over its spillway, and a family of ducks circling a group of reeds. It's an oasis of quiet—the quietest space I've found since coming north to this noisy city.

I close my eyes and inhale. The water doesn't smell like home—too clean, none of the pungent saltiness of the tidal plough mud—but the gentle lap of water against land, the rustle of bird wings and tall grass, and the sigh of the trees behind me all whisper "home."

"There's a bench over here," she says. I take another moment, then open my eyes and follow her.

"I come here to paint sometimes." She crosses her legs

beneath her as she sits down on a splintered park bench. "Or to think." The ducks note our presence and beat their wings against the water, racing over to Ella. She laughs. "And feed the ducks. Sorry, guys, nothing for you today."

The birds quack and flap their wings, two larger ones making their way onto land, waddling around her feet, inspecting the ground. Disappointed, they return to their flock.

I sit down beside her. "This is my new favorite place," I tell her. "Reminds me of home."

She stiffens at that, and I kick myself mentally for saying anything. "I wish I could remember more. How long was I there?"

"Eleven days. Your gram and uncle came to pick you up the day before Thanksgiving. Even though we said good-bye, I still didn't believe you were leaving for good, so I insisted on setting a place for you at Thanksgiving."

I don't tell her the rest—how for years I insisted on saving a place for Nora at the family table, how I'd scrawled pictures and made invitations that Mom would slide into thick envelopes and mail for me. It became the family joke, but I never laughed about it. Instead, after everyone was sated and leaning back, watching football, I'd sneak out, go down to the empty patch of land where the burned-out cabin once sat, searching the dunes for any trace of her, waiting for her at the ocean's edge until the sun set behind me and the moon rose.

"Eleven days," she echoes. "Why so long?"

"No one knew who your parents were. The police traced the car registration to your dad. His emergency contact was his partner."

"Darrin." She frowns.

"And he was out of the country, attending a conference in London. Your mom didn't list any next of kin other than your father, so it wasn't until the police tracked down Darrin that they knew about your grandmother and uncle."

She frowned at that. "Isn't that strange? That Helen and Joe weren't listed as next of kin? Didn't they realize my parents were missing?"

"Everyone thought your folks were on vacation, remember? And your gram and uncle lived in a small town in upstate New York—from the interview notes, it sounded as if they hadn't seen your parents in a while."

"Why not? New York's not that far for us to go visit them."

I shrug. "Maybe because you were just a baby? Too difficult to make the trip?"

She considers that. "Then why bother to take me on vacation? Why not just leave me with Helen?"

"I don't know. Anyway, my family is registered for emergency foster care, so we took you in. By the time Helen and Joe made it down, the police verified your parents' ID."

"How? You said DNA—from family members?"

"Your dad didn't have any family."

"My dad's dad died right before I was born. Heart attack. His mom when he was still in college. Cancer." Her face remains placid, staring out at the ducks, but her hands tighten over her knees. I can't even begin to imagine how painful this must be for her.

"The police in South Carolina called the police up here, and they went to your home, gathered toothbrushes, stuff like that with DNA. Also checked to see if there was any evidence indicating why . . ." I trail off, uncertain how to qualify what the investigators had been searching for. The reports used official language like "previous incidents or episodes of violent or aberrant behavior," but no way am I going to repeat that to her.

"So the DNA proved that they were my parents and after that they were able to notify next of kin. I guess it doesn't happen as fast as in the movies."

"No. Not with so many jurisdictions involved—it was too big a case for the local department to handle alone, so the state police did most of the work. Plus, tests take time, witnesses have to be located and interviewed. There are a lot of moving parts."

"Did I tell you anything about that night? Back then, I mean."

"You didn't say anything. I mean literally not a word, not the whole time you were with us." Eleven days she refused to leave my side—wouldn't even go to sleep until I threw a sleeping bag down on the floor beside her bed in the guest room. "Social services, a psychologist from the mainland, the cops—no one could get a word out of you. Even when your gram and uncle came, you kept hold of my hand, like you were in shock, didn't know who they were—"

"I'd just turned three, maybe I didn't. Not if I didn't see them very often."

"Anyway, they took you home. We never heard from you again." I hesitate. "I wrote you. A few letters that year, a few more the year after. Do you remember that?" What I really mean to ask is, *do you remember me?* But her answer would break my heart, so I keep silent.

She shakes her head. "I guess they were worried about the trauma, wanted to protect me? They never gave me any of your letters, I'm sorry. But I think I might remember something of that night. I remember running and hiding, a man shouting, being terrified that he was hunting me, that he'd find me. I remember the fire—and running to the water. But the man, who was the man? If someone else was there, then maybe—"

"They didn't find any trace of anyone else," I tell her. And immediately regret once again cutting off any avenue of hope.

"Maybe they were wrong," she snaps. Then she takes a breath, calms herself. "But we're starting fresh, remember.

Once you know who the victims are, where do you look next? The evidence?"

"Close associates. Family. Anyone with a motive." I steer her away from the forensic evidence—no way is she ever seeing those photos. And the evidence is clear cut: both victims killed by the same nine-millimeter pistol, the same pistol found in possession of the male whose wounds were consistent with a self-inflicted gunshot to the head.

"Motive. Right. Let's start there." She turns to me. "Family's out—you said they hadn't even seen us in months. And Darrin was in London, so it wasn't him. Why would anyone want my parents dead?"

That's a very good question, I think.

CHAPTER 24

Ella

"**Motive usually boils down to profit,** power, or passion," Alec tells me. He sounds so earnest, like a law professor or something. Much older than his years. "At least that's what my dad always says."

"Passion—like a love affair?" I'm shaking my head. "That's the one thing even I remember, how much in love my parents were. They—we—were happy." I'm trying to convince him, as if what Alec believes could change what dozens of professional investigators decided fifteen years ago.

He hesitates. "Okay. Let's skip that one." He leans back on the bench, one arm slung over his messenger bag beside him. But he doesn't need to get his laptop; it's clear he remembers everything about my parents' case. "Power. Guess that would be control of Cleary and Sons, right?"

"That's Darrin, but he was in London. Besides, he was

my dad's best friend. They were college roommates. And he's worked his butt off growing the company, basically rebuilt it from the ground up after my parents died. But according to their will, Cleary and Sons still belongs to me. So I can continue the family legacy." I hate the gray tinge of bitterness that colors my words, am thankful Alec is blind to it. My parents couldn't have foreseen how their final wishes bound me tighter than iron chains.

"The police verified Darrin's alibi." He frowns. "But maybe that's a motive for Helen and Joe? With you alive and your parents dead, they can access all that money."

I shake my head and roll my eyes, the idea is so ridiculous. "Right, the two people on the planet who want nothing more than to become hermits and lock themselves away from the rest of the world would conspire to be forced to raise a kid? No way. Besides, Darrin controls the money. He has to approve any expenses, like when we moved into town and bought the house here or redid the basement and turned it into a studio for Helen."

He frowns, his pool of suspects quickly diminishing. "Which brings us right back to profit. Follow the money. If it wasn't Darrin, Helen, or Joe, who else stood to gain from your parents' deaths?"

"That's easy. Me." Though I don't remember much about that night, I'm at least sure I had no hand in my parents' deaths—other than running away and abandoning them. "I get everything—the family trust, their insurance policies, even a special educational trust that Darrin just told me about. Now that I'm eighteen, I can access that money as well."

"No one else? Maybe at Cleary and Sons?"

"Darrin's the only one who still works there—after my parents died, he expanded the company, refocused it on targeting corporate clients, which meant new specialists, new staff. The only thing left of the old Cleary and Sons are a few document boxes in the attic at my old house up at the lake."

That makes me wonder about what else might be up there—maybe it's time I finally looked? The last time I was up in the attic at the lake house was back when I was twelve and Joe and I moved the bat colony to the dock.

Alec seems to be thinking along another direction entirely. "Maybe you should use the money. Leave, forget about all this, go to Paris." His tone has changed, is suddenly charged. "Why open up old wounds you didn't even know exist?"

Now it's my turn to become emotional. I stand up, turn to face him. "Why? It wasn't my idea to come bursting into my life asking about my parents."

He looks away, shame-faced. "I know. I know. I said I was sorry."

"What if it was someone like a serial killer? A random act of violence?" My aura is warm, shimmering like wet blood. "We can't let them get away with murder."

"It's a possibility, I guess. But no matter what we learn, we might find answers you don't want to hear. Are you prepared for that?"

Now I see what he's saying. He still believes the police. "You think if we can't find any evidence that someone else killed them, then it was my father. That he snapped, went mental, did that to my mom, to me—" I'm scared and angry and uncertain and my voice shakes beneath the weight of it all. "That *he* was the random act of violence."

Alec jumps up, places his palms on my arms, anchoring me. "It happens. Doesn't mean it's anyone's fault, or that it might—"

"Might happen again? Like to me? Because stuff like that, psychosis, severe mental illness, it's often hereditary, right? That's what you're really afraid of, isn't it? If we can't find a good reason why my father did what he did, then that's all that's left. And that means . . ."

I gasp for air, twist free of his hands, unable to finish the thought. Because what that means for me, I can't even begin to comprehend. "No. I don't believe it. There was a man. I heard him, saw him, he was there."

"Ella." His voice is soft, guiding me back from the brink. "Either way, it's okay. You're not alone. This is all my fault and I'm not going to leave you. No matter what, I'll see it through. I promise."

I whip away, can't stand looking at him.

"Maybe I don't want you here." I spit out the words and race down the path, away from him, away from facts and evidence and forensic truths. Running toward the only truth I know: home.

CHAPTER 25

Ella

Blinded by emotion, I don't even remember the drive home. After throwing my phone on the charger in my bedroom—mainly to have an excuse not to answer in case Alec or anyone called—I shut myself inside my studio, trying hard to relegate everything Alec has told me into something small and manageable that I can pretend doesn't exist, like a child playing hide and seek, covering her eyes to make herself invisible to the rest of the world.

I have no idea how long I've sat staring at my portrait of Rory when a timid knock on the side door comes. I get up and walk toward it, noticing that it's already dark outside. Uncle Joe waits, holding a plate and a glass of milk. "Nothing better than next-day birthday cake, right?"

He raises his offerings with a hopeful half smile. His aura bathes the cake and milk in a pale glow the color of bruised peaches. Not necessarily an ugly color, but it does make the food suddenly unappealing. Or maybe I've lost my appetite after everything that's happened.

"Darrin took your gram to meet with her new producer, so it's just us left to forage for ourselves." Joe skirts the canvases and bottles of pigment, managing only to topple and re-right one Mason jar of paint thinner near the space heater before he makes it to the chair nearest to my stool. He sets the food down, spilling milk on my sketchpad, but that's okay, as nothing I've been able to put to paper today is any good. He stands behind me, one hand resting on my shoulder. "Long day."

All I can do is nod.

"I like the painting. Is it Marilyn Monroe? Reminds me of Andy Warhol's portrait of her—like you went from the real woman to his portrait and then back to who she could have been if she had lived or something. Very *ethereal.*" One of his favorite words—tastes like vanilla, he says.

I almost laugh—his intention, I think, but I'm not sure. Joe is what I'd call "art blind." He loves talking about art. Trying to compete with Darrin, who's always bringing me catalogues from world-famous galleries and collections he's visited. But Joe can't appreciate the difference between a Warhol and a Kandinsky.

Once, years ago, me, Max, and Rory got together and bought a paint-by-numbers velvet Elvis that we all did together and gave him for his birthday. It was meant to be a joke, but he put it in an expensive frame, declared it was the best gift ever, and it still hangs above his fireplace in the lake house. Even had us all sign it. Thankfully, we're the only people who ever visit him, so I don't have to worry about being humiliated in front of strangers.

He's made me smile—it feels like my first of the day—and, grateful for the kindness, I hug him so hard that I'm almost crying again.

As I slump back onto my stool he says, "Oh, honey, I'm sorry. Did I say something wrong? You know me, I know nothing about art."

I shake my head, staring at the paint splatters on the concrete floor.

"It was that boy, wasn't it? He has no right, coming here, insinuating himself into your life, trying to hurt you."

I want to set him straight about Alec, but I simply don't have the words—not that I could get them past the boulder in my throat anyway. I feel miserable, worse than having the flu, when the fever drowns you in your own sweat at the same time it parches you from the inside out.

"Tell me the truth." I finally manage to find my voice again. "You knew Dad. Did you have any warning? Was he . . . sick?"

There are other words I want to use, gentler words like *troubled* or *depressed*, but I know they're words that will trigger Joe's synesthesia in a bad way, so I avoid them. But *sick* also doesn't feel right. It's much too small, too weak for what my father did—and why he did it. Something that horrific, that monstrous, deserves a word larger than life.

He pats the top of my head like he used to when I was little. "After he and your mom got married, after you were born, we never saw much of him—of any of you. They didn't come home for holidays, always had an excuse—work or other plans. A young family, both your parents working such long hours to build Cleary and Sons, a toddler at home, it made sense . . . until it didn't." He shakes his head so hard his hair falls into his face. "I don't know if there's anything we could have seen, could have done—it's something that will haunt us the rest of our lives."

"But surely you talked about it—after. Had he seen a doctor? Did Darrin notice anything at work?" I'm grasping at will-o'-wisps, searching for logic in an event that defies logic.

"No. Nothing. If only—" His sigh whooshes through the rafters above us. "Darrin, none of us, even knew he'd taken you and your mother away. With Darrin gone at that conference, your dad was meant to be at the office, running things." He stalks through the crowded garage, his pace stuttering. "I wish I had answers, but I don't. No one does."

His erratic movements send a stack of canvases cascading to the floor and another Mason jar of cleaning fluid spills, its fumes stinging my eyes. He turns back to me, fists raised, searching for a target. I've never seen him so agitated.

"We could go. Get away from all this," he says, the width of the garage dividing us. "Darrin told you about your trust, right? Let's change those tickets, go to Paris right now. If you ask him, he'll give you the money, I'm sure. He knows how miserable you are here."

"How much money is there? How does it all work?" I'm curious, but more than that I'm desperate to change the subject away from my leaving home. There's a strange tug of war pulling at my insides. I've dreamed of so many far-off places: the towers of New York, Chicago's old-school architecture, seeing a full moon over the ocean, and yes, even Paris. All so far out of reach that I've sequestered them behind mental walls as mere childish fantasies.

But now, suddenly, I have the chance. And part of me wants to take that chance. But there's that insidious whisper of dread overshadowing my dreams. That if I leave my family, run off to some strange, wonderful place, something terrible will happen.

I used to think that whisper was simple childish fear. That all I needed was to grow up, find someone else to look after Helen and Joe. But thanks to Alec, I know better. It's not fear of what might happen, it's terror over what *already* happened.

Joe does a quick calculation. Numbers aren't his thing.

"How much? Sitting there for fifteen years, compound interest, all that jazz, gotta be over seven million now."

"Seven million? Dollars?" I almost fall off my stool. Shades of iridescent green swirl through the air, practically filling the room with the allure of money.

"Yep. All yours. Well, once you're twenty-one. Until then, Darrin has to approve any withdrawals."

"I had no idea." I knew my parents had left my family fairly comfortable as far as money went—enough for us to keep the lake house for Joe, and when I started school, to move us here to the city, buy this house, help Helen get started with her voice acting career, pay the bills. But . . . seven million dollars? That was a kind of rich I'd never imagined.

"It's a lot of money. You'll need to be careful. Who you tell—not even friends."

He's right. Rory and Max would freak. I sober up fast. "Money like that changes everything."

"Exactly. But there's no reason not to use it. Let's take it out for a test drive. You and I." Hope sparks bright through his cloak of burnt umber doom and gloom. "Darrin knows how much you hate winter. Besides, you're just wasting time this year, waiting until you can go to college."

Technically, I could have graduated last year since I'd doubled up on my core academics to make more time for my art classes. There didn't seem to be any reason to rush—at least that's what I told Darrin and Helen. Really, I'm terrified to even start looking at colleges, for fear that I'll finally have to tell them the truth: I don't want to take over Cleary and Sons. I don't want to go to business school or become an actuary.

"No. I can't leave. Not now."

He doesn't understand, I can tell. How could he? I don't understand it myself. All I know is that running away isn't the answer. Not this time. I need to stay here, figure out my past, figure out my life.

"Drink your milk," he says, the words billowing with that same weird orange-yellow glow they had when he walked in. I'm not sure what it means, but it didn't exist before today. Guilt for hiding the truth about my parents? Worry about what I'm going through? It circles the cake and milk in a fog. "Enjoy your cake. We'll talk more later."

He's close enough to the door that he could just walk out. Instead, he surprises me, rushes back and gives me a big hug, almost toppling me from the stool, and sets me down with a gentle kiss on the forehead. "I wish there was some way to fix everything. Love you, kiddo."

He releases me and steps back, staring at me as if he wants to say something more. Instead, he simply hands me the glass of milk. He whirls and leaves, a canvas and easel rocking in his wake, but as he opens the door I hear him shout, "What are you doing here?"

Energy sparks through the air, bright red embers sizzling in the sunset's fading light. I slide off my stool to join Joe at the door, clicking on the outside lights.

"You need to leave. Now," Joe is saying, any sweetness in his tone gone.

Alec stands there, bathed in the too-bright light, hands shoved deep into the pockets of his coat, but head held high. He's almost the same size as Joe, I realize with surprise. Maybe even a little taller.

"I came to apologize again," he says. "If you'll let me." The last is aimed at me, his gaze tangling with mine as if Joe doesn't exist.

"She will not. You've caused enough trouble. Leave now."

Alec looks to me, his face so filled with remorse and anguish that I don't need to see his aura.

"It's okay," I tell Joe.

"No, it's not." Joe refuses to back down, tries to block my view of Alec.

"She can make her own decisions," Alec snaps. "She's not a little kid anymore."

"No, I'm not," I flare back, annoyed by their patronizing tones. "So both of you can stop treating me like one. Joe, thanks, but I'm fine. Alec, you have five minutes." I wave my hand, inviting one man inside and ushering the other out. Joe frowns and hesitates outside the door, staring at me until I shut it firmly.

CHAPTER 26

Alec

I step inside Ella's studio and stop to collect myself. Last thing I wanted was for her to see me unleash my anger on her uncle, but I couldn't help it. Not only did her family hide the truth from her all her life, they all seem to treat her more like a possession or a child instead of the smart, caring, thoughtful person she so clearly is. Something inside me wants—needs—to stand up for her, protect her.

She walks past me without even looking in my direction. Because of course she doesn't need protecting. Especially not from me, the guy who brought her whole world crashing down around her. My shoulders slump. Why can't I find the right words to explain things to her? It's as if when she's around, my thoughts and emotions get twisted up so tight they all just spin out of my control.

I have to get everything right this time. As I gather my

words, parsing each one, trying to craft the perfect speech, something bulletproof against my churning feelings, I look around the studio. Ella's perched on a stool in front of a large painting of a girl, her movement sending a paper sketch drifting down to the floor by my feet. I pick it up and all I can do is stare, my carefully collected words of apology forgotten.

"Who's this?" I ask, my fingers sweating, smudging the pencil strokes that cover the page in a furious, jagged scrawl. The figure is dark, his face hidden, a monster surrounded by flames. Is it me? Is this how she remembers me from that night so long ago?

Or is it how she sees me now? The obsessed madman who's shattered her life?

My hand trembles as I wait for her response.

"I told you, I saw a man that night. He was calling my name, looking for me."

I blink in relief. Once again, I want to keep quiet, let her hold on to her false hope, but the truth weighs too heavy and I can't help but set it free. "There was no evidence of anyone else there. Are you sure this isn't—"

She reaches out and yanks the paper from my hand. "It's not my father."

"How can you be sure when you can't remember?" I temper my words by placing a palm on her arm. I keep my touch gentle but firm, and I can feel her agitation. Like my own, it buzzes just beneath her skin.

She frowns. "You think I'm imagining, that these aren't memories? That I'm . . . delusional?"

The words aren't spoken as they hang between us both: *Like my father?*

"I'm sorry," I say. "Again. I promised you a fresh start on your parents' case. I shouldn't have dismissed your alternative hypothesis so readily."

"Anyone ever tell you that you're really good at saying you're sorry but not so great at actually meaning it?" Her words snap between us like a whip cracking through the air.

Words failing me—as they seem to so often when I'm with her—I hold my hands out wide. "Read my aura. Can't you see that I mean what I say?"

She stares at me, her cheeks flushing and her eyes flashing as if she thinks I might be making fun of her synesthesia.

I'm not. I'm curious, truly curious. "Seriously. What color is my aura? What does it tell you?"

"Stop it," she flares.

What did I do now? I wonder as I drop my hands back to my sides.

"I can't see your aura. Happy? So go ahead, lie, cheat, steal, do what you want, I'll never know."

Wait. "I don't have an aura?" That makes no sense. In everything I've read about synesthesia, each person's symptoms remain consistent. Curiosity crowds out everything else—including the reason why I came here in the first place. "Does that happen very often?"

She glances down at the sketch of the man crumpled in her fist. "Never. You're the first."

"But why? I don't understand. Why would I be special?"

She says nothing, simply shakes her head while huddled on the stool, obviously miserable. I try to make amends. "That must be strange. Like you can't trust me. But you can. You know that, right?"

"Sure. Because life has been so wonderful ever since we met."

I turn away before she can see my crushed expression. My motion makes the large canvas sway. I reach to save it from falling, rebalance it on the easel until it's perfectly square.

I study the portrait of the girl, comparing it to the other paintings. Ella's work is breathtakingly vivid—abstract swirling dervishes of pure color, emotion roiling off the images as if instead of looking at a static picture of a person or thing, I'm being given a chance to see into Ella's soul.

This is how she sees the world. So different from my reality, my truth. Her synesthesia tells a person's story to her, and it colors everything Ella sees—and paints. Her entire world, her idea of reality is based on her auras, colorful symptoms of a mis-wired brain.

No wonder she's always on edge around me. If she can't

see my aura, which she depends on as my truth, she must feel blind, lost. There have been moments when she relaxes, seems comfortable with me, but now I finally understand why those fragile moments have been so easily shattered.

How can I make her understand *me*? Words seem too small compared to Ella's vivid, larger-than-life colors.

As I stare at the portrait of the girl, one of the few that appear grounded in reality, Ella fidgets on the stool beside me.

"She gets her braces off after New Year's, so I thought this would be a nice Christmas present. Kind of a preview of things to come?"

"This is meant to be Rory?" I ask slowly.

"Of course."

I point to another painting, bright hues of color spiraling like a vortex in constant motion, a copper bright blossom at the top. "And this one?"

"Gram Helen." She hesitates and adds, "See? Her copper hair tangled in all her silk scarves caught in infinite motion. It's who she is, not what she looks like. I almost never do realistic portraits. This painting of Rory is an exception; I've tried to portray her true beauty as realistically as possible."

I hate the yearning in her voice—she wants me to reaffirm her vision, her version of Rory's truth. I despise myself because I can't lie to her. But the world she sees through her synesthesia isn't real.

"It's a great painting. Stunning." I say, bracing myself. Why is the truth so hard when it comes to Ella? Truth is meant to make things better, not worse. Yet every time I tell her the truth, I end up hurting her. "But it's not Rory."

CHAPTER 27

I frown as I scrutinize the canvas. How can Alec not see that this is Rory?

"What do you mean? Everything in that painting is Rory. It's as realistic as anyone could get." What's wrong with him, I wonder.

Alec walks from one side of the space to the other, observing the painting from every angle. I can't help but remember Joe's assessment. So far from the mark, I'd assumed it was Joe being Joe. But I know I'm right. This *is* Rory. From her wide smile to the gleam in her eyes and the glow that lights her up from the inside. It took me a dozen or so tries, but I captured it all, right there, in pigment and canvas.

"Why do you paint?" he surprises me by asking.

"Why do you want to be a journalist?"

"To find the truth. Too many people, all they want are

comfortable lies, entertainment. They've lost sight of what real truth is, of why people do what they do, of what they could be doing to make the world better. If you're living a lie, how can you create a better future?"

His earnest answer surprises me. I was expecting something different, less philosophical, more . . . cynical? Then he repeats his question. "Your turn. Why paint?"

It's a question I've struggled with all my life. Not because I don't know the answer but because I'm afraid my answer will sound foolish to anyone else. He's waiting, the silence taking on a life of its own. I expect him to turn away, change the subject, just leave . . . but he doesn't. His gaze never falters, holding me safe.

"I paint to find the heart of a person or scene, beyond what you think you see at first glance." I frown; my words sound childish and cliché. But I throw back my shoulders, standing by what I've said.

He nods. Turns back to my portrait of Rory once again. Staring at it with such intensity, I'm surprised the canvas doesn't singe.

"I think," Alec starts, then stops again, regroups. "Maybe because of your synesthesia, this is how you see, how *you* experience Rory. Like you said, you see her heart. But it doesn't look anything like the real girl."

Now I'm getting annoyed. "Well, of course I took her braces off—that's the whole point of it."

"Ella. You can't give her this picture. You can't ever let Rory see it. You'll break her heart."

His tone is so sorrowful it rattles my confidence. "Why? Is it that bad? Maybe I can ask one of my professors for help."

"No. No, that's not what I'm trying to say." He grimaces in frustration. "The painting is fine—more than fine. It's beautiful. But that's not Rory. Not the real Rory. You made her look like she's some Hollywood glamour queen. And she's just not. It's as if you painted who she could be in a perfect world, but that will only show her how far her reality is from that perfection. I'm not sure anyone's ego could take that kind of crushing comparison."

I've never come so close to slapping another person before now. Not because of his criticism of my work, but because of his criticism of my friend. "Rory's the most beautiful person I know. Everyone loves her."

His smile is both sad and gentle. "She is beautiful. But not this—not this artificial perfection. Like here, her eyes, they aren't symmetrical like they are in your painting. One is much smaller than the other, her right eyelid droops, and her cheekbones are crooked. And her smile—her mouth is too small for her face, but you've painted it wider than it really is. And her nose—"

I shoot in front of him, blocking his view of my masterpiece. "Okay. You've made your point. You think my best friend is ugly. And since she's prettier than I am, I'm not sure how you can even bear to look at me."

"No. No, that's not what I meant—" He raises his face to the ceiling as if searching for heavenly guidance.

"Whatever you meant, I'm sure I don't need to hear it. Maybe you should just leave." I stomp my foot against the concrete floor. "Now."

He raises his hands in surrender and backs toward the door, leaving me to consider the painting on my own. As he closes the door behind him, I can sense the gloom of rain in the air. Or maybe it's not from outside, maybe it's my own aura.

I think about Alec's words. Sink onto the stool across from my easel and stare at Rory's portrait some more. I'd tried so hard to be as realistic as possible—a huge leap for me as my work is always a loose expression of reality. Defying visual gravity, one teacher had described it. No idea what she meant by that, but I like the sound of it.

My agitation fills the air. I swear I see the batik streamers above me wave in the breeze as a chill wind blows through the space. It's gone so fast that I wonder if it was my aura, too frustrated and confused to settle on a single color, instead revealing itself as pure motion.

I thought I was seeing the truth beneath the surface, Rory's real truth. Thought I had a gift, that somehow I could bring that truth to life so others could see it as well.

Maybe my skills simply aren't up to the task of capturing the true essence of someone so close to me?

Or maybe, the way I see the world isn't the truth at all.

If that's the case, how can I rely on anything I see as being real? If I can't even see the truth of my best friend, what else am I blind to?

Like my family . . . all their emotions were true. My synesthesia didn't fail when it came to showing me what they felt, yet still their words were false. Fifteen years of well-intentioned lies and omissions.

My aura turns smoky, oily, so thick it drifts through the space, blocking the overhead lights. But then the lights flicker and sparks sizzle from near the door where the space heater is. I hop off my stool and race to turn it off but the lights go out before I make it halfway there.

Panic floods through me as I push my way through the darkness toward the door, toppling over easels and over-turning jars of brushes. All that fabric and paper, not to mention the cleaning supplies—one spark and it could all go up.

A glowing swirl of red-blue-gold fire shines through the canvases on their easels, a storm gathering intensity. Then, one by one the canvases burst into flames, blocking my path to the door.

I freeze, stunned by fear. The flames spread fast along the paint thinner on the floor, so fast that I abandon my initial plan of grabbing a drop cloth to smother them. Suddenly they're everywhere: racing up the drywall, dancing along the exposed beams of the overhead rafters, flaring bright colors as they devour my paintings.

Memories of a school fire safety class flood over me. It takes less than a minute for a fire to take hold. Two minutes and it will be out of control, filling the room with smoke.

Three minutes—maybe four if you're lucky—and the air heats up until any flammable material anywhere in the room, even if it's not in direct contact with the flames, spontaneously combusts into a ball of fire. A flashover, the firemen called it, showing us a video where a single stray cigarette in a trash can erupts into an inferno.

I drop to the ground, choking, the smoke so thick that if it weren't for the flames I'd be lost in total darkness. Pulling Helen's sweater over my mouth and nose, I turn and crawl toward the overhead door, the noise of my life's work screaming death knells as it burns.

CHAPTER 28

Alec

At first I pedal away from Ella's house, regretting that I'd ever come. I'd done enough harm already—destroying Ella's past by telling her the truth about her parents. And now, I've wrecked her faith in her art. I should never have said anything. That's me, always blurting out the truth, even when it hurts the people I love the most.

A good journalist examines all sides of an issue. That's where I went wrong; I'd been so focused on what I wanted, answers to a mystery that has plagued me for fifteen years, that I neglected to see things from Ella's point of view. Not only with the mystery of her parents' deaths but also with her art.

Halfway down her block, I stop. I need to call Professor Winston, let him know I've failed. He'll probably fire me from my research assistant job. Which means money is going to be even tighter.

But that's not what's worrying me. Not really.

I turn around and slowly head back toward Ella's house. Losing the story and the job and the once-in-a-lifetime chance at publication, that I can handle.

Losing her? Again? I can't take that.

I reach her driveway and sit there on my bike, trying to figure out my next move. I like Ella. I like making her smile and laugh, like arguing with her, like the way she sees the world so differently than I do. We had moments when the world felt balanced, right, calm . . . I want more of those.

Headlights from an oncoming car blind me. If I sit here much longer, someone will probably call the cops. The car pulls into a neighbor's driveway and the lights go out.

Maybe tonight's not the night. Dad always says I'm too intense, too focused. Says it turns people off, that I need to learn to give people space.

It's a lesson I wished I'd paid attention to before I met Ella. I turn my bike around to head back to campus. There's always tomorrow, I tell myself. She's not going anywhere. Except maybe to Paris.

The night air smells of rain and smoke. I look over my shoulder one last time before leaving. From this angle, I can see down the driveway to the old garage she uses as her studio. It's clouded by a haze that blocks out the stars.

A haze that sits much too low, far below the sky above. A haze of black, oily smoke. I pop my kickstand down and get off the bike, sniffing the air. The scent of wood burning is corrupted by an acrid chemical stench. A tongue of flame licks at the garage door windows.

Arms pumping, I sprint to the garage. I try to open the main overhead door, but it won't budge. The small windows lining the top of the door are almost totally black with smoke. Beyond the glass flames dance in warped configurations over the rafters as they devour Ella's canvases.

I race around to the side door. Ella's uncle is tugging at the doorknob, frantic.

"Is she still in there?" I shout at him, my words propelled by adrenaline.

Joe glances up, flames reflected from the window etching his face into strange angles. "What are you doing here?"

I barely hear the older man as I join him at the door and try the handle. Locked. "Where's the key?"

"I don't know!" Joe sounds panicked, desperate. "Did you lock it on the way out? Why would you do that?"

"It wasn't me!" I grab my phone to call 9-1-1. Why would Ella lock herself in? Obvious answer: to keep me out.

"This is all your fault!" Joe yells. "You had to come, meddle in everything, get her upset—" A wall of flame fills the window. Something inside explodes with a loud pop and the crash of shattered glass. Joe grabs a log from the woodpile.

"Stop," I tell him. "You'll just make things worse, give it oxygen."

He doesn't listen. He smashes the window. Heat and flames blast out at us. Smoke billows through the opening, thick, noxious fumes that have us both coughing as we take shelter.

There's no going in. Not that way. Which means Ella's trapped.

CHAPTER 29

I never knew fire could be so loud. Crackling campfires or a few logs tumbled into the fireplace on a cold winter's night, sure. But this? Deafening. The roar of the fire is ravenous, an ancient beast raging, searching for its prey.

For a moment, I'm transported back in time, to that terrified little girl hiding from the dragon-monster of smoke and flames blocking her path to her family. Tears cloud my vision and my throat burns as if I've been screaming.

I start crawling, my face pressed as close to the floor as possible, searching for the garage door. It seems much farther away than it should—have I gone off course? Blazing remnants of my canvases shower me from above. A few are heavy enough that they set the back of my sweater on fire and I take precious seconds to roll over, smother them. Others spark in my hair, forcing me to swat at them. Time and oxygen wasted, and I'm running out of both.

My fear is as alive as the flames surrounding me, wanting to devour me from the inside out. I force myself to breathe slow and deep, pretend I'm in the swimming pool and this is all happening above the water that protects me, all happening very far away.

It works until something angers the flames; they leap and caper and grow larger as a gust of air rushes into the room. I think I hear someone calling my name but it's very far away and I don't have the breath to call back—not that it would do any good, since the flames will smother any sound I make.

I hear the clatter of easels falling, stacks of material tumbling to the ground. My life's work gone, but there isn't time to worry about that. Somehow, I find the strength, now coughing even through my makeshift mask, noxious fumes gagging me, to reach the garage door. My palm slaps against its rough wood hard enough to rattle it in its tracks. The overhead door hasn't been used in almost a decade—not since I took over the garage.

I tear away the old blanket I keep shoved against its bottom gasket, blindly searching for the latch. Thankfully the door is locked from the inside; a mere turn of the latch should allow me to open it. A large canvas topples in the windstorm created by the fire, cracking me on the back of the head with the corner of its frame, engulfing me in flames.

Primal fear sets in and I forget all about staying calm and breathing slow as I battle the searing strands of canvas to free myself. My sweater starts to smolder, and then to burn, and in an instant, I'm on fire.

I roll, bouncing into the door, flounder in the other direction as the blankets also blaze to life, and somehow manage to free myself from the sweater's embrace.

In the dark, with my only illumination waves of flame washing down from above, it's impossible to orient myself—is the latch to my right or left? My breathing is now ragged, all pretense of controlling it long gone, and each coughing fit leaves me wanting to embrace the concrete floor and never move again. But I keep going until my fingers stumble against something metal. The latch.

I try to turn it. No good. It's been locked for years, is not about to relinquish its grip so easily. With my last ounce of strength, I push my weight against it. Slowly, painfully, it yields.

A coughing attack tears at my lungs and I collapse, my hands flailing against the door, fingers pushing past the rubber gasket at its bottom, trying to gain purchase.

Suddenly a second pair of hands from outside cover my own. I know without seeing that it's Alec. He gets his hands beneath the door and pushes up. I taste vomit in the back of my throat—linseed oil and turpentine and all the noxious smoke have gathered there, filling me up inside and out—but somehow manage to help push as well.

The door creaks and groans, its weight shudders up, grudgingly lifts a few inches then stops, refusing to yield. I collapse, embracing the tiny draft of fresh air coming in through the crack we've created. Exhausted, I can't move, it's all I can do to simply breathe. Alec's face appears mere inches away from mine, but all I can see are the flames reflected in his eyes. The entire ceiling is engulfed, the rafters dripping in fire.

Then he smiles, and suddenly that's my whole world. "I've got you."

His hands grip the door and I see his knees bend, hear his grunt of effort as he manages to raise it a few more inches. Then he slithers inside the inferno and throws his arms around my shoulders. Together we crawl forward, Alec shielding me from the flames with his own body. Once we're most of the way past the door, Alec rolls out into the fresh air as I weakly claw my way against the asphalt drive. Then he's there, reaching down for my hands, pulling me free from the fire.

We're both coughing and gagging, stumbling in a weird half-walk, half-crawl free fall down the driveway until we finally collapse onto the front lawn. Alec wraps his hand in mine but he's coughing too hard to talk. His face is streaked with smoke and tears. I'm sure I look worse. I feel worse, probably have burns and cuts that will awaken as soon as my need for oxygen eases, but we're alive.

He holds me close, fear quaking both of our bodies, neither of us able to talk as sirens fill the night along with shouts as neighbors come running. All I can do is close my eyes and breathe.

CHAPTER 30

Ella

It isn't until the paramedics bundle Alec and me into the back of the ambulance that the puking starts. The only consolation is that Alec is almost as bad off as I am, both of us clutching emesis basins and oxygen masks as the ambulance bounces and swerves, diesel fumes adding to my nausea.

Alec greedily sucks on his oxygen from the bench seat beside the cot where I'm strapped in. The medic has me on a big monitor and Alec on a smaller, portable one. Our heartbeats chime through the air, synchronizing except when one of us has a coughing fit. The medic's aura is a calm, reassuring cerulean, very relaxing.

"Where's my uncle?" I ask, not for the first time, as the paramedic trades my puke bowl—good thing I hadn't eaten dinner yet—for a wet wipe.

His partner answers from the driver's seat behind me.

"En route to the hospital. They found him collapsed. Chest pains."

"Chest pains?" My voice, already hoarse, breaks with panic. "Is he going to be all right? Did he have a heart attack?"

The medic can only shrug in answer. What if Joe dies because he was upset about the fire? Because of me? I couldn't bear it, I just couldn't. My eyes are dry and scratchy, unable to produce tears despite my anguish. "I need to call Darrin."

My words are muffled by the oxygen, and the medic has moved to stand between me and Alec as he examines my head wound. I, of course, don't have my phone—it's on its charger in my room—but Alec's hand slides between me and the medic, his phone at the ready.

I hold it like a lifeline until I realize I can't remember Darrin's number or which restaurant Joe said Darrin and Helen were going to. Cleary and Sons does business with several, and they're always ready to roll out the red carpet for Darrin and give him a quiet, private room so Helen's synesthesia won't be roiled by unwanted noises. I try to dial Rory but end up getting her number wrong, a gruff older man answering instead. I mumble an apology as the ambulance comes to a stop then begins backing up, and I realize we're at the hospital.

Alec's phone's home screen fills with a background picture of his parents flying a kite on the beach, their auras so bright with joy that it makes me blink. Wordlessly, I hand it back to him. He glances at the photo, his expression transforming as if just seeing their picture gives him strength, and then he slides it back into his pocket.

The next bit is like being a scrap of paper tossed into a tornado. Alec and I are separated, each given our own team of nurses and doctors. I'm undressed, examined, vampired—again and again, my arm for an IV and blood work, then my wrist for blood from an artery, which hurt more than the burns I was finally starting to feel—salved and greased and wrapped and stapled—turns out that bump on the head was more like a laceration—x-rayed, nebulized, examined again, and finally ushered into a separate room at the far end of the ER.

"Our observation area," the nurse tells me as she wheels me down the hall. "Everything looks good, but your carboxyhemoglobin levels are borderline high—that measures the amount of carbon monoxide in your system. We'll need to keep you on oxygen—flush it out, so to speak—and monitor you."

"For how long?" My voice is still raspy and my throat stings, but after the breathing treatment, my cough is pretty much gone.

"Just overnight. We'll redress your burns and send you home in the morning." She leans down to help me out of the chair—which I don't actually need, except I'd probably trip over the assorted paraphernalia that came along for the ride.

"I'll see if I can book the whirlpool for you in the morning. Best way to treat burns like yours. Much less painful."

The burns aren't serious, the doctor had assured me, but they are already rather painful. "Thanks. Have you heard anything about my uncle?"

"Waiting for his cardiac enzymes to return. I'll let him know you asked. It might be a while before you can see him, but he's doing fine."

"And my friend, Alec Ravenell? He was in the fire, came in with me?"

"Right behind you." Alec's voice rings out from the door behind me—observation rooms come with actual doors instead of curtains. "You decent for company?"

The nurse finishes tucking me in, shows me how to work the bed and the monitor and IV in case I need to go to the bathroom. "But the first few times, hit this button and call us. Don't try it alone."

Right. Like that's going to happen. She leaves and allows Alec to come in. He has a bandage on his wrist that matches mine. But otherwise he looks fine. Much better than me, I'm sure—in addition to the new staples on the back of my scalp, the fire singed my hair so it's all ratty and uneven, and I'm wearing an oh-so-lovely hospital gown. My clothes are gone. All that I have left are my shoes in a plastic bag dangling from the end of the bed, and my underwear.

"Are you okay?" he asks at the same time as I do. He smiles. "Jinx."

"They're watching me overnight. Something about carbon monoxide levels."

He holds up his phone open to a Google page. "Yeah, they checked me for it too. But you were in there so much longer than I was. Guess you're lucky it wasn't a lot worse."

"I held my breath most of the time." I don't really want to talk about the fire. If I do, I'm afraid all the terror I've been holding back will break free.

He settles into the chair beside the bed. "I'm sorry you lost all your paintings."

I can't help my sigh. "No great loss. I have it on good authority that apparently I suck when it comes to portraiture."

He looks down at his boots. "Actually, that was what I was coming to tell you. Why I went back. I was wrong."

"Excuse me? Mr. Truth Above All Else?"

"Maybe there's more than one kind of truth. There are the facts. But then there's the understanding of the why behind the facts."

"Which is why you're interested in my parents' case."

"Right." He glances up, meets my eyes. "I know the facts, but I want to understand them. But what you see, what you paint—that's a whole different truth. No less valid, maybe even more important."

"I don't understand."

"You see possibilities. What the truth could be—or maybe what it *should* be. Like that picture of Rory. It wasn't her as she is now, but even though the physical facts weren't accurate, it represented the woman she's destined to become. And anatomy has nothing to do with that." He worries with the tape binding the gauze to his wrist. "Does that make any sense?"

"No," is my knee-jerk response. His expression crumbles. "I mean, yes. It makes sense. But no, what you're talking about is a level of talent I could only hope to achieve. What you're saying is what real artists do—revealing a hidden truth not just about their subjects, but about the world." I shake my head and offer him a timid smile. "I love that you think maybe someday I could do that. It makes losing everything seem not so bad, like maybe I can do better next time around."

His smile meets mine, releasing a flush of warmth inside me. "No maybe about it. I know you can. You will."

Then I realize. "Rory! If I don't call her, let her know what happened, she'll freak."

"Already taken care of. She and Max are out hunting for your grandmother and Darrin."

"They went out to dinner with her new producer, but Darrin will have his cell phone turned off while he's with Gram."

"Right. Forgot about the family quirks."

We fall silent, the raucous sounds of the ER surrounding us, isolating us from the rest of the world.

"I asked them," I say. My fingers knot the sheet and I'm suddenly fascinated by the red glow of the oxygen monitor clipped to my ring finger. "About my parents. About why my dad did that. No one knew." I turn in the bed, facing him. "Do you really think you can find out?"

"I want to. I mean, I have all the facts of the case, and they all add up—except they don't."

"Same way I feel when I can't figure out a painting. Like something's missing."

"Exactly. Maybe if you tell me about your parents. What you remember. What were they like?"

I hesitate, gulping in more oxygen. The plastic smell of it is an oil slick on the back of my palate. I'm scared—who wouldn't be? All my life I've cherished these memories. They're all that I have left of my parents. Last thing I want is to bring my memories into the light and dissect them until they're empty corpses.

"It can't be all lies." His tone is encouraging. I'll bet he's good at coaxing kittens out of trees. "Maybe what I know isn't all of the truth."

"So you admit you might be wrong about what happened?"

His face twists. "I admit that there might be more to it. Maybe we can figure it out. Together."

I nod, the heartbeat monitor speeding up a bit. This is scary—in some ways more frightening than facing the fire.

"Let's start with your mom. I know she worked with your dad."

"She was actually at Cleary and Sons before he was. He was still at grad school when my grandfather hired Mom even though she didn't have a degree. Because she had a talent with numbers—a different type of synesthesia than mine, more like seeing them as a puzzle. When Dad joined the firm, she was already running their fraud department."

"But, what was she like?"

"She was . . ." I falter, pretend to adjust the IV needle to a more comfortable position. But really, I'm trying to separate what I really know with what I've been told over the years. "She was from Sarajevo. They lost everyone in the war." Not that anyone ever really talks about it. Certainly not Helen or Joe. I frown, struggling. "That's it. I just can't—"

Alec senses my distress. He reaches his hand to cover mine on the bedrail. "You were only three when they died. Most people don't have any concrete memories that far back. But I guess what I'm asking is, how did she make you feel?"

I lean back on the starched sheets and close my eyes. "I remember . . . I remember music, always music when she was near. Humming or singing or just tapping her fingers as she worked while I played in my crib beside her desk." I jerk my chin up, eyes popping open as the memory fills me. This is true, this is real.

"I can see her, she's so much taller than I am. Her hair is auburn, so long it reaches almost to her waist—her aura is the same color. When she leans down to pick me up, it falls around me, and it's like being caught in a shower of red silk. I like to grab it, feel it between my fingers, it smells so good." A wistful sigh escapes me. "That was Mommy. Warm and safe and soft as silk." I shake my head. "I'm sorry, I was just too young. That's all I can remember."

He nods and straightens. I know he's going to want to hear about my dad next, but I just can't face that—not if everything I remember is a lie. Not if the man I loved was the same man who killed my mother, who wanted to kill me. The heart rate monitor bleeps my distress.

"Could you check on Joe for me?" I ask. "See if Rory and Max found Helen and Darrin?"

"Of course," he says. I know he's disappointed, but he's been living with the fact of what my dad did for years—it's all still new and fresh and painful for me. "I'll be right back."

As the door closes behind him, I lean back and think of Dad. Who was he, really? Why didn't I know? Why couldn't I have seen it coming, in his aura if nothing else? Why wasn't I ever afraid?

Memories shiver through my vision. My oldest memories: music and light, each day adding another movement to the symphony that was our family. It grows and swells until it's difficult to contain, running through my mind in so many colors and variations, chasing a rainbow through the endless crash of ocean waves. My father and mother, one dark-haired, the other copper-bright as the sun. Together they dance in harmony, me cradled between them, so close I can feel their hearts beat.

I remember swimming—no, not swimming, a bath, joyously blowing bubbles, delighting in ducking beneath the surface of the water, painting pictures with the light shimmering down. My father's face, his hair a halo of black curls, his smile reflecting from the bubbles over and over again into infinity. I splash to the surface, begging for more, more, more and he holds me so safe and sound as I escape the cold air and plunge into the water again. I'm not afraid— how could I be, with his hands around me?

His laughter creates my universe. I'm at the center of it, the sun to his Earth and Mom's moon. Perfect harmony.

Or so I thought.

CHAPTER 31

Alec

I make it as far as the nurses' station when I see Ella's grandmother striding toward me from the opposite direction. Despite the incessant barrage of noise here in the ER, she seems fine. Unstoppable. A force of nature, even, with her bright silk caftan billowing around her. Her gaze lasers in to target me.

"That's him," she yells. A police officer and Joe are behind her as she storms down the hallway, pointing at me. "That's the man who's been harassing and stalking my granddaughter. He started that fire. She could have died!"

I back away, keeping my hands in the air so that the police officer, a white guy in his thirties, can see that they're empty. "Officer, I—"

"Don't you dare deny it," Joe says, waving a clutch of hospital discharge paperwork. "I heard you fighting with

Ella, saw you storm off. Next thing we know, the place is on fire. With her locked inside!"

"What's your name?" the police officer asks. Hardy is the name above his badge. I know the routine, tell him my name, hand over my wallet open to my student ID—and Dad's business card. He writes everything in a memo book while Helen and Joe watch.

"These are some pretty serious charges, Mr. Ravenell. I think it'd be best if we went down to the station and cleared them up." Hardy glances around the hospital ward, nodding to the nurses who're staring at us. "A better place to talk it all through, don't you think?"

It isn't really a question. My dad uses the same technique. But it calms Joe and Helen. "Of course, Officer," I tell him.

"You as well, Mr. Crveno. I'll need your witness statement."

Joe puffs up with importance. He turns to Helen and clasps both her arms. "You watch over our girl now. Don't let anything happen to her."

"Of course. I'll have Darrin meet you down there." She glares at me. "We'll make sure he doesn't get near Ella again. Darrin will know how—he'll get a restraining order. Whatever it takes."

Hardy nods vaguely and ushers me down the hall, Joe following. I ride in the back of Hardy's squad car. Joe drives himself.

I try to explain things to Hardy, now that we're away from the drama that seems to come naturally to Ella's family, but it's such a short ride to the police station that I barely have time to do more than answer Hardy's questions about where I'm from and the like. Meaningless chit-chat designed to get me to lower my guard—except I don't have anything to hide, so it's all a waste of time.

Once we're at the station, Hardy leaves me alone in an interview room—typical utilitarian furnishings, but no two-way mirror like they show on TV. Instead there's a camera overhead behind a black plastic bubble. The furniture is sparse: a desk with a chair that's too lightweight to be used as a weapon across from two upholstered chairs, too heavy to be used as weapons.

I slump down into one of the comfortable chairs. More waiting. I'm trying not to be impatient. After all, Ella's safe, and that's what matters most. But I can appreciate why police officers developed these tactics. Sitting here, alone and worried, definitely makes you want to confess, to talk about anything to get out, even if you haven't done anything wrong.

Finally, Hardy returns, taking the seat at the small desk while I remain in the relatively more comfortable chair. Another tactic—it doesn't feel as much like an interrogation when you're sitting in a comfy chair. I suspect that if I hadn't left my coat and messenger bag on the other chair beside me, Hardy would have sat there—more intimate, just two guys having a chat, nothing to worry about.

After a few preliminaries, Hardy explaining carefully that this is an interview and that I'm free to leave at any time, he asks me to walk him through the events leading up to the fire.

"I left Ella in her studio—the garage," I explain. "But about ten minutes later I went back. That's when I saw the smoke. Her uncle was trying to get inside but the door was locked. He broke a window, but that only made things worse, so I went to the front overhead door. After Ella got that door open, I helped her out."

Hardy nods. "Let's back up a bit. You were there at Ms. Cleary's invitation?"

"Uh, no. Not exactly. I went to apologize."

"You had a fight?"

"No. More like a misunderstanding." I hesitate. It isn't my place to tell the police the intimate details of Ella's family's history. "I just thought it would be the right thing to apologize, so I went to her place."

"You apologized and left."

"Right."

"Then why were you going back again? Had she asked you to come back?"

I force myself to sit still and not to squirm under the intensity of his carefully neutral expression. Dad uses that same look and I know it means trouble. "No. We had a bit of a fight—"

"Another misunderstanding? About what?"

"One of her paintings." It sounds lame. But if I try to explain, it will just dig the hole deeper.

"Okay." Hardy makes a note. "Let's go back. When did you first meet Ms. Cleary?"

"Yesterday."

"Where was that?"

"At the college. I needed help on a project for school. She was in the pool. Swimming." I'm rambling, and rambling is not good, so I pinch the flesh between my thumb and forefinger to get myself to stop.

"You'd never met Ms. Cleary but you knew who she was?"

"I wasn't stalking her or anything." Exactly what a stalker would say. "My father's a cop—a sheriff's deputy down in South Carolina. Believe me, I know about stalking. I mean that it's bad. I mean, I'd never—" I trail off.

Hardy keeps up his bobblehead impersonation, letting me hang myself with my own words. "So you've only known Ms. Cleary for a few days, and already you've had two 'misunderstandings' serious enough for you to go to her home and apologize in person?"

"Yeah, I guess."

"Her uncle states that after you arrived the first time, you seemed rather agitated and she was reluctant to allow you inside her studio, the garage. According to him, you and she argued, and several minutes after you left he saw the lights in the garage suddenly go out. When Ms. Cleary didn't appear, he went to investigate and found the door to the garage locked and the fire inside. Any idea how that happened?"

"I don't know. I didn't lock the door, if that's what you're asking."

"You didn't lock Ms. Cleary inside?"

"No, of course not."

"And you didn't knock over the space heater when you left? Or maybe pour some solvent into it?"

"No. I just left. I shut the door behind me and left. That's all."

"But you didn't leave. You came back." Hardy consults his notes. "Ten minutes later. Where did you go?"

"I started to ride my bike back to the campus. But then I changed my mind and went back."

"And why did you return to Ms. Cleary's studio?"

"I told you, to apologize."

"And that's when you saw the smoke?"

"Well, I think maybe I smelled it first. I'm not sure." I meet his eyes. "You said the space heater was knocked over? Is that how the fire started?" I remember the glass jars with cleaning fluids scattered around Ella's studio—it wouldn't take much to spark those fumes into flames.

Hardy doesn't answer my question. Instead he asks, "Were you surprised?"

That stops me cold. "Surprised?"

"By how quickly the fire spread?"

"I don't know when it started, so how could I be surprised by how fast it spread? Besides, I didn't really have time to think about anything. I saw the smoke and flames, saw that Joe couldn't get in, he said Ella was still inside, so I went in after her."

"You were trying to save her."

"Of course."

"Did you think by saving her life, she'd see you as some sort of a hero? Maybe it'd make up for all these misunderstandings and arguments you two were having?"

"No. You see someone in a fire, you go to help them. You don't think about it, you just do it."

Another nod. Another note jotted down. Another glance at the camera, making sure it's still recording. All of which does not bode well for me.

"Besides," I say, hoping to turn the tide before I drown, "I didn't save her. She ended up saving herself."

Hardy sits back at that, abandoning his pad and pen. "Son, this is nothing to joke about. Arson. Possible attempted murder. Stalking. These are some serious crimes. You might want to think about telling me what really happened and why you're so fixated on Ms. Cleary. Get it off your chest, help me understand. I'm sure appearances are deceiving—but I'll need your help to clear all this up."

Another ploy I recognize: make them think you're in this together. That's when I know it's too late—Hardy thinks I'm guilty.

"I've told you everything I know." I stand and reach for my jacket. "If you're not charging me with anything, I think I'd like to leave now."

Hardy frowns, seems to realize he's missed his chance. But he also knows he'll have other chances—it's not like TV where criminals are locked up before the commercial break. Real police know the value of taking their time, building a case.

"You can leave. But we'll be talking again—me or the detectives, depending on what the arson investigator finds. And if I were you, I wouldn't go anywhere near Ms. Cleary or her home again. Understand?"

I jerk my chin in a nod, grab my messenger bag, and leave, my head held high. It's sheer bravado, totally fake. And Hardy knows it.

CHAPTER 32

Alec

The police station is a little more than a mile from my dorm, and since my bike's back at Ella's house, there's no choice except to walk. It's just after midnight by the time I reach my building. I stop outside my door. Then I turn and leave again. I can't deal with my roommate—a guy I barely know even three months in. I need to be alone, to think.

My obsessing time, Mom used to call it, her laugh half genuine and half nervous. Burning up like a lit firecracker is how Dad describes it. But I don't know how to function any other way; once a problem or question or puzzle grabs me, I can't turn my mind off until I solve it.

This time it's more than plotting a way to spy on an osprey's nest or spending a week over summer vacation locking myself in my room until I'd finished reading—three times through—Ralph Ellison's *Invisible Man,* deciding what it meant to me as a black kid getting ready to start at a mostly white middle school, before moving on to devour James Baldwin.

This time it's life and death. Ella's life.

I retreat to the student union, barricade myself inside the same meeting room where I'd met Ella and her friends. The union is open twenty-four hours a day, but a Friday night like this, it's virtually empty except for a crowd on the other side of the building at the bowling alley and arcade. I remove my laptop from my singed messenger bag, holding my breath as I turn it on. The screen has a star-shaped crack—probably from when I fell helping Ella crawl out of the fire—but the machine comes on, no problem. Good thing, because it would take me a year to save up for another one.

I feel cut off from the rest of the world, isolated and alone in some desolate land where nothing makes sense and no one is who they seem to be . . . least of all, me.

What kind of person am I that the police imagine I'm capable of arson and attempted murder? How can I prove them wrong?

I spread my notes across the meeting room's table. If the police are right and someone set the fire, the only way to save myself is to discover who and why. If it saves Ella in the process, that's fine, but after being forced to examine my own actions as if I'm a criminal, I finally realize that she never asked me for help, never even wanted my help—I'm not even sure she needs my help.

Except . . . the fire. Who would want to hurt Ella? Maybe it was just an accident—her studio was a natural firetrap with all those flammable canvases and papers and solvents. Maybe she did it herself, is as unstable as her father. I frown at that, pounding the computer keys harder than necessary. No, out of all the possible theories, I can't bring myself to believe that one.

But where to start? That's easy—exactly where Ella said I needed to start: from scratch. Treat her parents like any murder victims.

One wall of the room is constructed of white boards, so I take advantage of the space to organize my thoughts. Suspects. Who knew Mia and Sean Cleary?

Darrin West is an obvious first choice. I shuffle through my paper files and use a magnet to stick a photocopy of Darrin's driver's license to the board, courtesy of Dr. Winston and his access to all sorts of investigative data-bases. Motive? Money, control of the company, control of Ella's trust as executor of the Cleary estate. Opportunity? No, he was definitely in London. Means? He could have hired a hit man.

I squint at the words. Try to fit their logic with the man I'd met, who'd seemed generous and kind. No, keep feelings out of it, the way Dad does when he's working a case. Stick to the facts. Who else? Sean Cleary had no other living family, so that left his wife's mother and brother.

The police back home had copied their New York state drivers' licenses when they had to prove their identity to claim Nora. I put them up on the wall beside Darrin's. Motive? Money, the universal motive—with the funds from the Cleary estate, they never had to work again. Sure, Helen had a successful career as a voice talent, but that was by choice, not necessity. She and Joe had all the money they needed while Ella was alive.

That stops me. I remember an investigator's note that if Sean Cleary died without heirs, the family trust went to charity. But what happens to the Cleary estate if Ella dies? And what about her educational trust fund, the one she said only opened up after she turned eighteen?

I don't have access to a copy of Ella's trust. I start to make a note to ask her—except I can't, can I? Not without being accused of being a stalker.

I sink into the chair. If the police charge me, I'll need a lawyer—which means money, which means asking my parents for help, which means telling them I'm accused of stalking and arson and whatever other charges the police dream up. If I'm not careful, Professor Winston will be using my own story in his next book. And there's a good chance it won't have a happy ending.

I stare at the crack on my computer screen. It's

asymmetric, just shy of center. I snap the lid shut. Close my eyes, concentrate on breathing. Focusing on the numbers, I count to four, breathe in, hold for four, breathe out for four, hold for four . . . now try five . . . six . . . I make it up to an eight count before my pulse finally smooths out, the tingling wasps beneath my skin calming down, returning to hibernation. I open my eyes, stare at my wall.

Back to Helen and Joe. They were obviously estranged from Mia Cleary since they hadn't been listed as her emergency contacts. It was Darrin who told the police where to find Mia's next of kin. Was it just distance? They lived in upstate New York while Mia and Sean lived in the house by the lake, about a half an hour outside of Cambria City. Or maybe Mia thought their synesthesia was so debilitating that they weren't reliable? Maybe that's also why Darrin was listed in their will as Ella's guardian instead of Helen and Joe.

Means and opportunity for the two of them? They'd claimed to have been home the night Ella's parents died, but the police never found any other witnesses—made sense since, because of their synesthesia, both Helen and Joe worked from home and rarely ventured out.

I frown, leave the chair, and draw two large question marks below each of their drivers' licenses. Hard to imagine a brother killing his sister that way, much less a mother committing such a heinous crime against her own flesh and blood.

How old was Helen? I glance at the date of birth on her license. Only sixty-six now, fifty-one when Ella's parents were killed. Younger than either of my grandmothers. My eyes move from one license to the other. Something's wrong here, something out of place, quirking and tugging at my attention, demanding to be seen, reawaking the electric wasps of my anxiety.

I stand precisely between the two drivers' licenses. Close my eyes. Breathe. Then open them. Immediately, my gaze falls on the date of issue, first for Helen, then for Joe.

The exact same date. Six months before Ella was born.

Frowning, I keep staring until my vision blurs. If these were Helen and Joe's new licenses after they moved to Pennsylvania to take custody of Ella, it would make sense— one trip to the DMV. But they weren't. These were their original New York state licenses. Maybe, because of their synesthesia and the way they lived such a sequestered life, they always went to the DMV together?

Could be as simple as that. I make a note to check to see when they'd moved to the address on the New York licenses. Then I take a step back and think about the fact that I only have three people on the list of potential suspects. Only three people were intimately involved in the lives of Mia and Sean Cleary?

That doesn't seem right. Were the Clearys recluses like Helen and Joe? After all, Mia did have synesthesia as well, even if hers was nowhere near as debilitating as Helen's or Joe's forms. And the Clearys had lived in a house halfway up a mountain on a secluded lake. Maybe that was why they'd been attracted to each other? Two introverts, content to raise a family in solitude?

And now these three people—three suspects—anchored Ella's life. Strange. I've lived most of my life on an island smaller than the size of this college campus, yet I probably have more experience with the outside world than she has.

I've never realized until now how isolated she is—Rory and Max are really her only friends. It's clear that other than school she rarely leaves the house—made even clearer by her fear of leaving Helen and Joe to go to Paris. She feels safe at home, maybe even content to stay in one place forever. Unlike me—I couldn't wait to explore the world beyond Harbinger Cove.

Yet, I sense the same longing for new experiences in Ella. Maybe because she had to care for Helen and Joe when their synesthesia became overwhelming, she became conditioned to accept her isolation as a way of life?

That brings me up short. Conditioned. Isolated. Sequestered. Little contact with the outside world. Solitary.

Why is it that every word and phrase I associate with Ella's home life conjures the image of a prison?

CHAPTER 33

Ella

Alec never came back. I wondered about that all night, even as Helen and Darrin fussed over me, reassuring me that Joe was going to be okay, was already discharged, then finally leaving to give Rory and Max five minutes before the nurse sent them home and gave me a sleeping pill. She said I'd be discharged the next morning.

It was afternoon the next day before I finally made it back home. Turns out "morning" means before dawn to doctors and nurses but more like noon to clerks processing discharge orders.

I also learned that most everything people tell you in hospitals is a lie, from "this won't hurt a bit" to "it's just like a bubble bath." The last came when they put me in a whirlpool to debride my burns—that's medical speak for cutting away your dead skin, exposing the raw new flesh below the charred old layer. Thankfully, the few blisters left are small enough that the doctor said I wouldn't need to do much until the dressing comes off in a week. It's some new bio-occlusive gel stuff that prevents infection as it heals. Only problem: no getting it wet. Which means no swimming, and I'm already desperate to return to my pool where I can find some peace and quiet.

When we get home, the still-smoking remnants of my studio are in sight at the end of the drive. Helen gasps and stumbles inside without a word to me, her aura a frayed and tattered shawl wisping around her. I decide she's in shock. Who can blame her? Darrin's babysitting Joe as he rests upstairs in the guest room beside mine. Panic attack, the doctors diagnosed, but his heart is fine.

While Helen retreats to her basement sound studio, I go upstairs. I start to knock on Joe's door but I can hear him and Darrin arguing. Darrin's telling Joe to trust him and be patient or maybe to be a good patient, but either way, I don't want to interrupt.

I go to my room and change out of the scrubs the nurses gave me and into soft fleece pants, an old T-shirt already splattered with paint so it won't matter if it gets yucky with medicine stains, and an oversized hoodie that won't press against my burns and scrapes and bruises. I'm definitely feeling the pain, head to toe, now that the medicine has worn off, but what surprises me by not hurting is the sight out my window: the remnants of my studio.

Every breath I take smells of smoke and destruction, yet somehow I feel hopeful. No, that's not quite right. Relieved? A tingle of anticipation at a chance for a fresh start on my art? I can't pinpoint the emotion with words, but if I painted it, it would be the color of Alec's eyes: vibrant aquamarine with enough energy to leap off the canvas.

Maybe this feeling comes from the talk we had before he vanished. Or maybe it's from the dreams I had last night, courtesy of the magic pills the nurse gave me.

I dreamed of my parents—real dreams, not nightmares. Almost memories, except in them I was older, as if I was seeing the future we could have had if they lived. Whatever they were, wherever the dreams came from, I'm looking forward to putting them on canvas in waves of ocean blue speckled by gold sunshine and soft, creamy foam whitecaps rushing over warm sand.

For the first time since I found out that Helen, Joe, and Darrin had been lying to me all these years, I realize it wasn't my synesthesia or auras that failed to reveal the truth. It was my perception of the truth that was at fault. Just like in my painting of Rory. Alec had been right; I'd painted the truth of what I wanted to see but not actual reality.

It feels good, having a way forward—thanks to Alec's perceptive insights. Because of him I now know how to take my art to the next level . . . and I know that instead of blindly trusting my aura to read the world for me as I observe from afar, it's up to me to learn how to connect with people. Like I have with Alec.

At least I hope I have. I wish he was here now. How ironic that his lack of an aura has helped me to learn so much about myself. I want to thank him—not just for saving my life but also for saving my confidence in my art—and continue our discussion, but he's not answering my texts or calls. Is he mad at me? Or maybe he has something more important to do? After all, he does have other classes and assignments besides working on my parents' case.

Perching on my bed, I stare at my silent phone. Maybe he's found something that proves my dad was mentally disturbed. Maybe a type of illness that runs in families. Maybe something so awful he can't bring himself to face me. No, that can't be it. Last we spoke, Alec agreed to start over with his investigation.

I'd assumed that meant starting over by working with me. But maybe he doesn't like dealing with all the drama that comes with me, including almost getting himself killed?

Thankfully, there's a knock on my door before I can leap down a rabbit hole into a universe of maybes. Rory bounces in. My breath catches and I examine her as if seeing her fresh and new—I feel like I'm seeing the entire world that way after the fire.

"How're you doing?" Rory asks, giving me a once-over inspection like she's one of my doctors.

"Fine," I tell her, figuring it's close enough to the truth. "I've been trying to text Alec, though—"

She plops down on my bed and takes my phone from me. I cringe as she reads my texts to Alec. I might not have dated much, but even I know how desperate they must seem. I've hidden behind my synesthesia far too long—I really do need to figure out how people and relationships work in the real world.

"Why are you tormenting him like this?" she asks. "You know he can't answer you."

"What? Why not?" Tendrils of fear leach through my aura. "Did something happen?"

"Didn't Helen and Darrin tell you? The police took Alec away last night, practically accused him of setting the fire."

"What? No way." I shake my head. "It was an accident. That old space heater went on the fritz, must have shorted out." That would explain the flickering lights that died right before I saw the flames and the way the fire blocked the door so I couldn't escape. "I'm positive Alec had nothing to do with it."

"That's not what the police said. Darrin told me they think Alec did something to the space heater when he left, maybe poured some of your brush cleaner into it—and once the fire got started, he came back to save you and play the hero. Only things got out of control." She turns to me, taking both my hands in hers. "You could have died."

I'm shaking my head, trying to deny her words. "It's not true."

"Helen told them he was stalking you. Monday, when the courts open, they're getting a restraining order against him."

"That's why he's not answering? Why he didn't come back to the hospital?" I lean forward, peering into her eyes. "Do you believe it? Do you think Alec could have started the fire?"

Her hesitation says it all even without her aura fading to a dull gray, the color of dashed hopes and dreams. "I don't want to believe it. You have to admit, he's pretty intense. We've only known him like, what, two days? And he basically dropped a bomb on your life."

"That ended up being true," I point out.

"Max says he promised to stay away from you, give you time to process what happened to your parents. But even after all that, he shows up not once but twice last night? Just in time for a fire to start and then in time to save you?"

I'd pretty much saved myself, although having Alec there to share his strength in opening the garage door helped. But that's beside the point. Rory's doubt is contagious. Could I have been as blind about the truth behind Alec as I'd been about the truth behind the lies Helen, Joe, and Darrin have been telling me all these years?

Could I be just as blind about my father?

CHAPTER 34

Ella

It's Saturday, so Max is working at his family's music store until three, but Rory texts him to come straight to my house and he arrives by twenty after, still wearing his employee nametag.

"What's wrong now?" are the first words out of his mouth, propelled by a cannon ball of red urgency. "Is it Alec again?"

"No," Rory answers for me. Her aura still isn't as bright as usual, but at least it contains a few muted colors instead of the dull gray it had faded to earlier. "But we've decided." She means *I've* decided, but as always, to Rory we're all in this together. I'm not sure she even knows any singular pronouns. "We need to find out what really happened to Mr. and Mrs. Cleary."

Max's expression darkens. "No. You don't want to see—"

"I know," I tell him. "But we can't trust only Alec's theories, especially if he . . ." I don't finish the sentence. I still don't believe Alec would try to hurt me, despite what Rory says the police think. They don't know him like I do. "No one in my family seems to know anything—at least not that they're sharing with me. Besides, after last night—"

"Last thing we need is to upset them more," Rory finishes. "Poor Helen hasn't left her studio all day. Darrin's even ditched meetings to watch over Joe. So . . ." She spreads her arms in a motion that makes her appear regal and in charge. "It's up to us. Max, you and I will take the actual crime."

"How?" Max asks, not at all convinced by this plan of action. "What makes you think we can learn more than the police?"

"Because," Rory says in her stern, listen-to-me tone, hands on her hips, "we're smarter than the police. We're going to examine everything, assume nothing." She pulls her keychain from her pocket and selects a small thumb drive from the ring. "And we have all of Alec's research to help us."

"How'd you get that?" I ask. I'd been sitting right beside Rory the whole time we'd been with Alec yesterday—she was nearest his computer, but still . . .

She rolls her eyes. "Not much to it, especially with Alec and Max threatening to beat each other silly."

Despite myself, I smile. Never underestimate Rory. If anyone should know that, it's me.

"You stole his files?" Max is shocked.

Rory outgrins any Cheshire cat, then breaks into laughter. "I can't believe you guys fell for that. First, I'm no thief. Second, I'm pretty sure it's against the law, breaking into someone's private computer. Third, do you have any idea how long it would take to transfer all those files?"

We stare at her. "Then how did you get Alec's research?" Max asks, an edge to his voice.

"I called him up and asked him. Told him I thought it would help Ella if she was able to independently confirm his information. He sent me access to his cloud before I even finished my sentence." She looks at me, ignoring Max's protective glower, which has everything to do with him not wanting her anywhere near Alec and nothing at all to do with me. Well, mostly nothing. I wish Rory could see that, but as usual, she's oblivious. "He wants to help, I'm sure. Just like I'm sure the police are wrong and he had nothing to do with the fire, even if there's no way he can prove it." For the first time since yesterday morning when we learned the truth about my parents, her aura blossoms with true, pure hues, bright as a rainbow.

"I still say we can't trust him," Max insists.

"I say we can," Rory counters, digging into her position defending Alec—despite the doubts she'd voiced earlier with me. Nothing has changed since then except she's listened to me talk about the fire and what Alec did to help save me. Somehow, despite the fact that Rory can't see emotions like I can, she's now convinced he's innocent. Even if we have no proof either way. And I'm glad of it. With the police and my family—and Max—aligned against him, Alec needs all the friends he can get.

"But there's no harm in verifying his info first, right?" She holds the thumb drive out to Max.

Somehow, I don't get a vote when it comes to Alec. Probably better that way. I'm certainly biased. Not only do I want to trust him, I wish he was here, right now, with me. With his reassuring way of nodding in solemn agreement, the gleam of excitement he gets when a new idea strikes him, even those silly glasses that make him look like an underaged professor.

Max looks down at his feet then back up at me. "Are you sure you're up for this?" he asks. "The answers might not be what you want to hear."

"Better than my imagination at this point. I can't spend the rest of my life wondering if my father was crazy." Or if I am too.

"Okay." He takes the thumb drive from Rory, slides his laptop from his pack, and takes his usual seat on the floor below the window between my bed and the desk where Rory sits. "What are you going to be doing, Ella?"

I grab my tablet and plop down on the bed. "I want to know my parents. As people. Even fifteen years ago, there was social media, chatrooms, bulletin boards, that kind of thing. They must have left some trail behind—maybe I can find friends or coworkers who knew them, someone who can tell me more."

"Darrin knew your father since college, and Helen and Joe—"

I cut him short. "They won't tell me the truth. They want to protect me. Besides, if my father did what everyone says he did, then he had another side he kept hidden, even from his best friend and his wife. But someone has to know the truth, someone must have seen something. I can't believe a person could just suddenly snap like that, not without good reason."

"I'd start with Cleary and Sons," Rory chimes in. "Both your parents worked there; maybe something happened at work."

"Then why didn't Darrin know?" Max argues. This is our usual rhythm. Debating, exploring, changing sides until we've examined every position.

"If it was something big enough to drive him to murder, then wouldn't the company have suffered?" I add, trying hard to be objective. I'm starting to sound like Alec—and I'm not sure if that's a good thing or not. "I mean, if my father had been caught stealing from the company or a client, there's no way that would have remained hidden after his death."

"I don't know; Darrin loved your dad. He would have done anything to protect him. Not to mention protecting the company from ruin would also protect you. Maybe he covered it up." Rory pauses, her aura shimmering her discomfort. This is hard to talk about. "Whatever 'it' was."

"So we're back to what could drive a man to murder." I think about that. "Maybe it wasn't work. Maybe it was something personal."

"Like an affair?" Rory frowns. "Seems kind of cliché, like something out of a soap opera."

"Besides, Ella was only three," Max argues even as he's rattling the keys on his computer. He's a great multitasker, something I have no talent for. I like to see the big picture, then focus in on what is important without having my attention diverted. "My little brother is around that age, and I don't think either Mom or Dad have had a chance to finish a shower or a meal since he was born. And that's with me and my sister helping out. No way either one of them would have energy for an affair."

Both Rory and I turn to stare at him. "So says Casanova. How the heck would you know how much energy an affair takes?" Rory asks. "Your idea of romance is a clean pair of socks before you show up to the spring gala."

"Exactly," Max says, unfazed by her referencing last

year's spring gala debacle—the one time they tried to do an actual date-date. Only Max didn't know it, thought they were going as just friends. As if a girl like Rory would take a mere friend to a formal. Guys can be so clueless. Seeing as how Rory hasn't asked him out again, I guess so can girls. I wish I could figure out a way to get the two of them together, but since I'm part of the problem—neither wants to risk hurting me if something goes wrong—it's been hopeless. "You've got to find the girl, then woo her—"

"Woo her?" I ask, holding back my laughter.

"Yeah, woo her. You know, pay attention to her hair and shoes and all that crap. And you've got to pay attention to how you look as well. And smell. And find interesting things to say and then places to go and things to do that keep her happy." He looks up at us. "You girls have no idea how hard it is to be a guy. Not to mention the time and money. To do all that *and* keep it secret from the woman you live and work with *and* find the energy after working all day and coming home to run around after a little kid? Trust me, your father was not having an affair."

He says it with such authority that both Rory and I are overcome with the giggles. Which of course brings on a fresh wave of agony as my muscles ripple and stretch beneath the burn dressings. But I ignore the pain. This feels good—not just finding something to laugh about, but knowing that I'm not in this alone.

"Okay," I say, wheezing. "For now, we'll believe you, Max."

Then we sober up as we realize there's another reason why my father could have done what he did. Instead of taking her place back at the desk, Rory unplugs the laptop and slides down to squeeze in between Max and the bed, sitting on the floor. As if she needs his warmth to fortify her. "Maybe he was sick." Rory is the first one brave enough to face the ugly truth that has crowded out our laughter. "Like a brain tumor or something."

"The medical examiner would have found it," Max answers without looking up from his laptop. He scrolls down to a document. "Nope, no evidence of any underlying medical problems. Tox screen was negative as well." I know he's reading from the autopsy report, and I can't help but shudder, my aura wrapping around me, hugging me like Helen's comfy old sweater had before I lost it in the fire last night.

Because that only leaves one answer. A disease that would have been invisible after my father's death.

"Maybe it wasn't a physical disease." My voice is low. Joe and Darrin are in the guest room next door and I don't want them to hear. "Maybe it was a mental illness."

"People don't snap just like that, do they?" Rory asks. "I mean, that's only in the movies, right? There must be warning signs, indications . . . something."

Max looks up, first at her and then at me. His aura sags from its usual dark red to burnt umber with hints of yellow ochre. Sorrow and fear. "Maybe there was. Maybe no one saw enough to put it all together in time. Like a jigsaw where you have the edge pieces and I have the inside ones and neither of us can tell what the picture should be."

"So where do we look?"

I think I have the answer. Or *an* answer. "There's nothing here. But when we moved out of the lake house, Darrin and Joe stored all of Mom and Dad's personal stuff in the attic."

I usually never think of the lake house as "my" house—Joe's lived there, taking care of it, for as long as I can remember. It's the gathering place where all of us, even Max and Rory's families, go on hot summer days when all you want is to leap into the crystal cool water and stay there forever. But now I'm seeing it in a new light. Not just as the house where I was born, or our vacation getaway.

Now it's the house where my parents lived and loved, the home they built together. If I'm going to find any answers, it will be there.

"Road trip," Rory shouts, as always finding the fun in any task. "We can head out first thing in the morning. It's so pretty up there this time of year with the leaves changing. We can build a fire, roast some marshmallows—"

"Search for evidence that Ella's father was homicidal . . ."

Max's tone is half-joking, half-serious, but his expression is all concern. "Ella, maybe this isn't a good idea. Why don't we wait, talk to Joe and Darrin again? After all, you're not a child. Once they understand how important it is to you, they'll tell you the truth."

"You didn't see how upset they were yesterday when I told them I knew." I cringe as I remember the inky black shrouds of fear and grief I'd awakened. "No." I hop off the bed, barely feeling the twinge of pain the movement brings. "You're right. I'm not a child. I don't need anyone to coddle me or sugarcoat the truth. Let's go. Right now."

Rory's aura flashes bright—not because she's happy, but because she wants me to be happy. Max's is dark with worry. And mine? My aura wafts around me like a fog bank rolling over sand dunes. I can almost hear the roar of the ocean—or maybe that's the roaring in my head as I realize exactly what I might find.

Because if my father was sick, sick enough that it drove him to kill . . . what's in store for my own future?

CHAPTER 35

Rory and Max talk me out of leaving right away for the lake. Turns out I couldn't have gone if I'd wanted. While we're still in the midst of our online sleuthing—and coming up woefully short—a knock comes on the door.

"Ella?" It's Darrin. He opens the door. "The police are here to talk to you. About last night."

Last night, I'd been asleep when they came to the ER, and I'd forgotten that they were meant to come back today. Rory and Max quickly pack their stuff, and we all walk downstairs together.

"Don't worry," Rory says as she hugs me, forgetting about my burns until too late. "We'll figure this all out. Let me know what time to pick you up tomorrow."

"Tomorrow?" Darrin asks.

"We're going to the lake house," she answers for me,

heading out the door. "Ella needs a change of scenery, don't you think?"

"Sounds good to me." He nods. "Joe will probably want to get back up there soon as well."

Max bumps my shoulder with his, a silent show of support. Then he jerks his chin in a nod and rushes to catch up with Rory.

Darrin leads me into the living room, where Helen and Joe are back in their usual positions on the couch. Joe still looks pale—his aura has faded like an autumn leaf left to rot. There's a police officer sitting across from them in the chair that's usually mine, but Darrin pulls a chair from the dining room over for me. I thank him with a glance and sit down, my back straight so my burns don't touch the wood.

"Ms. Cleary, I'm Officer Hardy," the policeman starts. "Like I was just telling your grandmother and uncle, these are only preliminary questions to see if there is a case here. If there is, I'll be making a report to the detectives and they'll take things from there."

I gulp and nod, not quite sure what he wants since he hasn't yet asked me a question. I decide to ask one of my own. "Did the fire investigator find anything?"

Hardy focuses on the small notepad he cups in his hand. He's also recording us on his phone, I see. As the silence lengthens, I decide the pad is just a prop, a way to help him control the conversation.

Joe jumps in to answer—he can't stand silence. "They think it's arson, honey. That someone purposely started the fire and locked the door—locked you inside."

"And we all know who that was," Helen says, her aura sparking with anger. "That boy, Alec. I knew he was trouble the moment I laid eyes on him."

I can't believe it. The space heater was ancient. And that door always stuck. Besides, why would anyone want to kill me? I couldn't be that wrong about Alec. I just couldn't.

"Alec didn't do this," I mumble. I want to say it loud and clear, leave no room for doubt, but I'm too overwhelmed, the emotions in the room suffocating.

"Why don't you tell me what happened," Officer Hardy says, never actually answering my original question. "Your family was telling me that Alec had upset you with some distressing news. That it was the first you'd learned how your parents died?"

I nod again, feeling like a dumb bobblehead. Helen answers for me. "We never told her, she was so very young. And that boy, he had no right to interfere. He only did it for the money—he's working on a true crime tell-all book."

"More than the money," Joe adds. "He's obsessed with Ella. Why else would he be stalking her?"

"Folks," Officer Hardy says in a polite tone, obviously exasperated by their interruptions, "I don't suppose there's anywhere I can speak to Ella alone? I just think we'll get through this faster, then can let her get the rest she needs after everything she's been through."

"Don't you need her guardian present?" Helen says in a righteous tone.

"She's eighteen," Darrin puts in. "So, no. But I'll stay. As her legal representative," he adds for Hardy's benefit. He doesn't mention that he hasn't seen the inside of a courtroom since law school and his practice consists solely of the legal needs of Cleary and Sons.

Helen and Joe aren't happy, not at all, but they finally bustle out to the kitchen, where they can eavesdrop without Hardy seeing them. As their auras swirl out behind them, I finally have air to breathe without their emotions choking me. Darrin's aura is his usual steadfast blue—almost a match to Officer Hardy's navy-colored aura, barely a ghost around his uniform.

I relax the tiniest bit and explain about using the garage as my studio and the set up—how I always kept the space heater near the door, away from where I was working so that I wouldn't risk spilling paint or water on it. How the door locked from the inside with a simple push of a button and you needed a key from the outside, but it was old and often stuck. How I'd been working on Rory's painting when Joe brought me a snack, and how Alec showed up to talk and, yes, Joe did hear us arguing and I was upset with him, but no, I hadn't thought it was anything serious. After all, I barely knew Alec, had just met him.

Of course, that led to exactly how I'd met him—Officer Hardy definitely grew more interested when I described swimming alone and Alec showing up. He grew almost smug when I explained about the fire starting, blocking my escape out the door, and Alec showing up again, just in time to help me get out.

But then he surprised me. "Sounds like the timing fits, but there's one other person who could have started the fire."

I glance up in surprise. "Joe? He was long gone." No way would he have snuck back inside the garage after Alec left—I mean, he could have, anyone could have, the easels blocked my view of the door and the space heater—but why would he? I remember the strange breeze I'd felt a few minutes before I saw the first smoke. I'd thought it was part of remembering my past, but maybe it'd been someone quietly opening the door?

The thought ambushes me, my aura flashing sick-bile green. No. Starting a fire? With me trapped inside? No one I knew could be capable of that, I'm sure. Especially not Alec. The past few days, the only moments of peace and security I've felt have been when I'm with him. Despite all the terrible memories he's brought to life.

"Not your uncle," Hardy corrects. Silence thuds between us as I realize what he's asking. "You, Ms. Cleary. You were upset. You'd just learned some awful things about your parents. Your uncle and Mr. Ravenell both describe you as agitated. Has anything like this ever happened before? Do you think you might have—not realizing how serious the consequences could be—could you have started the fire yourself? A cry for help, maybe?"

His tone is gentle and I understand why he has to ask—it's his job to pursue any possibility. What I don't understand is why Darrin not only doesn't look surprised, but is nodding as if he thinks Officer Hardy is on the right track. What did he and Joe and Helen tell Officer Hardy before I joined them? Something about my father?

Or something about me?

I slump in the chair, forgetting about my burns until pain spirals across my damaged flesh. "No, sir," I say, trying to sound calm and confident and, well, sane. "I wasn't anywhere near the space heater when the fire began. I don't know how it started."

Officer Hardy regards me with solemn brown eyes, his aura expanding as if it's sighing. He flips his notepad shut and tucks it into his chest pocket. "All right, then. I think we've gathered enough to get started." He stands. "Thank you very much, Ms. Cleary. We'll be in touch."

And then he leaves. But his presence isn't gone, not really. The doubts he's sown sprout like rotten apples strewn around the living room.

Darrin knew my father better than anyone. He knows me better than almost anyone. And he thinks I might have tried to hurt myself? That I'm unstable? What was the word Officer Hardy used—agitated?

That's when I realize I can't take the not knowing. Not another minute. As soon as I can sneak past Joe and Helen, I'm heading to the lake house. If there are answers there about my father, I need to find them. Now. Tonight.

CHAPTER 36

Alec

The clock on the wall says it's just past four. I have to blink twice and think about it before I realize it means four in the afternoon. Other than bathroom breaks and trips to grab overpriced junk food, I've spent almost sixteen hours in this windowless room. With precious little to show for it.

Throwing my glasses to the table, I rub my eyes. The laptop has too many open windows, forming a kaleidoscope of color. Each contains a single verified fact. Taken one at a time, they each make sense, a few even irrefutable. But put them all together and they form an incoherent mess.

I gave up on the murders a few hours ago, focusing instead on the fire I've been accused of setting. Who could have started that fire? Why? Who would stand to gain? Why would anyone want to kill or hurt Ella? She poses no threat.

At least not until she started asking questions about her parents' deaths. Thanks to a bumbling fool from South Carolina.

My phone rings and I jump, grabbing my glasses before answering. It's Dad. I swallow, my mouth murky with Dorito breath, and try to act casual. "Hey."

"Don't you 'hey,' me. Want to explain why the hell a Cambria City cop is calling me? Telling me my son is in danger of being charged with half a dozen felonies? What have you gotten yourself into up there?"

"Why did they call you? I'm nineteen—an adult."

"Courtesy call. It's what you do when you see some poor kid halfway across the country from his home getting ready to ruin his life. Thank the Lord this Officer Hardy called me at work, otherwise he would have gotten your mother."

"You haven't told her?" I exhale with relief. Facing Mom's wrath would be worse than any sentence a judge could hand down.

"Say the word and I'll take off work, head on up." Coming from Dad, this is crazy talk. The only time the man has ever used his vacation time was the day I was born.

The thought splashes cold against the fire of my worry, clearing my head. "Hardy doesn't think I did it," I say slowly, my thoughts trying to make sense of the jumble of facts I've been juggling. "Only reason why he'd call you before there were any formal charges." No cop would risk their case like that, showing their hand to a concerned family member of a suspect. Not unless that suspect wasn't really a suspect. "So what does he think happened?"

"He says the family thinks the girl might have done it herself. Says she's been acting erratic. Might need help." Dad pauses. "After what happened to her when she was little, wouldn't be too surprising. Maybe you stirring things up actually helped them to see how troubled she is."

It's the closest Dad will ever come to admitting that a civilian—Dad prefers the term *amateur*—investigating a case could possibly be a good thing.

"There's nothing wrong with Ella," I snap, frustration propelling me to my feet. My back and neck creak in protest, but I ignore them.

"You barely know the girl, son," he says. "You can't be sure."

"I think her family's up to something." I still haven't found any actual proof that Ella's grandmother, uncle, and godfather are involved, but they're also still my only suspects. Other than her father, of course. I start pacing, making a complete circuit around the table before a thought stops me. "If Ella is declared mentally incompetent, that would give Ella's family access to her money, right? In a way, it'd be even better than killing her since there'd be no investigation into an unstable teen trying to self-harm."

I stand in front of the white board with Helen, Joe, and Darrin's images while I wait for Dad to consider my theory. I can't believe I'm thinking this way—this is how psychopaths think, driven by their own selfish needs, giving no regard to humanity.

The three most important people in Ella's life conspiring against her? Cold and calculating to the point where they don't care if she lives or dies? People who'd lived with her for fifteen years, family who'd sheltered and protected her . . .

"Hard to believe." Dad echoes my own doubts. Although I'm also thinking that the timing of the fire, right after Ella's trust opened up, is highly suspicious. "What proof do you have?"

My gaze returns to Helen's and Joe's photos. Funny; other than their red hair, neither looks much like Ella's mother or Ella herself. Nothing too strange about that—I don't look like either of my parents, and instead take after my maternal grandfather. Just one more stray fact to throw into the chaos.

"No proof," I admit. "Just a lot of facts that don't add up."

"You know . . ." Dad's tone is the one he uses to break bad news. "There is another option."

I know exactly what he's talking about and I don't want to hear it. He's suggesting that Ella is as unstable as her father. No. Despite the turmoil of the last few days—turmoil I'd caused—despite almost dying, she hadn't broken. Instead, last night in the ER when we talked, she'd seemed stronger, as determined to find the truth as I was.

"She's not like her father." I'm stating a fact. "If her father even was mentally unstable."

"You don't have any proof otherwise." He makes a *hrumphing* sound, dismissing my amateur investigatory skills. "I'm coming up. And you're laying low until I get there."

"No." I can't remember ever using that word with Dad—not like this, not as an absolute. It fills me with a strange mix of pride and fear. Am I ready to be a man, stand up to whoever was threatening Ella on my own? Doesn't matter. With Dad so far away, he'll never get here in time to help—and what could he do that the local police couldn't? "No. Thanks, but I'm okay."

"You've got more to think about than yourself." Dad's tone holds a warning, or maybe a sermon: pride going before a fall.

"I know. And I'll ask for help if it comes to that, I promise."

"Sure now? I know how obsessed you can get, wanting to do everything on your own." Like climbing up to an osprey's nest or moving a thousand miles away from home to search for answers to a case the police had already declared solved. "This girl, is she safe?"

Exactly the question I've been wrestling with all day.

"I can't go near her, but the police are investigating, so the whole family is under scrutiny. And I called her friend, asked her to stay with Ella."

A pause as he considers that. "Is she worth it?"

That's easy. "Yes."

"Okay, then, son." Suddenly, Dad sounds older—or I feel older, I'm not sure which. "I'm here for you, you need anything. Just call. And be safe."

"Thanks, Dad." I hang up and slump back into my chair, staring at the phone.

I've never had a conversation with Dad like that—one that hovered on the edge of emotion rather than our usual commerce-like exchanges: what I need balanced by Dad's price. Need a ride to the mainland library on a Sunday when the buses don't run? It'll cost taking the next weekend off to help Dad paint Aunt Trisha's house. Want to buy a computer? Spend the summer getting up at three in the morning to go out with my uncle's shrimp boats.

But this time, I'm sure that Dad just now told me he loves me. More than that, he trusts me to do right by Ella. And it didn't cost me a thing.

I close my laptop—the crack in the screen is giving me a headache—and grab my notebook, flipping to a clean page. Time to circle back. Again. Find the right thread to pull and I'll unravel everything.

Dr. Winston always says to start at the beginning. Not

when the crime happened, but the real beginning, the why and how people ended up where they did. When the perpetrator felt he had no choice but to commit a crime. When the victim made the fateful decision that placed them in harm's way.

Then go back even farther. To the world around them that molded them both into the people who made those choices. Look for intersections. Seemingly random, inconsequential moments that were the first domino toppling, the start of the chain reaction.

But I've done all that and gotten nowhere. I hesitate—I'm trying to impress Dr. Winston, not convince him I'm some psycho-stalker who can't stay objective about a story—but he has resources I don't. So I call him.

"Alec, good to hear from you. Did you nail down that subject yet? Get her permission and the release form signed? I'm going to New York next week to meet with my publisher and I'd like to pitch your project as a standalone book."

"Really?" I'm stunned. Then I glance around the room with its whiteboards covered in scribbles, fast-food wrappers, notecards scattered across the table, and my own foul stench filling the air. "I'm not sure if I'm quite ready to create a pitch."

"Why not?" He always sounds so certain of himself. More so than Dad, even. I can only wish for that kind of confidence and authority. "My sources at the police tell me they think the girl started the recent fire herself—perfect ending. And timely as well. Two generations devastated by the tragedy of untreated mental illness. From homicidal maniac father to arsonist daughter."

"I'm not actually sure that's what really happened. I think someone else is behind it all."

"Really?" He sounds disappointed. "Like who? The police ruled out the business partner. He was in London."

"Ella's family. Her grandmother and uncle. There's something strange about them."

"Strange is good. We can use them as red herrings, increase the audience's empathy with the girl, then *pow*, hit them with the twist, that she's just like dear daddy. You know, if she's declared incompetent, we might be able to proceed without her release. I'll have the publisher talk to his lawyers." A woman's voice comes through the phone. "Sorry, got to go. My wife and I were just headed out to a function at the dean's house."

"Wait. Could I access that database you use, the one that does background checks?"

"Sure, no problem. I'll text you the login info. But kid, seriously, we've struck gold. Don't go stirring the pot, know what I mean?"

"Not exactly."

"A journalist has to know how to find the story—we've

done that. But he also has to know when to back off and lay low, protect his sources, until he gets the chance to tell it. Can't risk anyone else scooping us, right?"

"But if someone's life's at risk, we can't stand by and do nothing."

"Sure we can. That's rule one. Never become a part of the story. Objectivity, objectivity, objectivity. Have I taught you nothing? Oh, gotta go. Let's meet Monday, discuss your pitch. I might need to be the author on this one since you're now part of the story, but don't worry, we'll find another project for you. And you can still do some of the writing, it will be good practice. See ya."

I'm left staring at my phone. The answers I've been searching for all my life, the story I've been fighting to tell, it can't be mine because I'm too close? And Ella, her life will be torn inside out, shredded into pieces for public entertainment? Dr. Winston makes it sound as if it doesn't matter if I find the truth, only that I find enough of it to allow him to twist it into a bestseller.

Disappointment and anger wash over me. For the first time in my life, I'm doubting my ability to be a journalist. Because I don't want to always be objective. I want to get involved.

I want to use my words to help change the world. Starting with helping Ella.

But where to start? What was the first domino? When had everything changed?

Then it hits me. So hard I actually jerk away from the computer as I consider the ramifications. My stomach knots, not from hunger even though I skipped lunch, but from fear. I'm wrong. I have to be.

The text with Dr. Winston's credentials comes through and I log on to the database.

I'm not wrong. The facts are right there, if you know where to look. Or rather, when.

Not fifteen years ago on the night of the murders. Not even in the days or months leading up to them.

The Cleary killings were the aftermath of the dominoes falling. The first domino—once it fell, nothing would ever be the same for Ella's family. Eighteen years and seven months ago. The date on Sean Cleary's updated will and family trust. One month before Helen and Joe arrived in New York and applied for new driver's licenses. When Mia Cleary was pregnant with Nora. Ella. The girl who changed everything.

My hand hovers over my phone, hesitating, but finally I grab it and dial Max. If I can convince him, my greatest critic, then I'll know I'm right. Even if the proof is all circumstantial, nothing concrete. Not yet. "I know you'd rather punch me in the face than talk to me right now, but I think I've found something important. I need your help."

"Help with what?" His voice is shaded with suspicion. "Why should I help you?"

"I think I might have discovered why Ella's parents were killed. I'm at the student center, where we met yesterday morning."

Silence. I think about asking Max to bring Ella, but decide against it. She's safer with Rory. And if the theory I've come up with is right, then . . . She'll be devastated. Never want to see me again. No. She'll hate me. For ruining her life. For taking everything from her.

Maybe Dr. Winston was right. Better not to get involved. But I can't let the truth be buried, no matter how painful it is. I just can't. Not even if it means losing Ella forever.

She deserves to know the truth. No matter the cost. I owe her that much.

"All right," Max finally answers. "But this had better be good."

It isn't. If I'm right, it's bad . . . very bad.

The cabin is only about a half an hour from the city, and despite the switchbacks and unmarked roads winding up the mountain and through state game lands, I can drive it in my sleep. This trip, I spend the time trying to remember.

Who was my father? What was he like? Am I like him?

Of course, trying to force memories only leads to no memories. And a feeling I've fought all my life: as if everything I do is dictated by the ghosts of my parents. I need to live my own life, unfettered by guilt.

For once, I'm not running away, not hiding like the scared little girl who did nothing as her family died.

As I steer down the lane, through a cathedral of intertwined hemlocks and mountain laurel that in the summer are a riot of color and green, I'm glad I came alone. Yes, this is Joe's place now, but he's always made it clear that it's also my home. Rory and Max would have been supportive in their hovering fashion. Helen and Joe would have whisked me away, back to my safe, warm bed, and then Darrin would have returned to search on his own—probably never telling me what he found.

I'm tired of being protected, smothered by their fear. I need to face the truth, however bad it is, on my own terms.

The trees part and I'm rewarded with my favorite view in the world—so much so that I've never tried to paint it for fear of failing to capture its charm. I've arrived at the golden hour, the hour before sunset, when the curve of the mountains and ribbons of sunlight create the illusion that our small lake and house are nestled inside a crystalline globe filled with magic.

The lake is to the side of the house, its water inviting as it shimmers blue and gold. At its shore stand a small boat shelter where we keep a canoe and several kayaks, the bat house Joe and I built when I was in fifth grade, and a dock long enough to stretch past the muddy shallows where salamanders frolic and out to where the bottom drops off and the water is deep enough that even I have never touched bottom.

The cabin is unlit except for the glint of the dying sun reflecting from its windows. It's two stories, made of ancient logs that creak and settle like they're still alive. There's a metal roof overtop the peaked attic and a porch that wraps around the entire first floor.

I pull up beside the steps leading to the front door and leave the car. Before I go inside, I stop and look out over the water, filling my lungs with the scent of home. The sun has vanished behind the mountains on the other side of the lake, leaving in its wake velvet streams of purple and gold weaving across the sky like a little girl's hair ribbons. I touch my hair, wonder if maybe I was once that little girl. If I close my eyes, I can almost feel my mom and dad taking my hands, the wood of the dock scratching the soles of my feet as we race to the end and leap . . .

The memory is deliciously intoxicating. I want more, good or bad. Finally time to see my parents for who they really were, not just who I wished they were.

Eventually, I go inside. It's chilly and dark but I don't want to disturb anything—not because Joe would be upset, but because I somehow feel as if I'm balanced between two worlds, the past and the present.

My breath shallows as I sense my way upstairs and down the hall to the steps leading up to the attic. Here I do turn on the lights—no sense breaking my neck—but the bulbs are old and dusty and the illumination they shed is soft, doing nothing to break the spell I'm under.

This is my first time up here in years. After the whole bat incident, we pretty much never used the attic again—Joe has plenty of room downstairs for storage. I climb over a stack of ancient, frayed life jackets, cartons of Christmas ornaments that we never remember to bring down, plastic storage tubs of my old clothing—stuff I begged Helen to keep so I could use it for future art projects but of course never think of when I'm faced with one. There's some half-finished bookshelves Joe started until the bats interrupted him, and an assortment of other detritus, but nothing from my parents.

I stand, my head almost brushing the rafters, and scan the space one last time. The light is so dim that shadows crowd all around me. Except for a glimmer reflecting from a broken mirror in the far, far corner. I crisscross through the other remnants of my family's life to reach it. Beside it, under the eaves, I find a cardboard box labeled *Nora's Toys*.

Nora. That's me, before I was Ella. No one called me Nora except my mom and dad. And Alec, I remember with a smile. I regret not calling him to come with me. He wouldn't hover or smother—he'd let me explore my past, ready to offer comfort. I should have never doubted him. As soon as I get back home, police or no police, I'm headed over to his place and asking him out. And I won't take no for an answer.

My fingers tremble with anticipation as I pry open the folded sections of the lid. The box is bursting with pressure, and as soon as the flaps separate, a blue hippo leaps into my hand. Hippo! How could I have ever forgotten him? He seems so small now, barely filling my palm, instead of the massive creature who once rode the waves of every bath. I was so enamored with the rubber beast that I'd often take him from bath to bed, snuggling with him.

Holding Hippo tight, I peer into the box, imagining treasures upon forgotten treasures, given the way it was overfilled. But all I find are old sheets and a quilt I don't recognize. No toys. No treasures.

I flip the box over, examine the handwritten label. Its confident, bold printing can only be my father's. I've seen it before on the framed poem he wrote to propose to my mother—that and a few photos are the only things we brought from this house to the city when we moved. The poem uses numbers as puns with lines like "may two march forth together as one," and even after all these years it radiates an aura of the most beautiful alizarin crimson, a pure red that could only mean true love.

Disappointed by the lack of any other childhood treasures or clues about my father, I hug Hippo to me. His playful squeak is gone, and instead of collapsing when I squeeze him, my fingers meet resistance as if he's stuffed with something.

Curious, I roll him onto his back and pry at the button inset into his belly. I chip a nail in the process, but finally the button pops free, releasing a wad of toilet paper. There's no writing on the paper. Despite the protection of Hippo's waterproof skin, it's brittle and tears as I tug it free, leaving something more substantial behind. I shake Hippo, feeling a thin rectangle. It takes me a few minutes to position it to where I can push it through the squeaker hole—so long that I even consider taking Hippo down to the kitchen and finding a knife to gut him. But finally I hold my father's legacy in my hand: a computer flash drive.

Somehow the house doesn't feel as empty when I creep back down the stairs. I turn on the lights as I go, the spell already broken beyond repair, and head to the living room where Joe's computer waits.

He's left it on, so it only takes a few seconds before I see what's on the drive. Folders labeled with strange names that are vaguely familiar. I think they might be clients of Cleary and Sons that Darrin has mentioned. When I click on one, it opens to reveal documents labeled by date and spreadsheets I can't begin to fathom.

I return to the main menu, scanning past the folders to find the sole text document. It's labeled: For Nora. Now I'm blinking so fast, the screen blurs. As I click it open, I hold my breath. The text fills the screen. It's dated the day before my third birthday, the day before we left for the beach.

The day before my parents died.

Dear Nora,

If you're reading this, then I am dead. And if I'm dead, and you found this, then your mother must be dead as well and you are alone.

First, you need to know: It's my fault. I wish I had the words to make you understand, but everything is my fault.

Your mother . . . I should have listened to her. So much more practical than I am, she saw this coming. If it wasn't for her, we might never have had a chance to escape, to get you to a safe place. But if you're reading this, then she failed to reach the FBI. We've both failed. All because of me.

I stop and re-read the last. Wait, what? The FBI?

I trusted too much. I should have seen this coming from the very beginning, long before you were born, before I met your mother. Your mother. Somehow she knew, she always knew, she never trusted him, not like I did. Our only argument was when we made him your godfather, but who else was there? After all, Darrin had been my friend since we were roommates in college. My father trusted him, I trusted him, how could I listen to your mother's doubts? To her worries that Darrin wasn't who he pretended to be, that he was a thief, a con artist, maybe even a killer . . .

By now I've stopped blinking, scrolling down the page as fast as I can without missing a word. Darrin? A killer? Maybe my parents' killer? No. How was that possible? He was in London at the time.

But I didn't believe your mother's instincts. It took her almost two years to gather the proof and convince me of the truth. And now we're out of time—he suspects that we suspect, I know it.

I don't know what happened to your mother and me, but if you're reading this, then you must be old enough to understand how dangerous it is.

Take this flash drive to the nearest FBI office or police station. Trust your instincts, and be safe. Don't make our mistakes—run now, and don't look back.

Just know that we both love you with all our hearts. Forever, in this life and the next.

Love,

Dad

Trembling, I slide the drive free and return it to its hiding place. Without the paper stuffing, Hippo is deflated. I keep the air squeezed out of him as I reinsert the plug sealing his belly. Now he's thin enough to fit into my inside coat pocket. Somehow, having Hippo with me makes me feel safer. But even with him in my pocket, I'm shaking, terrified of what I've just read.

Darrin. Could he have been the man on the beach that night? The one chasing me? No, the police checked his alibi—it was airtight. Maybe he hired someone? With my mom and dad gone, he was executor of their estate, got to run Cleary and Sons, got to control the money that came to me.

I wonder at that. Why hadn't Dad gone to Gram Helen or Joe? Why didn't he mention them at all? His letter made it sound like he and Mom had no one to turn to for help, no choice but to run. Were they afraid Darrin would target Helen and Joe? Use them as hostages? But then why not warn them, take them along when they ran?

Maybe it was me. Maybe running with a toddler already made them too conspicuous, maybe I slowed them down.

Theories and scenarios pummel me from all sides, none of them making any sense. I'm reading the letter again when a sound at the front door has my heart squeezing my throat tight. I whirl away from the computer in time to see a man's silhouette darken the other side of the glass.

Darrin. He's found me.

CHAPTER 38

Alec

The meeting room door bangs open as if a SWAT team is kicking it in. I glance up from where I'm working. It's only Max, venting his anger, but he's still polite enough to catch the door before it hits Rory.

"We're here," he says. "But this had better be good." He takes a position against the wall, arms folded across his chest.

I ignore him. "Rory, I thought you were with Ella. Is she okay?"

"The police are with her—they made us leave."

I can't really argue with that, but I don't like it. I shuffle my notecards one last time before squaring them up and centering them in front of me.

"Stop stalling," Max says.

"This isn't easy. Bear with me, please. I'm going to try to work backward, put everything in some sort of order, but there are places where I can't be certain of the chronology—and things where you might be able to help me fill in the gaps, since you've known Ella and her family for so long."

Max simply narrows his eyes, braced as if for an attack, while Rory nods and says, "Go on."

I haul in a breath. Part of me hopes I'm making a fool of myself, that they'll quickly point out where I went wrong. Most of me is dreading being right. "You know I came here to learn more about Ella's parents' murders."

"Right, for your tell-all book." Max rolls his eyes.

Rory waves him to silence. "You said murders. Plural. You don't believe Ella's dad killed her mother and then himself?"

"I think it's not as black and white as the police report says. I think what happened in that beach cottage was set in motion years beforehand. And I don't believe Sean Cleary suffered from mental illness. I think everything he did was to protect his daughter. Including killing himself."

Even Max seems interested at that.

"What if," I continue, "this was never about Mia and Sean Cleary? What if it was about the company, Cleary and Sons? Specifically, the family trust that owns the company."

"Aren't they all basically the same thing?" Max asks.

"Not if this all began with Sean's father and his death."

"Ella's grandfather?" Rory asks. "He died right before Ella was born. How could he have anything to do with it?"

I slide a piece of paper over to them. Samuel Cleary's

obituary. "Survived by his only son and daughter-in-law. No other relatives to inherit the company."

"Not until Ella was born." This from Rory.

"Exactly. So if your business is insurance and finance, and your father just died and your wife is pregnant with your first child, what do you do?"

"Make out a will," Max says. "Protect my child's interests in case anything happened to me or my wife."

Rory's head bobs as she pieces things together. "Wait, wait, if you think someone killed Ella's parents so they could take over the company, then why wait until she was three before murdering her parents? And why not kill her as well? Or do it before she was even born? And . . . whoa . . . are you saying it was someone they knew?"

"Where's Darrin in all this?" Max puts in. "He's been running the company since they died—actually, since before Ella's grandfather died. He started at Cleary and Sons while her dad was still in grad school, was like second in command under her grandfather."

"I looked it up. Chief Financial Officer and Executive Counsel, to be precise. And, don't forget, he's executor of Ella's parents' wills and the trust fund they left her." I pace along the narrow space between the conference table and the wall. They're asking the right questions even if I don't have all the answers. Yet. "But you're right. Why wait three years before killing her parents?"

"Oh." Rory bounces in her seat, raising her hand before catching herself. "Not just that, but if it's about insurance money, then suicides don't pay out, so why make it look like her dad killed himself?"

"That's actually not true," Max says. "Some insurance companies will still pay out after a suicide if the person held the policy long enough. I know because that's what happened with my aunt."

I glance his way, ready to say something sympathetic, but the rigid set of his shoulders warns me off. Instead I return to the few facts I have. "He's right," I tell them. "Usually you have to hold the policy for several years. And of course, being in the business, both Mia and Sean Cleary had excellent insurance policies. Which they supplemented after she became pregnant and his father died of that sudden heart attack."

"Are you suggesting Ella's grandfather's heart attack might have actually been murder?" Rory asks.

"Or coincidence. I'm not sure. But it's something to keep in mind."

"I'm still not buying it," Max puts in. "The cold-blooded murder of three people? Doesn't seem like much of a payoff, not with the risk of getting caught. I mean, Darrin already had control over a lot of the company and made a ton of money. Besides, the police cleared him—he has an alibi, right?"

"He was cleared. He was in London when Ella's parents died." Now for the part that's a hard sell. "Someone else working with Darrin did the actual killings."

"You mean, like, he hired a hit man?" Rory's eyes grow large.

"I think his partners are closer to home. Who gains the most from Ella's parents' deaths?"

"Ella, of course, but she was only a baby. You said Darrin was executor of the estate, so that leads right back to him."

"Okay." I try again, fighting back a glimmer of hope that maybe I am wrong. "Think of it this way. Who profited from Ella staying alive all these years to inherit her father's estate? And who stands to profit if she dies now, like maybe in a suspicious fire?"

They both furrow their brows in disbelief. Rory shakes her head in denial. "You mean Helen and Joe. No . . . they love Ella. They gave up their whole lives to come and take care of her."

"Besides," Max chimes in, "why would Ella's mom's family kill her? They have plenty of money from the company."

"Exactly why no one ever suspected them. My research was so fixated on the details of the crime and why Sean Cleary might have killed his wife, I never looked into Mia's past. I don't think anyone did. Honestly, there's not much there. Mia Crveno, daughter of Helen and Joseph Crveno. After her father was killed, Mia fled Sarajevo in 1992, began at Cleary and Sons in data-entry, where her unique skills from her synesthesia allowed her to quickly rise through the ranks to head of the fraud division. Then she drew the attention of the founder's son. They married and the rest is history, right?"

Both Max and Rory nod, waiting for the inevitable twist.

"Except for one thing. I can't find any records of Helen or Joe Crveno existing here in the US before eighteen years ago. The first I can find are when they moved to New York—around the same time Ella's mother was pregnant with her and her grandfather died."

"They were war refugees," Rory says. "Maybe their records from before were lost."

"No." Now it's Max arguing my point. "Then they'd have records here. Just like Ella's mom did." He frowned. "So where were they all that time between leaving Sarajevo and arriving in New York? What were they doing?"

"Maybe the question isn't where or what but *who*? Who were they before they moved to New York?" I wait for the implications to sink in.

"You think Helen and Joe aren't really Ella's family?" Rory asks, her voice breathless. "How did they get custody?"

"Easy. They had legal identification with the names of Helen and Joseph Crveno. By that time they were well established at their New York state address. Plus, the executor of Mia's will—Darrin—identified them as the legal next of kin. Why would the police in a small town a thousand miles away, their hands full with a murder-suicide that was the crime of the century, ever question it? Not to mention that in both Mia's and Sean's wills, Darrin is named not only executor but legal guardian of their children in the case of their deaths. Which was kind of strange if Mia had relatives living here in the States, right? Technically, the police were obligated to give custody to Darrin once social services cleared him. Which means no one ever did a complete background check on Helen and Joe. Because whoever Darrin chose to help with childrearing was up to him."

Max and Rory look at each other, eyes wide. "So no one even looked?"

"No one even looked. They had no reason to," I answer. "But once you knew where to look—or rather, when—it wasn't hard. I found two people from New Jersey who legally changed their names to Helen and Joseph Crveno eighteen years ago before moving to the small town in upstate New York where Mia's supposed family lived. From then on, they were legally the Helen and Joe you know."

"No," Rory says. "You're forgetting, they both have synesthesia. It's hereditary."

"Right. A rare disease that affects each patient in a unique way, one that could reveal itself in a myriad of symptoms. One that there is no easy medical test for."

A long pause as Rory and Max exchange wide-eyed stares. "It wouldn't be hard to pretend to have synesthesia," Rory suggests in a hesitant tone. "I mean, I guess."

"The medical literature has articles on people who live their whole lives acting as if they have synesthesia, but when they test them with MRIs and PET scans, they actually don't. So, if someone wanted to fit in with a family with synesthesia or wanted a way to excuse themselves whenever conversations got too tough or the wrong questions were asked—"

"It makes for the perfect con." Max's tone is bitter. "All those times I've been extra nice to Helen when she complained about a migraine, or the way we tiptoe around words to protect Joe—what a laugh they must have had."

"Not just us. Think of Ella," Rory says. "They're her only family—her entire world revolves around them. This is going to crush her. If it's true."

Neither of them is calling my bluff, telling me I'm wrong. Instead, they're buying my theory, crazy as it is.

"Darrin, he's the one who planned all this?" Max asks. "To get access to Ella's inheritance? Then why not take a big insurance policy out on her and kill her? Why all this trouble, not to mention the expense of raising a kid?" He starts pacing around the room. "Fifteen years is a long time to be faking all this. And, as soon as she's an adult and starts to check into her parents' finances and the company, the gig is up. Why bother with raising her at all?"

Rory interrupts him. "Is that why the fire started? They were trying to kill her? Before she's old enough to start working for the company and putting the pieces together?"

"I think so." My voice drops, weighed down by guilt. "And I might have sped up their timeline, coming here and asking questions."

"No. Not just you," Rory says. "I know why they waited until now. Ella told me this afternoon. She inherited more than the family trust that came with Cleary and Sons. Her parents had a separate trust funded by their life insurance so she wouldn't have to worry about education costs. She gained access to it when she turned eighteen."

"How much?" Max asks cautiously.

"She didn't say—which makes me think it must be a lot. Otherwise she would have told me."

The final piece of the puzzle. I stop, my breath frozen. I force myself to exhale, breathe in, and exhale again. But still the weight on my chest doesn't budge. "Which means Ella's fair game. Kill her now and they get everything."

CHAPTER 39

Ella

Before I can hide, the cabin's door opens. I have my finger on the button of my Howler, the sonic alarm Max gave me for my birthday last year. It's guaranteed to stun any attacker long enough to let you escape.

A man steps out of the dark and into the light. Not Darrin. Joe.

I almost run to him in relief, want to tell him everything, but then I see the pistol in his hand. Aimed at me.

I pull up short. His eyes fly wide at the sight of me. He glances around the empty cabin. "You're alone. Good." He sees me staring at the gun and jerks his body back from his own hand as if holding a snake. He fumbles it into his jacket pocket. "Sorry. I saw the light. Didn't know who was in here."

"Why do you have a gun?" I've never seen Joe with

a weapon—not even to hunt, which just about everyone around here does. He wouldn't even bait my hook with worms when he taught me how to fish. Instead, he used rolled-up bread balls for bait.

He shrugs, walks past me to the computer that's bright with my father's last words to me still open in the word processor. I curse myself for not having enough time to close it out and delete it, but it's too late now. Darrin is Joe's best friend—does he have any idea what Darrin did? Is that why Joe has a gun?

I say nothing but edge closer to the door as he reads. At least he won't be able to see any of the folders from the thumb drive—all I did was look at their titles, and the letter was the only one that opened all the way in a computer program, so I think I'm safe. Then I realize: safe from what? From who?

"Should have known your dad left you breadcrumbs. Darrin always said he was smarter than the average rube."

I stare at him as if he's speaking Martian. His posture is different, straighter, taller, and his accent has changed as well: more flat and nasal, far from the mountains of central Pennsylvania.

He glances over his shoulder, sees me staring, and grimaces. "Guess it's time to tell you everything. I was trying to find the right time—it's why I wanted you to come away with me so we could figure out a plan. One that hopefully doesn't get us both killed."

"What are you talking about?" My words are a strangled whisper as he turns his back to me to start the gas logs in the fireplace.

I return my keys to my pocket—after all, I came here to find answers, so using the Howler and running away will do me no good. Besides, although he seems different than the Joe I know and love, he doesn't seem threatening—his aura is more sorrowful, filled with regrets, not violence.

If I'm going to stay and listen, though, I want to make sure help is on the way, just in case. I slide my phone into my hand, half-hidden in my pocket, gripping it tight since it's the best weapon I have, but I'm not hopeful about making any calls. There's never any cell reception up here. But with Joe's Wi-Fi, I should be able to get a text out. Worth a shot, I think as my fingers type silently.

"Well, for starters, I'm not who you think I am." He moves to plop into one of the leather chairs in front of the fireplace, legs spread wide, relaxed. "Legally, I really am Joe Crveno, just like it says on my driver's license. Have been for eighteen years. Before then I was Jimmy McCray." He taps his forehead in a fake hat tilt. "Pleased to meet ya."

"My dad said Darrin—you're working for him?" No, that can't be right. "Helen, she, she's not your mother?"

"She's my aunt. And Darrin's mother. We're a twisted bunch, our family." He laughs at my confusion, but it's not a cruel laugh, more one of self-deprecation. "I know this is confusing, a lot to take in. But I promise, I'm not here to hurt you. I want to help. Sit down, ask me anything."

My family isn't my family—it's Darrin's? I want to stay where I am, near the door and its escape, but my legs are quivering, and I know even if I run, he'll catch me easily. So I move to the chair and slide it back, away from his. Before I sit down, I take the fire poker from its stand. It's just there for decoration, left over from when the fire took real logs, but its cold iron heft feels good in my hand.

Then I start. "My dad wasn't crazy."

"Nope. Not even a bit. Your mom, though, she was the tough one—her synesthesia made it almost impossible to fool her once she got her hands on the books. She's why Darrin changed gears and instead of fleecing the company, he decided to fleece the family legacy: you."

"I don't understand. Darrin knew my father since college."

"Yep. Only one of the family to go. Got a scholarship. Well, actually, he stole one. Applied for a bunch under a variety of stolen identities until he got a full ride. See, that's the family business: grifts, cons, scams, whatever you want to call them. Up and down the Jersey shore, that's our territory. Or was, until Darrin came up with this game." He shakes his head in admiration. "Longest, most profitable con in family history. He's a true genius."

"Con?" I ask, although I think I'm finally understanding.

"After Darrin met your father, he realized that Cleary and Sons was a proverbial pot of gold. False insurance claims, skimming off the top from clients, and a bunch of gullible folks who wouldn't think twice about trusting him with their life savings. So, Darrin decided to learn everything he could about the business. Graduated with honors. Your dad went on to grad school for his MBA and got Darrin a job at Cleary and Sons. But Darrin knew he needed to get close to the old man, your grandfather, earn his trust. So he went to law school in his free time, proved himself. I mean, seriously, the work he put in was astounding. Had the rest of the family laughing at him, thinking he'd gone straight. Should've known better. By the time your father finished his MBA and returned home, Darrin practically ran Cleary and Sons."

I can't help it. I lean forward, entranced by his story despite the fact that I already know its ugly ending. "Darrin planned this way back in college?"

Joe nods. A hint of a proud smile plays across his face, though it's quickly chased away by fear. He glances at the door, but the only sound outside is the wind. "Darrin thinks big, I'll give him that. Once he got himself exactly where he wanted, only thing he had to do was bide his time, wait for the old man to die and then take care of your dad. But he got greedy. And the whole thing blew up in his face."

"My mother. She found out what he was doing."

"Almost ruined everything. Kept finding inconsistencies

in the books—that's why he moved her to work fraud, let her ferret out the clients who were trying to screw the company instead of stumbling over Darrin's thefts. But then she met your dad, and it was love like in the movies. Suddenly they were married and she was pregnant, and now he had an heir to Cleary and Sons to deal with instead of an old man and a clueless son."

Joe runs a hand through his hair. "Darrin did get one lucky break when your grandpa died. But by that time, your dad had already redone his will and the family trust. It didn't leave Darrin with many options, not if he wanted full control of the company and the money."

My mouth goes dry. I have to struggle to get my next question out. "He killed my parents?"

He glances down at the fire. "No. He really was in London. I know because we had to scramble to set it all up once we realized what your mom had done. She'd been gathering evidence, finally convinced your dad she wasn't paranoid, that he had been betrayed by his oldest, closest friend. She'd arranged to take the evidence to someone in the FBI as soon as they got you to safety. Of course, she had no idea Darrin had her house and car bugged, was two steps ahead of her."

He makes a sad sighing sound, the fire blazing behind him. "Darrin. Always thinks of everything. He's the clever one. They only brought me on board because of my hair—red like your ma's. I had no idea what I was getting myself into. Family calls, you answer. Period."

His aura is the same orange as the tips of the flames and flickers, as if he's actually burning. I push back in the chair, his new voice suddenly all too familiar: the fire demon who's haunted my dreams.

Fear paralyzes me. Despite the fire, my face goes numb. Because if Darrin didn't do it . . . "You followed them to South Carolina? *You* killed my parents?"

My grip on the poker tightens. Then I'm standing over him, surging across the space between us so fast I nearly don't stop. "I saw you. Out on the dunes. Looking for me."

His expression morphs into sorrow. "Worst night of my life. I had no idea what I was getting into. No idea what she was going to do—"

"She?" Who? My mother? Then it hits me. *Helen.* "Helen killed my parents?"

"Only way to protect her family—her son." Darrin. He's talking about Darrin as if a lying, cheating thief's life is worth more than my parents'. "You gotta understand, I thought it would end after that. Figured we'd take off with what Darrin already skimmed, forget the rest. But then the cops called Darrin, asking about who your guardian was, if there was any next of kin, and next thing I know, we're back on. He couldn't have planned it more perfectly if he tried, especially with him being out of the country."

Joe glances up at me, regret plain on his face. The only time I see fear in his aura is when he glances toward the door or the clock. "We're running out of time. We should get going."

"I'm not going anywhere with you." Contempt colors my voice, but it's an act. Inwardly, I'm a quavering mess, trying to sort through the ramifications of everything he's told me. All my life I've been driven by the guilt of running from my parents when they needed me most. The certain dread that if I ever abandoned Helen and Joe, something just as bad would happen to them. Like everything was my fault.

I guess it was. By merely being born, I'd sealed my parents' fates.

Joe's voice cuts through my confusion and despair. "Don't you see, Ella? I've been trying to save your life."

"By butchering my parents and pretending to be my family and stealing my money and . . ." My voice rises with every syllable. Then it drops to a whisper. "Did you start the fire last night?"

He shakes his head, *no, no, no.* "I was out there trying to get you to leave, before Darrin and Helen got back, remember? And then I was trying to get in, to save you." Despite his words, guilt colors his voice.

"Don't lie to me. You know you can't lie to me." There's menace in my voice, and I hold the fire poker higher. I don't even recognize myself.

"I'm not lying. Not really. See, that trip to Paris in the summer—that's when you were meant to die. Some kind of accident far away—I never wanted to know the details. Darrin was going to take care of it. Then we'd divvy up your inheritance and life insurance and what's left of the company and be on our merry way. At least that was the plan."

My stomach clenches. "Then why did someone try to kill me in the studio?"

The bilious green of his guilt deepens; not even the flames behind him break through. "I didn't start it—" he finally says, and I know the other half of his sentence before he says the words.

"Darrin did," I finish, still not quite believing that we're having this conversation. It feels like something out of a nightmare.

"He found out that kid, Alec, his dad is a cop down in South Carolina. Same place where the murders took place. When you wouldn't run away with me and that kid came back and both of you seemed so upset—I called Darrin, told him. He said he'd take care of everything." He shrugs as if we're not talking about my life and death. "He left Helen to cover for him at the restaurant, snuck back to the house, and started the fire. You die, the kid makes for an easy patsy. If you live, we blame it on you, lock you away, have you declared incompetent, get control of the money. Told you. Darrin's a freakin' genius, right?"

I don't even have words to answer that. It's all so . . . outrageous. I feel like the stupid girl in the horror movies who opens the basement door. Only it's my life that's devolved into a Hitchcockian bloodbath.

"It's not what I wanted, believe me." Cowardly yellow shame swirls through Joe's aura—shame mingled with fear. "I didn't even want Darrin to send you to Paris. I told them, she's eighteen now, the trust is open, let's clear it out then clear out ourselves. But no, he had to have it all. Not just the trust and the company—there's another five million in life insurance riding on you being dead. That's why if Darrin finds us, he'll kill me as well. Because he thinks I'm trying to make off with the golden goose. But all these years, watching you grow, seeing how talented you are—I love you, Ella. Like you were my own kid. I can't let anything bad happen to you."

Stunned, I step back, slamming into the forgotten chair behind me. I sink into its embrace, the poker dangling from my fingers. He's telling the truth. I don't need my synesthesia to know that. But suddenly the truth is worse than the lies I've been living.

"My parents. Tell me about my parents. How did they really die?"

The door flies open. Helen stands there, silhouetted by the porch light, her aura cascading around her like a flowing cape. It's a color I've never seen on her before: a boastful sunflower yellow. It takes me a blink or two to spy Darrin standing behind her, her aura is so blinding.

"Good work, Joe. Stalling until we could get here," she says. "I told Darrin you'd never let the family down. And I was right, wasn't I?"

CHAPTER 40

Ella

Helen's words slap me into action. I spring from the chair, poker raised, ready to strike. Then I see the gun in her hand. Aimed at me. Gone is my gram, the woman who guided me through adolescence, who helped mold me into the person I am now.

Before I can swing the poker, Darrin steps forward, and in one swift movement he wrenches the poker away from me and strong-arms me back into the chair.

I land with a gasp, staring up at them. "Was any of it real?"

Joe answers, "Yes. Of course it was." Earning him a glare from Darrin, who stands beside Helen, between me and the door. I can't tell if Joe's lying to me or them or himself. His aura is a muddle of colors, as confused as he is.

But I can't miss Helen's shushing motion with her hand

hidden from Darrin. Signaling Joe to shut up and follow her lead. Maybe, like Joe, she's had second thoughts about killing me? If so, if I can convince them to take action, we can overpower Darrin.

"Does it matter?" Helen says. "The past is nothing, we need to focus on the future." She eyes me. "A future that we now need to rearrange."

"A slight alteration," Darrin adds as if I'm not even there. "Everyone knows how upset she's been—even the cop saw that. Like he said, mental illness often runs in families."

Helen nods in approval. "Like father like daughter? That could work. Forensics will be trickier this time around."

"Another fire? The police already believe she began the one last night."

Joe is scowling, focused on them as if reading a book written in a foreign language. His aura is the same burnt umber that surrounded him last night when he wanted me to leave with him. Concern, fear, worry . . . for me? Or himself?

He rises and positions himself between me and the others, his hands thrust deep into the pockets of his jacket. I remember his pistol—will he use it on his own aunt and cousin? I'm desperate to find a way out, but there's nothing behind me except the wall and fireplace. No weapons, no escape, only this chair to shield me if they begin shooting.

How has my life come to this? I don't have time to

wonder or worry; I need to focus on a way out. I tap my phone, blind-texting Rory again, hoping against hope that my message makes it out. Not that it will do me much good—no one can make it here in time.

I'm alone. But not helpless. I grasp my keychain with the Howler inside my pocket. Would it be enough to keep them from shooting? Or would the noise startle them into pulling the trigger? They're so close, there's no way they could miss me, so I decide to save it as a last resort.

I examine the auras of the three people I once thought I knew best. Darrin's is his usual inky indigo but Helen's ebbs and wanes as if reflecting the flames of the fire beside me. Despite her fierce words, could it all be an act? What would persuade her to let me live? What do I have that she wants?

"I can sign over the money," I say, marveling at how calm I sound. All three of them turn to stare at me. "I know Darrin controls it now, but what if I signed it over to you, Helen? Surely you're tired of waiting for him to dole out your share after he gets the first piece of the pie?"

I stand, slowly, making myself seem meek, no threat. I focus on Helen—or whatever her real name is—and not the archway beyond Joe that leads into the rear of the house. If I can make it past him, I can get out the back and down to the lake or into the woods. All I need is a chance.

Helen nods slowly, almost as if she's hypnotized by my offer. Her expression shifts, and remorse shines through

THE COLOR OF LIES

her aura. Is this all just an act for Darrin's benefit? Have I convinced her to help me? "Exactly what your parents offered. Your father, he begged me to spare you and Mia. Said he'd pay anything, sign anything, even take his own life to seal the bargain if that was the only way to save you both."

But then she shakes her head, her aura turning to guilt-tainted ochre. "That's when I killed Mia. And I told your father if he didn't kill himself, you'd be next."

I stare at her in horror. Who is this woman? How could I have ever loved her?

"Nice try." Darrin laughs at my pathetic attempt to win over his mother. "We might be crooks, but we never cheat each other."

"Because family is off limits. We never treat family as marks," Joe puts in. His aura morphs into a desperate shade of puce, and I realize he's trying to save us both. "And after fifteen years, isn't Ella family? Maybe we should hear her out."

I sidle the tiniest bit to the side, edging behind Joe and toward my escape route.

"That's rich, coming from the man who almost cost us everything," Darrin tells him. "Did you really think you could hide Ella from us? You're such a sentimental fool, trying to save her." He shakes his head.

I glance at the clock. It's been almost long enough since

I first texted Rory for her to get here if she sped—but now I don't want her anywhere near the lake house. Not with this new Darrin, this bloodthirsty stranger before me.

"How many years have we been planning this, and you risked it all for a girl who's not even blood?" Helen scolds Joe. She steps forward, and for a second I think she's going to slap him.

But then she stops. I freeze, looking at her past Joe's shoulder, thinking she knows exactly what I'm doing, edging toward an escape route. She's going to shoot me, I just know it. Set the stage of my insanity before Rory can arrive—she and Darrin will happily make my friends witnesses, use them to build the case against my mental stability.

Joe knows it as well. His aura goes from fearful brown to defiant red as he steps in front of me. "Stop. You don't have to do this."

"Relax, cousin," Darrin says. "You'll get your fair share, just like I promised." He turns to Helen. "I'll check the barn. There should be a gas can out there. You'll take care of the rest?"

Helen merely nods. Goose bumps crawl over my flesh as I realize they're talking about me.

Darrin leaves. Helen waits until he's crossing the space between the house and barn before she speaks. "What am I going to do with you?" She's addressing both Joe and me.

"Can't you see? Even if Ella signed over the money, Darrin could still go to jail if she ever changed her mind and set the cops on him. I have to protect my boy."

I can't help but notice that she's speaking of me in the third person as if I'm not standing right there. Not just third person—past tense.

"But we're family too," Joe insists. Both their auras are clouded by conflicting emotions and I can't tell if he's getting through to her or not. "There has to be a way."

"Darrin's put his whole life into this. I can't let him down now."

"What about your idea of having Ella committed?" He's between me and Helen, acting like a negotiator. He turns to me. "We'd find a nice hospital, peaceful, in the country, you could do your art. You'd only be there long enough for us to get free and clear, create new identities." Then he faces Helen. "All those countries, no extradition. What's the one you're always talking about? The Maldives, beautiful beaches just waiting for you. Don't you deserve a rest after all these years of hard work?"

As he's talking, I keep edging toward the archway leading to the back of the house. But Helen spots my movement.

"Stop!" She raises the pistol but Joe is partially blocking her aim, so I take my chance and turn toward the rear of the house. I only need to make it four steps, just four steps . . .

She fires. The sound is deafening. I jump, thinking she's

hit me, but when I look back I see that Joe has lunged toward Helen. His hands are raised, fingers spread wide as if they can magically stop a bullet. His face is wide with shock because of course the bullet keeps going, though his hand and into his neck. Blood sprays out even as Helen screams, "No!"

His aura darkens and he crumples to the ground.

Then she turns to me and shrieks, "You did this! You killed him!"

This woman is no one I've ever met before. A complete stranger, her eyes dark as coal, the cheerful light that usually illuminates them dead and buried. She aims the pistol at me, and this time there's no one to stop her from pulling the trigger.

CHAPTER 41

Alec

It takes a while, but finally Max and I are in Rory's VW, speeding up the twisted mountain roads to Ella's family's cabin by the lake. While we'd been dissecting and debating my theory, a bizarre text message from Ella's phone had propelled us into action: *Laker sooss*.

"I still don't trust you," Max tells me after we drop Rory off at the police department, armed with my research. She let us use her car since neither of us have one of our own. Rory argued that she should come with us, but someone had to explain to the police what was going on. After the fire, there was no way they'd believe me, and there was no way Max was going to leave Rory alone with me, so after a few seconds of emotional calculus, Max finally agreed to let me come with him to Ella's lake house.

"Who's to say you didn't fake all that so-called evidence,"

Max continues, almost elbowing me as he whips the steering wheel around, taking a steep curve too fast. "That's just as likely as people I've known practically all my life turning out to be murderers and thieves. I mean, who could do that? Kill two people—"

"Can you just focus on the road?" I put in, my hands braced against the dash as we speed around a corkscrew switchback. Who designed these crazy roads?

"I know what I'm doing. Anyway, who could kill two people, then take over their lives and wait all those years for the payout?"

"It's called a long con. There was almost no risk that they'd ever be caught—at least not until someone examined the trust fund accounts or checked to see if they'd changed their names. Other than Ella, who would do that?"

"You. The one thing they didn't factor into this devious master plan of theirs." Max still doesn't sound convinced of Ella's family's deception. "We're getting Ella and getting out of there. You can tell her your story on the way to the police station, and then you're out of her life unless she decides she wants you in it. She and the police can figure things out. You will not call, text, email, drop by, or contact her again without her permission." Max's voice grows serious. "Understand? You leave her alone."

"As long as she's safe, I don't care." It isn't the whole truth, but it's what Max wants to hear.

Because I do care, very much. So much that I can barely force words past the fear choking me. A garbled text message doesn't mean Ella is in danger. Rory said she often went to the cabin to think. She could just be upset after everything that happened. We'll probably arrive to find her crying, expecting Rory responding to her text, upset when two guys barge in on her private grief.

At least I hope so. But as Max steers us off the narrow, nameless, two-lane road and onto a gravel drive that winds through a massive gathering of hemlocks and rhododendrons, my dread worsens. The trees give way to a clearing, a sliver of moon reflecting on a small lake that spreads out beside the house and continues behind it. The cabin is larger than I expected, two stories tall with a peaked tin roof. There are lights on inside, but what worries me the most are the other cars parked behind Ella's Subaru.

"Joe and Darrin are already here," I say. "We should call the police." Really, I want to call Dad, but what could he do, a thousand miles away?

"No cell reception up here," Max says, his door already open. I cringe away from the light from the overhead dome that backlights Max. I reach up and flick it off before opening my own door and quietly easing it shut.

"Wait," I urge Max, my voice a low whisper across the car's hood. "Let me check things out. If there are any problems, you can go get help." Nothing more valuable than good intel, Dad always says.

"You wait," Max snaps. "I'm going to get Ella. She's my friend, not yours."

Before I can stop him, Max strides down the drive and up the cabin's porch steps. A woman's silhouette appears at the door. Helen. I creep forward, using the other vehicles as cover, keeping out of sight.

"Is Ella here?" Max asks in a polite but firm voice. "Rory sent me to get her—she needs her help with a school project."

Not a terrible lie, I think. And if Darrin and his cohorts are playing it safe, they'll let Ella go with Max. After all, they have no idea what I've found or that Rory is sharing it with the police. From their point of view, they still have time to cover their tracks.

I almost relax. Until I realize that Darrin, Helen, and Joe wouldn't have followed Ella up here unless they're suspicious that their con is in danger of being exposed. After all, Joe is supposed to be resting at Ella's house, and Darrin was meant to be headed back to Philly.

Inching my way closer to the house, I strain to hear Helen's response.

"Come on in, Max," she says in a cheerful tone. "We need to talk."

I slump against Ella's car in relief. Then a twig snaps behind me. Before I can turn around, the muzzle of a gun touches the back of my neck, coming to rest directly over my spine.

"You'd best come inside as well," Darrin says, grinding the pistol into my flesh. "Ella's waiting."

CHAPTER 42

Ella

I drop to the floor, beside Joe's body. "Joe!" There's no pulse. It's too late.

"Help him!" Helen's face turns crimson. "Why isn't he moving? Is he dead? He's dead, isn't he? This is all your fault!" She paces back and forth but never takes her aim off me. "What am I going to tell my sister? Why did he do that? Move right in front of me. He was always too sentimental. You're not worth it."

She raises the pistol, aims directly at my head. She doesn't know about Joe's gun, but there's no way I can get it out of his pocket in time, so instead I back away and slowly climb to my feet. If she's going to shoot me, it's going to be while I'm trying to fight back. I won't be helpless like my parents.

Before I can make a move, a knock on the door startles us both. It has to be Rory or Max. Helen places a finger over her lips as she holds her pistol at her side, out of sight of the door. Then she somehow rearranges her posture and her face until suddenly it's my Gram Helen smiling as she turns to greet our visitor. Fifteen years of practice have honed her acting skills to an Oscar-winning level.

It's Max. I'm helpless to do anything except watch—a word of warning and she'll shoot him. She invites him inside, standing so she's at his back when he steps into the living room and sees Joe's body. By the time he whirls around, she has the gun aimed at him. The door opens once more and Darrin shoves Alec inside, also at gunpoint.

"Well now," Helen says. "Isn't this a nice little party? Our distressed damsel, her over-protective friend, and our friendly neighborhood stalker." She glares at me. "Maybe Joe's death isn't in vain. I think we can make this work, don't you?"

"Absolutely," Darrin says, placing Alec in a chokehold, his gun in his other hand. He doesn't even give Joe a second glance, that's how heartless he is. How could I have ever have thought he loved me like a daughter? "But it's best to immobilize the hostages."

Before any of us can protest, Darrin shoots Max. He's hit in the leg and goes down on one knee. To my surprise, he doesn't make a sound, although his face and aura blaze white with pain.

I rush to Max, who has fallen beside Joe's body. As I

cradle him, I inch his hand until it's on top of Joe's jacket pocket where his pistol is hidden.

"When I run, use it," I whisper, assessing both Helen and Darrin's auras. Helen's is murky with grief and anxiety, but Darrin's flashes red with victory—the most emotion I've ever seen from him. If Helen or Darrin follows me, it will give Alec and Max a chance to fight back, and Max will have a weapon to defend them with.

It's a desperate plan, but the best I have. I meet Alec's panicked eyes as Darrin applies pressure around his neck, enough to make Alec gasp for air but not enough to knock him out. He's as helpless as Max. It's up to me.

Blood stains the floor below Max. We don't have much time. I have to move. Now. Helen turns her aim on Alec. He kicks out, knocking her to one side before Darrin can rein him in.

For a split second, no one is looking at me. I dive through the archway into the dining room, spin to my feet, and am racing through the kitchen and out the back door when I hear a gunshot.

"Come back or your friends are dead," Darrin calls after me.

I pray that isn't true, but I know going back won't save any of us. Our only hope is that they want me more than they want Max and Alec. I'm already off the porch, ducked down in the azaleas that line the path down to the dock, when Helen appears at the back door, her aura spiked with sulfur—fear and anger mixing in an ugly ochre that oozes all around her like a witch's brew.

I creep through the shadows toward the water. Exactly where she'll expect me to go. Helen turns on the porch light but I'm already beyond its reach. Then she starts down the path to the dock, holding her gun in both hands.

"Come out, come out wherever you are," she calls, trying to sound confident, but her voice can't fool me. Not with those whiffs of uncertainty coloring her aura.

She reaches the dock as I sidle into the trees beside the bat house. I grab a stone and toss it into the water, the splash drawing her down the dock.

"Of course you'd hide in the water. But you can't stay under forever." She scans both sides of the dock, even bends down to look below in the area around its pilings.

I can feel the rustle of the bats above me—it's not yet cold enough for them to be hibernating, but this time of year, they'll be gathered for warmth in their cozy house, preparing for the winter. I hate to do this to them, but it's my best chance.

I slide my keychain free and activate my Howler. Helen whips around, gun aimed in front of her. She can't see me through the bushes, but that doesn't matter.

The bats swarm out of their house, away from the piercing noise, directly toward Helen. There's no escaping their vortex of angry wings whipping through the night. She screeches, raising her hands to cover her face as she moves in the only direction she can: down to the end of the dock.

That's my cue. I rush forward, ducked down below the whirl of bats, my speed enough to rock the deck's planks as I tackle Helen and throw her into the water.

CHAPTER 43

Alec

I'm not sure what Ella's plan is, but I know for certain that she's not running out on me and Max. She's trying to play decoy—and might just get herself killed. When Helen rushes after Ella, I struggle against Darrin's chokehold, but he throws me to the ground and steps back to take aim.

Nowhere to run, nowhere to hide.

Then Max comes through. He sits up, somehow having found a gun of his own, and fires at Darrin.

The shot goes wide, but it's enough to force Darrin to take cover—which he does by ducking out the front door, leaving me alone with Max.

Max is ghastly pale and panting, but he keeps both hands on the revolver he has pointed at the door. He doesn't even blink, despite the fact that his leg is gushing blood and his hands are shaking so bad he'd be lucky to pull the trigger again.

I gently remove the revolver from his hands.

"Good job," I tell him. Max gives me a nod and weak smile then slumps to the floor. I check the revolver. Five shots left. I keep it close to hand and position myself where I can keep an eye on the door and front windows, but Darrin has vanished.

Outside comes a shriek of noise so loud and high-pitched, it makes me wince as it fills the air. Max manages a weak smile. "My Howler. And she laughed when I gave it to her."

I use the noise as a distraction while I take my belt and wrap it around Max's leg, above the bullet hole that keeps filling up with blood. "This is gonna hurt," I warn him.

Instead of crying out when I yank the makeshift tourniquet tight, Max goes white and faints. But at least the bleeding slows.

There's no way I can carry Max out to the car without risking us both getting shot. I check my phone. Still no service. I glance around the room. There has to be a landline. I make sure the tourniquet is secure and leave Max to search the place. I find a phone on the wall in the kitchen. I lift the receiver and am rewarded with a dial tone.

The 9-1-1 operator wants me to stay on the line, but I can't leave Max defenseless, so after giving her the basics, I leave the phone off the hook and return to the living room. Max hasn't moved—his coloring is gray and his eyes are closed.

I'm about to try to drag Max to better cover when the sound of another gunshot sounds outside. The Howler's shriek fades then dies. But then a second shot cracks through the night.

Max's eyes flutter open. "Help Ella," he gasps, one hand flopping against my arm.

I'm torn, but he's right. Ella is alone and unarmed up against both Helen and Darrin. Holding the revolver, I edge my way carefully through the door and head around the side of the house in the direction of the shots.

As I near the path to the dock, I hear splashing and Helen shouting. Helen's in the water. Darrin is on the dock, but instead of helping Helen, he's aiming his pistol at the other side of the dock. Bats whirl overhead, filling the night with a noise almost as teeth-jarring as the Howler's piercing scream.

Helen paddles toward shore, disappearing in the shadows of the overhanging trees. I focus on Darrin—he's the greater threat. I use the bushes lining the path as cover, creeping forward, hoping to get the jump on him. Darrin stops, peering down at the lake's surface from the far end of the dock, and I see moonlight glint off pale skin as Ella emerges just long enough to take a breath.

"Ella, no!" I shout. I sprint toward the water and fire a shot at Darrin, even though I have no hope of hitting him from this distance.

Too late. Darrin takes aim and fires . . . and Ella vanishes below the surface.

CHAPTER 44

Ella

Water has always been my safe haven, but I guess it's too much to expect it to deflect bullets. After Helen and I tumble into the lake, I push her off me and quickly swim below the dock. She thrashes and sputters in the cold water, eventually ending even farther away from shore.

I duck below the surface and quietly kick my way to the other side of the dock, expecting to glide to shore out of sight. But I haven't counted on Darrin arriving so quickly. I manage to avoid his first shots by diving deep, but eventually I have to surface. When I do, I'm totally exposed.

His indigo aura is so strong it blocks the crescent moon behind him. Time slows and I can see the bullet, its path a blaze-orange comet streaking toward me, but I can't move fast enough to avoid it.

It hits my arm just below the shoulder. Pain spikes

through me as my arm goes dead and flops to my side, trailing blood that glints on the water's surface.

Thankfully I don't need both arms to swim, but Darrin keeps shooting. Bullets fly through the water, silver moonlight glistening in their wake. One grazes my calf as I'm twisting, trying to dive deeper, seeking the protection of the lake's depths.

The pain is overwhelming. I sink, ribbons of blood swirling with my every movement, my body laced with pain that burns like ice, my skin frozen numb from the cold water as my chest heaves, fighting the need to breathe.

I touch bottom, silky fronds caressing my body, clinging to me as if they want me to stay there forever. I'm half tempted to. My body is so very heavy, I doubt I'll ever be able to force my way back to the surface.

Then I remember Max and Alec are still out there, and any chance of giving up vanishes in a blood-red haze as my need for oxygen almost has me trying to breathe water. I push away from the muddy bottom with my good leg, trying to kick to the crescent moon reflected so far above me. Too far. But I don't give up, not even when a black form splashes through the moonlight, careening toward me.

Panic grips me. Darrin has come to finish me off. But there's no indigo cloaking this swimmer. Then he comes closer, his body rippling through the moonlight, and finally I can see his aura—it's as clear as the finest crystal.

Alec's face turns toward me as I stretch out my good arm, but I'm too far away and begin to sink once more. He blinks, and I see his luminous green eyes.

Even as I'm falling away from Alec, all I can think is how wrong I've been. It's not that he has no aura. Or even that his aura has no colors. Rather, his aura is like a prism, a crystal capturing all colors.

Bubbles of laughter escape my lips as my last bit of air convulses from my lungs. Then everything goes black.

CHAPTER 45

Ella

The next sensation I feel is my parents' hands clasping mine, keeping me safe, never letting me go. I don't know how I know it's them—I still can't see anything—but I just know. Somehow, with my parents with me, I'm no longer haunted by that night so long ago. It's gone fuzzy and frayed and I'm relieved to be here at the end. At least I think it might be the end . . .

Some distant, quiet part of my brain realizes now is my time to decide once and for all to stay or leave . . . surrender or keep fighting. It's my choice—maybe the first one that was ever mine alone.

The whoosh of air escaping my body goes on and on, a sigh echoing in eternity. My body is weightless and far away, drifting down, down, down, embracing the caress of the water.

My parents feel so close, I can almost see them . . . if only I could open my eyes . . . I ache to stay with them, to never leave this warm embrace of memory.

I decide. My life belongs to me, and I'm not going to be driven by fear or ghosts or lies any longer. I want to wake up. I want to wake up. I want to—

Warm breath brushes against my cheek. Then fingers pinch my nostrils tight, and dimly, I sense lips pressed against my own. I feel arms wrapped around me, legs kicking beside mine, hauling my body through the water, someone forcing air into my breathless lungs.

I choke and cough and sputter, my body convulsing upright and almost immediately sinking into the water. I open my eyes. Alec is supporting me and we're near to shore, my feet mired in the silty muck. He helps me onto dry land, where I collapse and vomit into the grass, narrowly missing him.

Alec holds my hair away from my face, his other hand cradling my cheek, so warm against my skin.

Finally, I stop retching. He sinks down beside me in the mud and wraps an arm around my shoulders, sharing his warmth despite the fact that we're both shivering violently.

"Thought I lost you," he murmurs, then clears his throat. He's lost his glasses and is squinting, trying to focus even though I'm right beside him, only inches away.

"Max?" It takes all my strength to utter the one syllable.

"He's okay for now. Help's on the way."

I can barely raise my head to glance around. We're just below the bat house—now empty of the creatures who saved my life. I look across to the dock, see Darrin's motionless body at the far end. "I heard you shouting at him. Before—"

"I needed him to stop shooting at you," Alec says.

"By making yourself a target?" I can't believe Alec did that for me.

"He finally ran out of bullets—I tackled him before he could reload." Alec shifts, and I see a bruise starting to form on his face. "Used his own designer tie and belt to hogtie him. Then when I realized you still hadn't surfaced—" His voice breaks.

We both turn as sirens sound. I can tell they're close from the way the noise echoes across the lake and bounces back from the mountains on the other side. I inch closer to Alec, seeking more than just his warmth, and something hard nudges me in the side. Hippo. I pull the toy out with my uninjured arm and press it into Alec's hand. My other arm is beginning to thaw, pain flashing down my nerves and blood oozing beneath my wet clothing. But I'm too exhausted to deal with that right now.

"Everything you need to know is in there." My throat is scratched raw but my voice is strong. "My mom figured out what Darrin was doing. She and Dad were going to the FBI—that's why they fled to South Carolina, wanted to be far away where Darrin couldn't find us when the police came for him."

"That's why Helen and Joe had to improvise. They couldn't wait for Darrin to return to deal with things. They had to act before your parents handed over their evidence."

"It was Helen. She killed my parents. Started the fire to cover her tracks." I slump against him, exhausted. "Where is she?"

"Not sure. Last I saw her, she was running into the woods." Both of us are still shaking with the cold, too exhausted to move. Despite the pain stretching from the burns on my back, along my arm, and all the way down to my leg, I feel strangely calm.

Alec pats his jacket. "I lost the gun. But the police will be here soon. They'll find her."

Lights blaze up the drive, screeching to a halt in front of the house. Two police cars, men jumping out and rushing inside. They haven't spotted us, hidden down here in our safe haven by the water.

The bushes across from us rustle and Helen emerges, her face ghastly white in the moonlight. Or maybe it's her aura that's gone so deathly pale. I'm not sure, because all I can focus on is the pistol in her hand.

"You ruined everything," she accuses us. "You killed my boy." She aims the gun at me. Almost pointblank range. This close, she can't miss.

Alec pushes me aside, leaping to his feet to stand in front of me. Just like Joe did. The thought of Alec suffering Joe's fate propels me into action.

I'm not sure how I find the energy to fight against gravity, but somehow I'm standing, moving my body between Alec and Helen.

"He's not dead," I tell her. She shakes her head, denying my words. "Alec tied him up. Darrin's fine. But the police are here."

Alec has his arm wrapped around my waist, squeezing against my injured arm, though he's too busy trying to move me out of the line of fire to care. Helen hesitates, glancing at the dock.

Somehow Alec reads my mind—or I read his, I'm not sure—because in that split instant we both launch ourselves against Helen, tackling her to the ground. With one arm out of commission, my only weapon is my body weight, so all I can do is hope that Alec can see clearly enough to grab her gun.

A shot rings out, making my ears shriek, it's so close. My head fills with a roaring noise as I risk glancing up. It was Helen's gun. But it was aimed toward the lake, away from either of us. Alec wrenches her pistol free from her grip just as policemen swarm down the path behind us.

"Show us your hands!" they shout, their auras tinged with the electric red of adrenaline. Alec and I both raise our hands even as we're sitting on top of Helen. My arm screams in pain, but I swallow it down.

Alec glances over his shoulder, not at the men with guns running toward us but at my face. Even without his glasses to magnify them, his eyes glow with warmth. He gives a tiny smile—one that I return. The worst is over, and we survived. Together.

Two weeks later . . .

I peer through turquoise water up to a cerulean sky that reaches out so far and wide that I feel as if I'm alone in the world . . . no, alone in the entire universe.

Until Alec splashes in my face as he dives below me, kicking up bubbles that turn my blue-green world into a diamond-specked kaleidoscope. He emerges on my other side, treading water and gasping for air, waiting for me to surface.

Just because I can, I take my time before finally arching my body upright, my face breaking through to the air, water cascading down behind me.

"Show off." He splashes me, leaving more of a wake with his motion than the gentle tide that buoys us up. "Aren't you cold?" His lips are blue, but he's trying to be manly about it. November in South Carolina means seventy-eight degrees, though to me the water feels as warm as a bath—certainly warmer than my lake back home.

"Wimp." I spin around by kicking one foot, my other leg still aching deep in its muscles. Same with my arm and the burns on my back, but the doctors finally cleared me for swimming—said it would be therapeutic.

I'm in awe of my surroundings. Not to mention the way Alec's family has welcomed me as if I'm a lost relative, gone but never forgotten.

"Seriously, though," he says. "Dinner will be ready soon. We can't keep Mom or Nana waiting."

The beach is empty as far as I can see, the horizon dotted with tiny cottages at the edge of the dunes. I sigh with something close to contentment. Helen and Darrin are behind bars. I wish the paramedics could have saved Joe—despite everything he'd done—but Max is fine, loving Rory's attentions as she nurses him back onto his feet. Turns out that maybe she didn't really want all those other boys after all—she had everything she needed right beside her all along.

"Are you sure?" I ask him. "I mean, Thanksgiving—it's time for family."

I've left everyone I know back home for the week and now am having second thoughts—well, to tell the truth, two thousand and eleventh thoughts. My heart pinches as memories of past holidays riffle through my mind. There had been so much joy in my family. How could it have all been lies?

"I told you, my mom and aunts and Nana cook enough for an army. People will be coming and going all day— friends and neighbors, deputies going in to work the night shift, families of the ones working days. Everyone's family on Thanksgiving."

After meeting his parents and grandmother last night when I arrived, I have the feeling that everyone is family to them any day of the year. Just like they'd taken in a lost little girl fifteen years ago, they've embraced me once again with open arms and hearts.

"You go ahead," I say as his teeth chatter. "I'll be right there."

"The ocean isn't going anywhere. It'll still be here tomorrow." His grin promises me many tomorrows—for the first time, my future is mine and mine alone.

I smile and watch as he paddles back to shore and grabs his towel. Then I submerge once more, letting the water wash away the world outside, and along with it, my doubts and fears.

As I spin below the surface, drinking in the endless blue sea and the endless sky above, I realize that I can go anywhere, do anything. *Anything.* I can go to the Rhode Island College of Design, or Savannah College of Arts and Design, or NYU, or even . . . Paris. And my parents would be proud, of that I'm sure—as long as I stop hiding from the world, from myself.

I break free from the water, kicking toward shore where Alec waits, shivering despite the jacket he's slung across his shoulders. I reach him and he holds a towel for me. I feel a tingle of déjà vu, remember the first time we met. After I'm wrapped in the towel and bundled into a coat, we still don't head back to the house. Instead, we remain silent, staring not at the water or the dunes but at each other.

I reach for his hands. He pulls me to him and his hands slide free of mine to wrap around my waist, his skin warm against mine. And the colors our combined auras create! Beautiful ribbons of light spanning the spectrum.

"I'm not going back," he tells me, watching for my reaction. "I don't want to be a reporter, not like Professor Winston."

"What do you want?"

His gaze goes distant, filled with possibilities. His eyes are like looking into rare opals, sparked with light. "There's this columnist who travels around the world, really gets into people's lives, gets involved. He writes these profiles that expose why people do what they do—good or bad. His stories really make a difference. And," he hesitates, "he's taking on interns. Teaching them how to do what he does."

"And you want to work with him?"

"Thanks to you and all the publicity, I have a good shot."

That's the worst part of what happened, having my life exposed for the world to comment on. But if it helps Alec . . .

"But?"

"But he's in New York City." He pulls back, watching for my reaction.

I smile, relief making me feel buoyant. Because, although I'll always treasure the lake house, Cambria City is the last place I ever want to see again. "You know . . . I hear there are some really good art schools in New York."

His laughter fills the air. He squeezes me tight, his body humming with energy, and I know it's taking all his restraint not to twirl me around—he's still cautious about my wounds, despite the fact that they're mostly healed.

Then he stops. Looks down at me with solemn eyes, asking a silent question. I know he's going to kiss me. I nod my permission, anticipating, wondering what I'll see in our auras. Fireworks blazing? Maybe a riot of wildflowers scattered on the wind as hummingbirds soar to the heavens? It has to be something beautiful, something right and true. It just has to be.

Images soar around us as our lips touch, embracing us, too crystalline to be clear in the sunlight, so I close my eyes to better see. But then I feel guilty, reveling in this joyous beauty that Alec can't share.

My eyes pop open. He pulls away. "Is something wrong?"

"Absolutely not." This time I kiss him.

The ground beneath me is steady. Not because he anchors me. Because I've finally found my footing here on solid land.

Our lips part, just enough to allow us to breathe—and I'm surprised by my sudden need for oxygen. I'm not sure how long I've been holding my breath, but it's longer than I ever have before. The world around me has exploded into color—bright and golden and utterly, utterly perfect.

"What did you see?" he asks, tracing my lips with his thumb. "In our aura?"

"It was beautiful." I nod and shake my head and laugh all at once. Then I place a palm on either side of his face, guiding him back to me. "I don't have words."

"Someday you'll paint it for me." He's not asking but I nod anyway, certain he's right. I think I'll be painting this moment for a long, long time to come.

Finally, we're both shivering, and we walk hand in hand toward his home. I wish Rory and Max were here. They'd love this, swimming in November, walking barefoot on the beach. I miss my friends. But for now, I need to figure out what my future looks like without my past to guide me.

My life. My choice. Whatever I decide, I'll be on my own, yes. But not alone.

The sun is as warm as my mother's kiss, the breeze carries me as gently as my father's arms.

Never alone.

Acknowledgments

Dear Readers,

Like every book, this one is the result of countless hours of work behind the scenes, beyond my writing the actual words on the page.

I'd like to thank the entire editorial, marketing, and production team at Blink. Special thanks go to my editor, Jillian Manning, who first fell in love with Ella's story and worked tirelessly to bring it to life. Also thanks to Katelyn VanKooten and Jacque Alberta for their input.

Also thanks to my agent, the incomparable Kristin Nelson, for her hard work and guiding hand.

Lastly, thanks to you, my readers, for sharing your thoughts and helping to spread the word about my books to your friends. Without you, everything would be for nothing!

Thanks for reading!
CJ

DISCUSSION QUESTIONS FOR

The Color of Lies

1. Because of Ella's synesthesia, she is able to determine people's emotions at a glance. Would you like to have this ability? Why or why not?

2. Early in the story, Ella says, "I'm not used to taking anyone's words at face value—I've never needed to." At which points of the story did you notice what Ella saw and what she believed were in conflict? How did these moments make you see each character in a different light?

3. Both Alec and Ella have been struggling with a childhood memory that changed their lives. How did each character help the other uncover the real truth of what happened the night Ella's parents died? And how did what each initially believed to be true change their approach to the mystery?

4. Throughout, Ella feels the need to stay close to her family because they need her and they are the only ones she can rely on. How much of this compulsion do you think was due to Ella's natural worry over the only family she had left, and how much may have been due to how Helen and Joe wanted her to feel in order to keep her close?

5. Fire and water both play a large role in the story. How do you see the author using these as a symbolic technique at different points in the story? Which usage do you feel was the most successful, and why?

6. Ella's friends Rory and Max are very different—with Rory being effervescent and light, and Max being more cautious and sometimes brooding. How does each personality help Ella (and Alec) grow as a character? Which one did you most relate with? And do you think Rory and Max will stay together?

7. Throughout, Ella's and Alec's ways of seeing the world are very different—most evident in how each sees Ella's painting of Rory. Do you agree with the comments Alec made, that Ella is idealizing the people around her and missing the facts? Or do you side with Ella choosing to focus on the inner "truth" she can see in each person and

rely on her gut? Or is the secret something in between the two?

8. As you read the book, who did you think was behind the murder once you finished the first half of the book? What about after the fire in Ella's studio? Were you surprised by the final reveal? What clues did the author drop throughout the book that tied everything together once the book was done?

9. At the close of the book, Ella returns to the same location where she last saw her parents alive. What emotions would be going through your mind if you were her?

10. What do you think Ella will do next with her life—will she go to art school in New York, as she hints to Alec at the end, or do you think her final decision will lead her somewhere else?

© Kellie McCann Photography

About the Author

Pediatric ER doctor turned *New York Times* bestselling thriller writer CJ Lyons has been a storyteller all her life—something that landed her in many time-outs as a kid. She writes her Thrillers with Heart for the same reason that she became a doctor: because she believes we each have the power to change our world.

In the ER, she witnessed many acts of courage by her patients and their families, learning that heroes truly are born every day. When not writing, she can be found walking the beaches near her Lowcountry home, listening to the voices in her head and plotting new and devious ways to create mayhem for her characters.

To learn more about her Thrillers with Heart, go to www.CJLyons.net